Razarkha's Rise

Matthew J. Dave

Table of Contents

Prologue	2
1: Malcontent	5
2: Subterfuge	17
3: Vanishment	32
4: Redemption	45
5: Tracking	60
6: Upheaval	71
7: Connection	85
8: Investigation	102
9: Justification	119
10: Execution	137
11: Duplicity	153
12: Betrayal	169
13: Desolation	182
14: Disruption	197
15: Confrontation	209
16: Ensnarement	226
17: Commitment	245
Epilogue	257
Appendix I: Map of the World	264
Appendix II: Races of the World	265

Special Thanks

Thank you to Jimi Simmonds, for making the map and creating this vast world alongside me.

Additional thanks to Luna, Milly, Sara and Nino for your enthusiastic following of this book's creation, and a further thank-you to Nino for creating the cover.

Prologue

Count Rani Fel'thuz kept a tall, poised gait as he exited the delivery room through the chilly, ore-like halls of Castle Selenia. Black, flowing clothes hung off his lithe body as they would from a hanger, and black makeup hid the creases beneath his eyes while bringing out the crimson in his irises.

To Rakh, his only son, he was immovable as a rock. The spellbinder boy tottered after him, his coordination not yet matching his mobility. Looking up, he broached the unbroachable.

"Is mother going to die?"

"I don't know," the count replied. "Your baby sister is alive, so that's one small blessing."

"She didn't look like a normal baby," Rakh said. "Her nose was all bent and her tail looks crooked."

"Thankfully for her, Tei is a spare child. Her life will be her own. Her deformities, while not ideal, are irrelevant to the Fel'thuz lineage."

Rakh paused. "Because I'll be marrying Razzie?"

"Because you'll be marrying Razarkha, yes," the count said, his tone shortening.

"Razzie doesn't like me. How do I make her like me?"

The count faltered just enough that his son noticed. "You'll be able to enthral her just as your mother and I enthralled each other. Remember to hone your magic constantly, always compete with her, make sure to push each other's limits. If you're always a challenge, you'll always engage her."

"So, I just need to be strong and always win?"

"Win or lose, what's important is you keep a sense of friendly rivalry. While your duty to the family will make her your wife, remember that first and foremost, she is your big sister."

* * *

Countess Terreza Fel'thuz lay in a bed of blood, holding a framed portrait of herself while a human wetnurse tended to her monstrous third child. In the painting she was glorious, wearing a sleek dress with spiny accoutrements front, back, and centre.

In the delivery room, she was broken. Wisdom Waldon, human fool that he was, assumed her misgivings were mere hysteria, that all she needed was poppy milk for the pain, but spellbinder women were not made to be brood mares like their short, fat, tailless cousins. Her hips were narrow even by her race's standards; the fact she'd survived her first two births was a miracle on its own. It certainly wasn't anything Waldon did right.

"Mother?" a girl asked in a quavering voice.

Terreza returned to the room and swept her gaze from her former strength to the start of her decline: Her eldest daughter.

"What is it, Razarkha? I'm not in the mood for your neediness."

"Are you well, mother? You haven't stopped looking at your picture."

The countess closed her eyes in gesture equal parts wince and sigh. "No, I'm not well. I'm dying."

The girl stared absently towards the window. "I thought so. Is this my duty to the family too?"

"It is. You'll have to marry little Rakh and bear his children, like I have with your father."

"Rakh hates me. How do I make our marriage good?"

"Of all the pointless questions to ask a dying woman—"

"Please, mother," the fuchsia-eyed girl demanded. "I want to bring glory to the Fel'thuz family. I want to be a good countess."

Terreza's breathing became laboured. "You must be impressive whenever an opportunity arises. You must bedazzle and beguile. Make Rakh doubt his standing whenever possible. Unlike me, you're blessed with being the older sibling. Remind him of this fact, make him struggle to match you in magic and acumen. That way, every time you try for an heir, he will feel honoured to have shared that intimacy with you."

"I just have to be powerful and mean? That's all there is to it?"

Terreza Fel'thuz's body emptied itself of air. "Not quite…"

Razarkha, a girl of eight, could only stare as her mother fell limp. When the portrait slipped from Terreza's hands, the young spellbinder glowered at the stocky human feeding her newborn sister. There was an open window nearby, there was a pot she could shatter into shards, there was a cold, hard, ilmenite floor. As her stare intensified, the wetnurse's hold on Tei tightened.

"You're lucky my father's still alive," the little girl muttered, and with that, she ran from the room.

alcontent

Count Rakh Fel'thuz slouched on the chair his father once occupied. It lay close to the end of a long table made of the same grey, shiny material as the walls: Ilmenite allegedly from the moon itself. Three of the walls bore dark blue banners with silver crescent moons, and upon the fourth, surrounding the only window in the room, were sky-blue banners with red-eyed white rabbits.

Beyond the building lay the only consistently good company Rakh had: The common folk of Moonstone. Within the room, the only friendly face sat directly across from him. Wisdom Erwyn Yagaska was an elven biologist whose silvery hair made it unclear how old he was, though his gaudy choice of monocle and cravat made one assume he was a well-kept forty-something.

Heading the table at his right was an exceedingly beautiful high elven woman whose hair was black as a starless night. While she was taller than most humans, she was still short compared to Rakh's kind. His dear sister-wife would call the woman obscenely curvaceous, but in truth she was slender even by elven standards.

This was Overlady Kagura Selenia, though due to her position as an unmarried daughter of a Selenia lord, dead as that lord may be, she preferred to be known as Kag'nemera, after her father, the late Lord Nemeron. She sat straight, her glassy maroon eyes staring through the petitioners sitting opposite her as other members of Moonstone's council deigned to address them.

The visitors were, in appearance, united only by their flowing, black-and-white robes with sleeves large enough to hide myriad vials of poison in. One was a human, wrinkled and large-nosed, another a spellbinder with looming height offset by a thinness bordering on frail, the third a high elf with wide shoulders and a hard glare.

Rakh ceased his apathetic scanning of the surroundings when said glare met his eyes. "I don't think certain members of the council are taking these spiritual matters seriously."

Wisdom Erwyn tapped Rakh's hand from across the table and cleared his throat. "Count Fel'thuz takes the Church of Eternity as seriously as any enrichment to the lives of Moonstone's common man."

"Of course!" Lady Selenia jutted in. "We're really, really concerned about the— that is— what are they petitioning about?"

Moonstone's Chancellor of Vaults, a sunken-eyed human woman in her fifties, spoke with all the mirth of a funeral director. "We're discussing the Church of Eternity's substantial losses over the previous moons."

"Oh, well that's easy, just ask the people for more money," Kag'nemera said with a dismissive wave. "I donate two gold every time I go to the church, if everyone gave that much, it would be fine, wouldn't it?"

Rakh covered his smirk with a portion of his illusionism, projecting a sincere face as he briefly enjoyed the out Kagura's bottomless stupidity offered him. After his moment's respite, he spoke up.

"Lady Selenia, two gold may seem like an appropriate amount of money to give weekly for you, but that's more than a moon's wage to the average man," Rakh pointed out, then looked to the high elven priest. "Father Aguron, was it?"

"Was it? You don't bother to remember the name of your city's spiritual leader?"

The spellbinder petitioner tugged at his collar. "He *was* correct."

Aguron sighed. "Yes, yes. What is your question, Count Fel'thuz?"

"Can you attribute these recent losses to anything of note? An event, a controversy, a rival faith gaining traction, perhaps? Churchgoers don't stop donating unless something's changed."

"Ah, insightful as always, Count Fel'thuz. There is a certain thorn in our side to consider," the spellbinder priest said, prompting eye-rolls from his fellow clergymen.

The human priest continued to explain. "The Order of the Shade has become especially popular with the dark elves of the city, but poor people of all races are becoming enamoured with the vile cult."

Rakh's interest was finally piqued. The Order of the Shade were a mage supremacist group as far as he knew; when the local Sergeant-at-Arms tried to recruit him and Razarkha, his pitch was offering them the respect spellbinders of their purity and power deserved. Even Razarkha had refused, likely because wilful submission to any kind of order repulsed her as opposed to any ethical qualms.

Despite his own experiences, Rakh had drank with enough commoners to know how the lower classes viewed the Order. To them, they were helpful recruiters of the downtrodden, helping hands for those with nobody else. Using supply roots passing through God-knows-where, they gave away plates upon plates of free food to the homeless and starving. The Eternalist Clergy, by contrast, were soft-handed, well-fed old men who preached that blessings came to the virtuous and misfortune was visited upon sinners who deserved it in some way.

"Poor people tend to be more sympathetic to organisations that don't brand them as sinners for having jobs they can't feed their families with," Rakh remarked.

"What do you mean by that?" the human asked.

Numerous councillors murmured, and Wisdom Erwyn shot the count a sharp look. Rakh silenced himself, and the wisdom spoke for him.

"The House of Selenia's council acknowledges your concerns and apologises for the curt nature of Count

Fel'thuz," Erwyn stated, adjusting his monocle. "Unfortunately, there are no means to force the population to increase their religious donations that wouldn't violate the Religious Donation Independence Act drafted by King Silas Godspeak. The law states that in exchange for religious organisations in the Arkheran Isles keeping *all* donations in non-taxable income, nobility are in turn not obligated to maintain their upkeep through financial assistance or other disclosed—"

"You may not be obligated to help us as a religious organisation, but as your *lender* we may have a few things to say," Father Aguron broke in.

Kagura once again found her tongue. "The Church of Eternity is a lender? But I thought the Eternal Word said something about usury being an evil deed—"

"Regardless of their hypocrisy, what they're saying is true," Chancellor of Vaults Enva clarified, shuffling papers in her hands. "We're currently in— one moment— fifty thousand gold's worth of debt to the Church of Eternity, largely due to Lord Nemeron Selenia's excessive oil painting commissions."

This was somehow enough to extract another world-changing insight from Lady Selenia. "What's excessive about father's oil paintings? I think they're really nice, especially when they're of me. I was such a pretty girl. I still am!"

"And nobody's doubting that, my lady," Wisdom Erwyn said. "I believe I understand the situation."

"As do I," Rakh said, bringing the murmuring to a tense silence. "Because of the late Lord Nemeron, the Church of Eternity wants us to pay for *their* alienation of the people. Have any of you drank with a man who clears snow for a living? How about making love to a peasant girl whose only options are to marry somebody rich or pray the town hall has another demeaning receptionist role? Do you think any of these people have money spare?"

"If they're drinking with nobility, they do," the human priest remarked.

"As though I wouldn't cover the pittance a round of drinks are to me. If you think these people, with what little disposable income they have, will spend money on priests who despise them, you're delusional. We shouldn't have to pay for your failure to connect with your churchgoers. That's entirely your fault."

"And we shouldn't ignore Lord Nemeron's debts, but we do," Father Aguron said. "I say we make up for our deficit by claiming something back."

"These are unrelated favours! We shouldn't have to —"

"Rakh," Erwyn snapped. "You're getting agitated. As it stands, they're the ones with leverage. Stop antagonising the clergy. If you can't, please step out."

"It's not as though he was invested to begin with," Father Aguron said, folding his deceptively muscular arms. "Slither off and do whatever you snakes do, far from where the decisions are made."

The spellbinder priest and Erwyn were the only people in the room displaying a modicum of discomfort. Rakh clenched his fists, then steadily unfurled them. Noblemen weren't supposed to take such open insults lightly. Razarkha would have probably threatened to kill the man then and there. Tei would have likely found an equally cutting insult to throw back.

Rakh was neither of his sisters. If there was one thing the common man taught him, it was that self-importance was the death of improvement. A man that resorted to insulting his opponent's race was likely not worth arguing with. Taking a deep breath, he stood up.

"I trust you to make a rational decision, Erwyn. I'll see you later."

Erwyn's cheeks flushed for a moment, and he tugged his cravat as he looked away. "Thank you for not taking this personally. Goodbye for now, Count Fel'thuz."

Rakh made to leave, but the uncomfortable silence was pierced by the innocent din of Lady Kag'nemera.

"What about me? You trust my final decision too, don't you?"

"I trust you to do what you always do," he answered, and with that he left the council chamber of Castle Selenia.

The area beyond was a winding hallway of doors, oil paintings, and entrances to staircases of varying safety. The sound of Rakh's footsteps alternated between the clacking of shoe against rock and the light thud of sole on rug. At some point, a phantom solidified in the spellbinder's peripheral vision.

She was almost his mirror image in a dress; she had the same small nose that resembled serpentine nostrils, the same black hair infused with purple-dyed highlights, as well as a similarly ring-studded tail. Pale white foundation contrasted with the dark makeup forming starbursts about her eyes, a light purple lipstick accentuated her smirk, and a hanging off her willowy, tall body was a black dress so minimalistic that it was almost incidental to the myriad lilac-lined spiky accoutrements attached to it.

"Razzie. I thought you might have been listening in."

"*Razarkha.* I'm certain you call me that just to irritate me further," the countess said.

"A stunning insight," Rakh said in a flat tone.

"It's good to see you have *one* skill, seeing as you're a completely worthless count," Razarkha remarked, making to lead Rakh down a staircase, only to stop when she noticed he wasn't following.

Rakh waited for her to catch up, then answered. "Of course you'd believe that."

"It's not a belief, it's a fact," Razarkha said, barely obfuscating her grin. "Even your best friend in the world, Wisdom Erwyn the Inverted, knew you were a liability. It's not the first time he's betrayed you for the sake of objectivity."

"He's a wisdom. He wouldn't be doing his job if he let friendship affect his judgement."

Razarkha gave Rakh a vibrant fuchsia glance. "Even when he could have lied to bolster your fragile ego and shut me up, he stuck to the facts. Remember the—"

"Of course I remember the little arcana test. Possession of greater natural magical power doesn't make you superior, you realise that, don't you?" Rakh said before turning right to walk down a nearby staircase.

Once again, Razarkha attempted to go her own way. This time, there was a considerable wait before she audibly, but invisibly, rushed down to join her brother.

"Asking a question and running is cowardice," Razarkha said as she reappeared.

"I engaged you enough that you wanted to follow," Rakh explained.

"You're not engaging, clever, or magically empowered."

"That's like a logger telling an archer he's physically weak. While a logger is a burly fellow who could beat an archer in a wrestle, all a logger manages to kill is trees. An archer shoots down people despite lacking sheer bulk."

Razarkha made mouthing movements with her hands. "Yes, yes, very intelligent. It's amusing to hear this from the man who so loudly endorsed the Order of the Shade to an Eternalist priest's face."

Rakh turned right at the bottom of the staircase, heading through another silvery hallway towards a ruby-studded door. "I don't believe in the Order's philosophy, no sane person does. If might makes right flourished as an ideology, there'd be killers and little else at the top."

Razarkha scoffed. "And you call yourself a Fel'thuz? We're *Plagueborn Ilazari* by blood, dear brother. Ilazar is living proof that nations *can* be run by might makes right."

Rakh opened the door, revealing a bedroom with a double bed, a pair of wardrobes, one marked with an oil painting of Razarkha and another marked with a simple rabbit insignia. Count Fel'thuz slipped into the room, hung his cloak in the latter wardrobe, and sat on his bed, rubbing his temples.

"I can't say I know how functional Ilazari is. I know my rationale, however. When I argued with the clergymen, I wasn't arguing for the Order, or for might makes right. The Church of Eternity openly despises its followers, yet the clergy grows fat from their generosity. They receive support despite offering nothing of substance in return, and now that support has rightly dried up, they demand income from another source.

"Meanwhile, the Order, regardless of their motives, are supporting some of the most vulnerable and needy in this city. I believe the well-fed can fend for themselves. Those at the bottom who have no-one else to turn to, they're the ones who truly need help. The debts the Church intend to levy are likely going to force Erwyn to raise the taxes again, and to protect our business owners the taxes are going to hit the working poor hardest of all. They don't need the extra grief."

Razarkha stood at Rakh's doorway, her smirk dying for once. She allowed the words to linger in the air for a moment, then abruptly burst into laughter.

"Why *wouldn't* we exploit the poor? Businessmen can mobilise private militias and force embargos. What can regular peasants do? Riot and get murdered in scores by guards?" Razarkha said. "You're an idiot, Rakh. Your caring act doesn't fool anyone. How can you preach kindness and morality when you openly admit to sleeping with women who aren't your wife?"

Rakh narrowed his eyes. "Shut the door, Razarkha. I know you want to make this argument into a show, so I'm stopping you now."

His sister-wife held her posture and sneer steady. "Make me."

"I don't need to."

Rakh raised his hand, and all beyond the doorway became a flickering, purple-black void. Razarkha folded her arms and her expression withered.

"Very funny. I could counteract that and broadcast our argument to the entire castle."

"Go ahead and try."

Razarkha rested against the wall while Rakh watched, the sides of his mouth tugging themselves upwards. Naturally powerful or not, sound-based illusionism was a weak spot of his sister-wife's. According to the scant books on illusionism in Arkhera, the components of visual and auditory illusions were similar in concept but extremely different in mechanics, and only the former came naturally to Fel'thuz illusionists.

Rakh had read further into the specific differences in two books written by the Soltelle Empire's Imperial Engineer, Hildegard Swan. As far as he knew, Razarkha hadn't bothered to do the same; Yukishimans were incapable of magic, and to her, the unmagical had no say regarding magical abilities.

"Have you set us up yet?" Rakh asked.

"Shut up."

"I'm just asking a question, dear sister. I wouldn't want to start the argument before you're ready."

"I said shut up," Razarkha muttered.

"Oh, let's just get started anyway. I'm sure as the superior mage you'll be able to multi-task."

Razarkha clenched her fists. "I'm going to kill you one day, Rakh. Mark my words. One day, you'll be dead by my hands."

"That's nice. So, you took issue with me fucking other women? Remember when we made that little agreement? Accepted there's no love in this marriage?" Rakh said, his tone embittering with every word he spoke. "I even agreed to never fall for any of the women I made love to. They're all strictly one-night because of our agreement, and believe me, I've met *so* many women I wanted to break that rule for. But I stick to it. You're free to have other men, I even said you're free to fall for them if you are capable of such a thing. You agreed to those terms just as I did, but you never took advantage of it. How is that *my* problem?"

"I— I just haven't met a man who meets my standards. They're all inferior to me," Razarkha claimed. "You're just indiscriminate. *Humans, elves,* your taste is utterly degenerate."

"How does any of that concern you?"

"You're the head of the Fel'thuz family, even though it should be me. You're disgracing *my* house. I'm the eldest child and I'm far stronger than you'll ever be."

"How's the amplification going?"

"Shut up! My— my point is, you're a weak leader and this gaffe at the council chamber proves it. With that idiot Kag'nemera at the top, House Selenia needs a strong advisor. She needs a Fel'thuz who can make her decisions *meaningful."*

"And I suppose you're far more qualified than me because you came into this world earlier?"

"I have three years more experience than you. That's a better reason than the thing dangling between your legs."

Rakh paused. "You have a point. How about—"

"Do you know why we both favour the colour combination black and purple? Why our parents and their parents before did?" Razarkha asked.

"I was going to offer a resolution, but I know you're not listening," Rakh droned.

"I thought you didn't. The founder of this house may have been Fel'thuz of Ilazar, but he was an albino who liked the colour blue and, for some reason, rabbits. Hence our official colours, an albino rabbit on sky blue. However, we all wear purple and black. That is because the person who truly helped this lumomantic immigrant achieve greatness was his Arkheran wife, Rina, who was already an associate of Moonstone nobility. Her preferred colours?"

"Yes, yes, black and purple, very interesting, can we—"

"So even though Rina wasn't the House of Fel'thuz's official head, her notable influence on her children meant that the true legacy of colour was hers."

"Fascinating. If she was able to be so influential without being the official head of the family, what's stopping you?" Rakh asked, smirking as Razarkha's face scrunched.

"What are you saying?"

"I've heard this a thousand times. You talk about all these great women, most of them legitimately wonderful people, and imply that because you're a woman, you somehow have everything in common with them and should therefore be head. It's frankly insulting to every woman in existence. Being head of this house won't make you feel any better about yourself, if that's what you hope."

"You don't know that."

Rakh's brow furrowed. "I've known you my entire life. You're doomed to be a dissatisfied, miserable little person for all eternity. That's why I'm confident in offering what I was trying to offer for the past few minutes."

Razarkha's blood could be seen through skin and foundation alike. "Fine. What's your oh-so-generous offer?"

Rakh clicked his fingers, and the world beyond the doorway faded into view. "I agree that it isn't fair that I have headship over this house simply because I was born a man. So I'll play by your rules. Let's battle, no fatalities, but otherwise a standard Ilazari honour duel. One on one, no-holds barred magic usage, public visibility, minimal collateral damage."

Razarkha's eyes lit up. "You're joking. You're going to fight me for headship of the family? But you only stand to lose! At best things stay as they are. You're an idiot."

"From my perspective, it's the other way around," Count Fel'thuz said. "Not that I'd expect you to understand. Is it a deal, then? First one to knock the other unconscious wins. The winner of the duel shall gain headship of the Fel'thuz family and will therefore become Overlady Selenia's advisor."

His sister-wife grinned unreservedly. "It's moments like this I despise and love you all at once. I don't care what trick you have up your sleeve, I will overcome it. Consider the duel agreed-upon."

Rakh stood and offered his hand. "Good. Because I broadcast the agreement to the entire castle. Erwyn's probably written the terms down already."

Razarkha shook her brother's hand, but while her body portrayed enthusiasm, her eyes were bloodstained ice.

"You love to be adored by those insignificant peasants, don't you? I can't wait to humiliate you in front of every person you hope to play hero to."

Subterfuge

The mirror mocked Razarkha Fel'thuz as she powdered her face. Today was the day her brother-husband finally submitted to her power, even if he didn't know it yet. Razarkha had tailed her male doppelganger throughout the weeks of preparation, and to her irritation, he hadn't been practising as much as she'd expected.

He'd gone to the Yookietown to prepare a jazz band, asked Erwyn to send letters to the local nobility and the Royal Electorate to secure a set of powerful witnesses to the upcoming fight, and of course seduced a few filthy, tailless cows along the way. There were a few times the Rakhs setting matters up proved to be fakes, vanishing once they were done communicating, but aside from that, he'd been a lazy excuse for a mage.

Razarkha straightened out her capelet's upward-turning collar, first the backing, then the spines that extended beyond it, and silently beheld the window through the mirror. Rakh should have been here, in their bedroom, getting ready with her. It was his duty as a husband to at least try for an heir, yet almost twenty years of failure had driven him away.

She was the purest of Fel'thuz stock, naturally powerful, beautiful and lithe, unlike that misshapen wretch that killed her mother. Why did fate taunt her with beauty and power if there was no way to pass it on? Razarkha stopped admiring her face and doubled over, supporting herself on her dresser.

The first was a shapeless, bloody mass that came out of her. The second was recognisably a baby, yet small and twisted. The third was another spatter of red. The fourth was Razander; he was carried to term, and despite his birth almost killing her, he refused to breathe when Waldon delivered him. That was the last insult Razarkha could take. Moonstone needed a new wisdom, and Erwyn Yagaska, a biologist by speciality, was a fine replacement. Despite this, he still couldn't conjure any successful pregnancies from Razarkha.

"Shut up," the countess told herself. "Shut up, Rakh, I can hear you mocking me, I said *shut up!*"

Rakh refused to speak or make himself visible. Razarkha straightened her posture, slipped a dagger into her garter, then checked that her dress sufficiently highlighted her thinness and expanded her silhouette simultaneously. Once that was done, she took a moment to calm herself before the fight. It was to start at noon, with the opening speech from Lady Selenia happening half an hour before. She still had another hour to kill.

She sat on her bed, alone with *Ilazari History: The Twisted Past of the Isle of Dreams*. The book contained tales of how the Isleborn Ilazari welcomed the immigrant community known as the Plagueborn, led by the man who'd become the Plague Emperor. It went on to explain how the Isle of Dreams freed itself from the Golden Galdusian Empire, and how during its war against Galdus, it became a centre for the production and spread of myriad magical artefacts.

The most famous of these were the seven plague obelisks, huge towers of nasite, a slick, black rock with an uncanny ability to drink the light from its surroundings, and the seven soulstealers whose locations were largely hidden. According to the book, six of the seven were unaccounted for, but since the book's publication, a Parakosi orc named Antique had found three throughout the world.

It was a shame such powerful relics were rotting away in the vault of an ape-man incapable of unleashing their potential. Worse still, when she braved the Parakosi sands to offer him her personal fortune for the artefacts, he told her they weren't for sale. Razarkha threw the book away and huffed; her ploy to relax had only dug up resentment she swore she'd buried.

She checked the pendulum clock upon the wall and with a deep sigh, stood. She left her room and drifted through the glimmering, yet colourless halls of Castle Selenia, sporadically forming afterimages, distortions, and copies of herself.

She was so lost in her last-minute practice that she nearly walked into Lady Kagura on the way down the stairs. As tempting as it was to push the idiot down the stairs, Wisdom Erwyn was beside her as a trusty babysitter, and he was not the sort to tolerate assassins. A recent memory of one such attempted assassin tickled Razarkha enough to make her smile authentically at the pair of elves.

"Ah, I see you're behind schedule too."

Erwyn's expression flattened as it always did in Razarkha's presence, while Kagura Selenia maintained her usual level of gormless pleasantry.

"Oh, hello, Countess Razarkha. I'm ever so excited to be an announcer for a real spellbinder duel," the overlady babbled. "You know, even if your people are ugly and noseless and have those strange rat tails, your magic is really fun to watch."

"You're ever so kind for a small, fat, tailless, pointy-eared imbecile," Razarkha replied in a sickly-sweet tone.

Lady Selenia's voice faltered. "I'm not fat! I'm a pretty woman, I'm pretty, you must apologise! I'm your *lady!*"

Erwyn cleared his throat. "My lady, you *did* insult Razarkha's race too. If she apologises, you must as well."

Razarkha took a moment to construct a fitting response. "Oh, my lady, please accept my humblest apologies. You're not fat at all."

"It's all right," the womanchild replied. "I'm sorry I said your people are ugly. I really like all your dresses though, you spellbinders are perfect models for extravagant clothing!"

Countess Fel'thuz frowned. This woman was like an animal, completely incapable of grudges or rational thought. She scanned Lady Kagura's Wrenfall-style kimono, a blue-black affair with a tilted obi knot and a skirt-like lower half. Embroidered throughout were silvery moons and constellations.

"Your kimono has nice embroidery," Razarkha haltingly said.

Erwyn hid his mouth with a hand, and when Countess Fel'thuz made to snap at him, his lady started filling the air with blether once more.

"I'm really jealous of you. Your parents gave you a brother to marry before they went to the moon. And he's a nice brother too, he's willing to let you be head of the house and play games with you! I don't think my brother will be like that when he comes down from the moon."

Erwyn's expression tightened, and Razarkha rolled her eyes. She'd heard this moon nonsense from Kagura before and hearing her use it to compliment Rakh added insult to injury.

Yagaska raced to get the first word in. "Before you say anything—"

"Quiet, wisdom. Lady Selenia, are you saying you're attracted to my husband? Because if so, I may take issue."

"Oh, heavens no, I'm not one of his commoner women! Besides, he looks like a snake. Still, he's ever so fun, what with his dancing and his willingness to challenge you like this. If my brother is born soon, I'll ask Rakh to foster him with you. That way you won't have to feel so bad about all the miscarriages."

Razarkha stopped walking just as they reached the exit of Castle Selenia. Before her lay greenhouses and winter-blooming flowers. Beyond that were the gates and stinking masses. All this environmental trimming blurred as one thing sharpened into focus: Lady Selenia's delicate head. It would be so easy, especially with the ice on the floor. She slipped a hand beneath her dress and touched her garter, but upon remembering Erwyn and the fact that they were surrounded by armed patrolmen, she settled for stabbing her lady with words.

"You know you're the reason your lord father killed himself, don't you? He was living with the knowledge that his only heir would be a soft-headed, moronic woman who isn't even prepared for the reality of death. Who could live with such a future? I know I'd want to leave the world if, upon having a living child, they turned out like you.

"You're utterly worthless, you lack any semblance of leadership skills, and you insult people without even knowing it. If you're going to mock people, at least do so deliberately, for God's sake. You're an utter disappointment, and so you know, your parents aren't on the moon, they're in the ground, of value only to maggots and mushrooms. Your oh-so-anticipated brother-husband? He'll never be born. You're an idiot for believing your father. You sent your sisters away for nothing."

Erwyn's face reddened. "Countess Fel'thuz, be silent this instant. Your conduct is unacceptable. You're speaking to the Overlady of the Forests of Winter, and you'll treat her with—"

"I'm sorry, father!" Kagura wailed, running back into the castle.

Razarkha covered the lower half of her face, but despite her efforts, a chuckle slipped out of her. For some reason, Erwyn, the beleaguered slave to Lady Kagura's every whim, stared at his liberator with disgust.

"Are you happy?"

At this point, all restraint fell from the countess. *"Happy?* Of course I am! Now she's almost certainly going to be late because she'll be too busy crying like the overgrown baby that she is. You'll probably have to take over her duties, as usual. Don't act like you don't enjoy being the true lord of Moonstone."

Erwyn took his monocle off and exhaled. "Lady Kagura is soft in the head. She can't help herself. You, on the other hand, can. You're a decade her senior, and while you're missing critical parts of what makes a person decent, you're hardly wanting for lucidity. You simply lack a soul."

Razarkha laughed uproariously. "If souls make even the most objective of people play pretend with twenty-something womanchildren, then I consider souls overrated. Go on, little wisdom, run after your charge like the foster parent you are."

Erwyn put his monocle back in place and turned from Razarkha, running after his meal ticket. He didn't even bother to get the last word in, a mistake Rakh would never make. A nearby guard in full plate armour and a blue cloak turned his visor-clad gaze to his countess.

"What are you looking at, brawn? There's a reason we have you lot wear helmets. It's so thugs like you can't stick your noses into noble business."

"We watch you when you sleep. At least your brother understands that," the guard said, giving his pike a casual lift.

"Don't threaten me, human scum."

"Or you'll tell your good friend Lady Selenia? Fuck off and lose to Count Rakh. Nobody's rooting for your victory, I hope you know that."

"Then I look forward to proving everybody wrong," Razarkha said in a low tone.

The greenhouses of Castle Selenia's grounds refracted light in a way that enabled Razarkha to continue experimenting with her powers as she walked. She cast a copy of herself through the greenhouse, focusing specifically on unrefracting it so it would look natural from the other side. Her abilities would be enough, especially given Rakh was under the impression this would be a non-fatal duel. Razarkha would need to compose herself before she reached the arena, lest her powers run amok.

Beyond the gates was the city centre of Moonstone. It was a snowed-upon plaza with numerous brick buildings, mostly clay, but the more affluent buildings, such as the town hall and the Church of Eternity, glimmered even in the grey sky with their smooth ilmenite exteriors.

The latter impaled the sky with twisting spires and reached impractical heights only fully scaled by their long-suffering bell-ringers, yet it still failed to match the utterly pointless size of Castle Selenia, whose spires marked each of its corners, along with a set of dark blue banners and flags portraying the silver crescent moon of the ruling family.

It was obvious where the arena had been set up; the only other time peasants swarmed to wooden scaffolds so eagerly was during a hanging. Razarkha cloaked herself and continued forward; she wasn't about to let a peasant halt her with whatever mind-numbing problems they had. Atop the scaffolding was a podium, a fenced-off area where Rakh waited, along with a gallery containing a set of musicians in dark glasses. Some of them wielded unusual Yukishiman instruments she couldn't care less about, but from what she could recognise, they had a mouth organ, a piano, and a trumpet. Razarkha slipped invisibly onto the stage and took a good look at her mark.

Dearest Rakh looked especially handsome today; he'd fully embraced Rina's colours, dyeing his entire fringe a tasteful dark purple and using it to cover one of his crimson eyes. His body was imperfect as ever, unfortunately; he'd spent so much of his time seducing lesser races that he'd added ugly musculature to his form to impress them. Still, his face was as pure spellbinder as they came, small-nosed and marked with eye-bags he'd neglected to enhance with makeup. Instead of his usual flowing robes, Rakh had decided upon a pair of tight trousers and a purple-pink feather boa topping a black leather jerkin.

Razarkha revealed herself and leaned on a nearby fence. "You have such good natural looks. A shame you squandered them with such grotesque meatiness."

"I was wondering when you'd appear," Rakh said. "Are you excited for the opportunity to become head of the house?"

"No, I've been bored the entire time," she replied. "Why get excited when the outcome is so obvious?"

"Your world must be exceedingly grey," Rakh remarked. "Do you ever acknowledge people that aren't directly interacting with you? Do you take pleasure in *anything* for its own sake?"

"What's bringing this up? Do you need some form of superiority to cling to after I destroy your credibility in front of all these people you love to 'acknowledge'?"

"I just thought that you might actually enjoy this if you knew who's watching. Unfortunately, I don't think you operate in terms of 'people', more 'titles' and 'value'. Thankfully for you, there's a few nobles over there," Rakh said, pointing to a set of elevated stands amidst the crowd of peasants.

Razarkha squinted to evaluate the worthy few. There was a blonde-haired human with a green-dyed streak surrounded by guards in white cloaks, a spellbinder-like behemoth of a woman surrounded by 'protectors' that amounted to bards and servant girls, along with a pair of spellbinders, one man, one woman, who flanked a keffiyeh-wearing human in purple that spent his time scribbling notes into a book.

"Who are they and why should I care?"

"One of them is Wisdom Yugen of Parakos, guarded by his masters of ice and fire. Mal'gan and Yukei,

I believe they're called. He's a historian, so he'll write down what happened while the masters of ice and fire are probably here to judge you for your wasted arcane power. The blonde human is Lady Gemfire. Odd that she hasn't brought her bastards."

"She's even worse than you," Razarkha said. "I've only read of her, but she's just as disgusting as I expected."

"I'm not sure how you reached that conclusion from a distance. Moving on, the chubby spellbinder over there is Quira Abraxas. I'm sure I don't need to introduce her," Rakh said, picking a nail out of a nearby piece of fence.

"Her tenure as royal advisor must be stressful if she's gained so much weight. Doesn't she use her powers?"

"She's always been like that from what I know. She likes cakes. We all have our little vices, and the only person she's harming is herself," Rakh said with a laugh, but upon glancing back to his sister-wife his mirth died. "You really don't care about anyone, do you? Why then, do you care about this title?"

Razarkha trembled. "You're— you're trying to get in my head. You're trying to make me lose my nerve before the fight. I'm onto your little tricks."

"Oh, of course, I couldn't possibly be trying to understand my angry, confused sister."

"Don't pity me."

"Fine. I couldn't possibly be trying to understand my monstrous, evil bitch of a sister. Is that better?"

Razarkha hushed her voice. "You're going to fail in front of everyone you value. I don't care what they think, but you'll lose everything you love here and now."

Rakh had nothing to say to that, and so Razarkha begrudgingly scanned the nobility once again. Royal Advisor Quira Abraxas was engrossed in conversation with one of her servants, a black-hooded girl with a short stature and what seemed to be a tail hidden beneath a cloak.

She shifted around Rakh to get a better look, but her stream of thought was blown away by an obnoxiously loud fanfare that heralded the arrival of Kagura Selenia and her wisdom. The lady's eyes were red around the edges, but otherwise her prior crying fit was hidden by makeup. Razarkha's resultant scowl birthed a smirk on Rakh's face.

"What happened? Did you try to insult Lady Kag before she arrived? It's futile, we all know she's too stupid to catch a cold."

"Shut up, I— I broke her, I—"

"Perhaps she's stronger than you thought."

"Impossible."

Lady Selenia finished her ascent to the podium, and the fanfare stopped. Erwyn Yagaska cleared his throat, then projected his carrying, level voice.

"All will remain silent for Overlady Kag'nemera Selenia's introduction to the honour duel between Count Rakh Fel'thuz and his wife, Countess Razarkha Fel'thuz."

Kagura cleared her throat in obvious imitation. "People of Moonstone, while you may think that I'm a genius who makes all of the best decisions for you people, in truth, I have a set of advisors who I hold very dear to my heart. They help me make all the important decisions, because being a lady is really, really hard. Dearest of all are my wisdom, Erwyn Yagaska, and my advisor, Count Rakh Fel'thuz.

"The Selenias and Fel'thuzes have a close, intertwined history. From the moment Fel'thuz came from Ilazar and joined Oberon Selenia's council, the families have entrusted each other with the responsibility of ruling Moonstone. Hence, whoever is head of the Fel'thuz family is really, really important. I like Rakh a lot, but sometimes he gets angry about things I don't understand, and Razarkha sounds really smart but she's mean most of the time.

"Razarkha, despite being a daughter when there is a son, wants to be head of the Fel'thuz family, and therefore become advisor to me. I would have helped with the decision, but instead the two have agreed to an Ilazari honour duel! This is— this is…"

She paused, whispered into Erwyn's ear, then he whispered something back. After an uncomfortable silence, she smiled warmly and continued.

"An Ilazari honour duel is traditionally to the death. It has only two participants and would normally happen on the Battle Isle of Azraiyen to avoid collateral damage, as this is an island without… collateral things. Anyway, so this isn't quite a real honour duel, because Rakh and Razarkha are only going to fight until the other is knocked out. They'll stay within the confines of this fenced-off arena, that way no collaterals will be damaged. My concern and love for you is paramount, even if the fight is sure to be amazing."

The Lady of Moonstone paused, then looked down on the arena. "You two, are you ready?"

"Of course. When you're done, I'll have the jazz musicians start," Rakh replied, his form slightly rippling.

"And you, Countess Razarkha?"

"It'll be over quicker than you expect."

"I don't understand. Oh well. I suppose as the adjudicator, I must start the fight. All right, you two, the duel will begin… *now!* Go, go, I believe in you Rakh!"

The lady leapt about like the overgrown child she was, and the crowd was already cheering for her brother-husband. Razarkha swung a punch at her brother, who clicked and vanished, prompting the Yukishiman band to play their jaunty, syncopated nonsense. Razarkha stumbled from her overcommitted strike and nearly hit the fence, which was somehow missing a board already.

She found her footing and cloaked herself, then projected multiple false renditions of herself. The true

Razarkha slipped back into view once a good six false ones were there to take the hits, and she called out.

"Come out, dear brother, you can't stay invisible forever! Why don't you dance to this music? You were the one to request it, after all."

An echoing, confident voice answered her. "Good idea, dear sister."

In moments, seven Rakhs appeared to answer Razarkha, swinging their bodies about in a semi-choreographed manner, meeting each of the Razarkhas in turn. When the real Razarkha met her Rakh, she raised an eyebrow.

"You expect me to dance along with you?"

"Why not? Give these folks a show."

The Rakh offered his hand, and surrounded by the music, the synchronised jiving illusions around her, Razarkha's eyes twitched. This was his attempt at mockery, wasn't it? Or perhaps he genuinely hoped to connect with his sister. The thought amused Razarkha enough that she decided to grant him this concession. After all the women he'd danced with, it was almost fitting that his final dance would be with his rightful wife.

She made to take his hand, but he snatched it away, making backward steps that meshed with the beat. Razarkha begrudgingly went along with him, moving her hips and legs with the constantly shifting beats of an irritating, improvised tune. If their forms made contact, their tangibility would be irreversibly tested.

And so, the projections danced in a troupe, pairs mingling and teasing each other, but refraining from contact. When they overlapped, they vanished, and pair by pair, the truth drew closer. Razarkha's eyes lit up as the third pair vanished; Rakh seemed to be struggling to track her true self down.

The Rakh Razarkha was dancing with gazed into the eyes. "It's time."

Razarkha's breath became heavy. "This'll be the first time you've held me with passion, won't it?"

"That's not true."

"I don't think your other copies spoke to me. Best of luck," Razarkha said as she spun towards him, keeping one of her hands close to her garter.

She ended her manoeuvre with an overt lean backwards; either this was a false Rakh, unable to catch her, making the true Rakh too far away to capitalise on her fall, or the man before her was real enough to hold her, in which case, the duel was over.

She didn't hit the ground.

Rakh's body leaned over Razarkha's and offered her a playful smile. Her back was more supported than she could have imagined, and for a moment, she enjoyed his touch. She couldn't afford to bask, however. She swiftly hiked up her dress and took the knife from her garter, then swung around and drove it into Rakh with swiftness even she didn't anticipate.

The first strike caught his shoulder, causing him to scream as his precious supporters gasped in horror. As he backed away the dagger slipped out of his body so slickly that it remained in Razarkha's hand, allowing her to stab him again, this time hitting his gut. Blood poured from his wounds like waterfalls, and his other illusions crumbled from sight. He fell to his knees, gasping as he clutched himself.

Razarkha checked her knife, which was practically shimmering with blood, then flung it to the floor. After a moment of shaking, her brother collapsed, allowing her to loom over her fallen foe.

"Is there anything you want to say, Rakh? A little dying speech for all the peasants you love so much? Perhaps you have something to say to your better?"

"I—" Rakh began, before choking on some fluid, then continued. "I underestimated your depravity. I knew you were many things, but I didn't think you were a kinslayer. You win. You're head by default. I hope you enjoy what spoils it affords you before the people rise against you."

With that, Rakh expired, and the rabble finally shut their mouths. They stood in horror, while Lady Kagura cried for her count. Erwyn, meanwhile, was frozen in muted terror. Even one of Quira Abraxas's little servant girls was in tears. Razarkha swaggered to the arena's edge and leaned over the people.

"Finally, you understand. Whatever Rakh was to you, whatever he did, no matter how kind he was, *kind* doesn't get results. You know what gets results? Cold-blooded murder. Anyone who crosses me will meet a similar fate! Moonstone will learn to fear me! *Me!*"

The people did not quail in fear as expected. Instead, they erupted into a maelstrom of outrage, only the occasional phrase gleanable from the cacophony.

"Fuck you, lady, the battle wasn't supposed to be fatal!" one fat old human yelled.

"I *loved* Rakh!" some elven girl said.

"We'll put your head on a spike!" an impassioned young dark elf promised.

The Royal Advisor whispered something to her three female bards, whose backs burst open to reveal writhing, purple-red tentacles, and in moments, the masses were very much relevant. She backed into the arena and scanned the surroundings for an escape, but guards were at every plausible exit of the stage. Finally, she shifted her gaze to her fallen dagger.

It was clean.

Behind her, something materialised; a slightly toned, leather-clad spellbinder. In one clean smack with the missing fence board, Razarkha Fel'thuz swivelled on her feet, then collapsed. As her vision blurred, Rakh Fel'thuz stood over her, his expression dour.

"I knew you'd try to kill me."

As the crowd bloomed into relieved applause, Razarkha checked the noble visitors' stands one last time. The hooded servant girl wasn't there.

Vanishment

Rooms with naught but the sound of slow, quiet breaths were familiar to Wisdom Erwyn Yagaska. While not technically in his job description, it would have been remiss of him not to tend to every injured person in Castle Selenia. Most of the time, the person sleeping in his spire's recovery bed would be a hard-working servant who'd hit his head falling down a poorly maintained staircase or slipping on a rug.

This time it was an attempted murderer with fortunate circumstances of birth. Her target being the most passionate man Erwyn knew hardly worked in her favour. Rakh had picked his sister up and invisibly withdrew from the outraged public, then once his fellow nobles were safely within the castle, he begged Erwyn to watch over her as she came to.

The high elven wisdom took out his monocle, blew on it, and wiped. Only Rakh would make such a request. In turn, Erwyn would accept such a request from him alone. Within the recovery room, numerous shelves filled with emergency ingredients stood, along with a recipe book by his mentor, Wisdom Melancholy of Thornwrit Heath. Despite his promises, despite the ethics he allegedly upheld as a wisdom, the book's back pages beckoned to him.

Melancholy maintained that manufacturing poison was easier than medicine, and as Erwyn flicked through his old teacher's findings, it was hard to deny the stance. Compared to the multi-step remedies throughout most of the book, the poison recipes at the back were laughably simple.

Death was, in a way, the natural state of living matter; as time wore on, beings didn't become more alive, they neared their demise. It followed that it was easier to bring something closer to their inevitable end than it was to tug them back from it. Nonetheless, dragging people back was Erwyn's duty as a wisdom.

A concentrated dose of acacia extract treated with a suitably noxious solvent would easily be enough if not for the distinctive scent, but with some ingenuity he could make it look like an accident. The wisdom looked to Razarkha Fel'thuz's sleeping form and sighed.

Rakh would know. It was a tap on the head, not a savage beating. The outcomes were his count believing he was a kinslayer or believing his wisdom was a cold-blooded killer. Erwyn shut the book, opened the window, and looked over the crowds gathering outside the castle gates. From the spire they were like a bubbling broth, roiling about with the occasional droplet vaulting the gates only to be swiftly cleaned up, by guards in this case. He had no choice but to leave Razarkha alone for a moment.

Wisdom Yagaska rushed to the first floor of Castle Selenia, where the Fel'thuz siblings' ruby-studded bedroom door lay. He knocked the gaudy structure twice, then called out.

"Count Fel'thuz, are you there?"

"Before you say it, yes, I can see the people outside the grounds," Count Rakh's voice said through the door.

"You know what they want," Erwyn stated.

"I'm not going to do it. Razarkha may be a kinslayer, but I'm not."

Erwyn rubbed his forehead. "Rakh, this isn't about your pride anymore, this is about preventing a riot. Either you can pacify them in a way I can't think of, or we have no choice but to give Razarkha over to them."

There was silence, then Rakh opened his door. "She's still alive, isn't she? You're not pushing this because you've done something irreversible, please tell me you haven't."

The wisdom tugged on his cravat. "I— I'm not going to act like I haven't *considered* poisoning her for everyone's sake, but I assure you, I've respected your request not to harm her. She's still unconscious, but she's alive."

"I'm ready to talk to her now. Don't worry, Erwyn, I have a plan. I can leave you to pacify business and political interests, but when it comes to the people down there, let me handle it."

"You overestimate yourself," Erwyn said. "You know me. I can't abide the violent and emotional nature of the average citizen. Yet I agree with them. I don't think that monster should live. Leaving her unattended is enough to make me nervous."

"I can defend myself."

Erwyn sucked air through his teeth and sharpened his tone. "That's brilliant, can you defend me as well?"

"Enough, Erwyn. Leave this one to me."

"If you fail, know that I'm not going to advise the castle guard to act as Razarkha's escort."

Rakh moved past his wisdom and gave him a smile that softened his harsh, thin face. "I know. I don't expect you to. If I fail, do as you want. You're not wrong for wanting Razarkha dead. I'm just hopeful that there's a better way."

Erwyn turned from his count and shook his head. "I hope for Moonstone's sake that you're right."

* * *

Erwyn's recovery room was marked with a ghoulish face halved vertically, scarlet on the left and deep blue on the right. Rakh opened the door to find Razarkha lying in the patient's bed, tossing and turning. Despite everything, seeing her alive and well filled him with relief. He opened the window and beheld the enraged public.

She didn't deserve his loyalty. It was only the spectre of Count Rani Fel'thuz that told him to spare her.

He knew Razarkha held no love for their father; she'd have killed him as readily as she tried to kill Rakh. He was protecting a monster.

"How did you do it?" a woman's voice asked.

Rakh briefly cloaked himself, sidestepped, then assessed the situation. Razarkha was sat up in bed; there were no daggers in her hand, no tell-tale ripples or glimmers in the air that gave away her laughably predictable illusionism, nothing to indicate this wasn't his flesh-and-blood sister.

Satisfied, he returned to visibility and walked to her bed. "How are you coping?"

"Perhaps you didn't hear me. I asked how you did it," Razarkha insisted.

Rakh covered his face. "You don't understand the situation you're in, do you?"

"Well, I'm not dead. If you wanted to kill me, you had your chance. Evidently something else has happened," she pointed out.

"Your life is in my hands. The people want you dead, as you well know."

Razarkha dabbed at her under-eyes, smudging off a bit of makeup. "You won't let them. That's why you're here, talking to me. To negotiate some sort of deal so I can walk away from this with my life."

"I don't want to see you in this city or this kingdom again. I've prepared a letter for the Royal Advisor, authorising your ejection from the Kingdom of Arkhera as soon as you are physically able."

"And how will the Crown enforce that all the way from Deathsport?"

"I'll make you tantamount to vermin in every city. Don't think that because I'm not stooping to your level that I'm not angry."

Razarkha put on a mocking tone of voice. *"Don't think because I'm not stooping to your level that I'm not angry*. Do you hear yourself? You're saying this while promising to exile me from the only place I can call home."

"You tried to kill me."

His sister-wife had nothing to say to that. They lingered in the recovery room, waiting for the other to say something. Rakh examined the painted face of the girl he grew up with, hoping to find a shred of remorse. As his search became increasingly futile, bitterness welled up within him.

"I'm glad our children never survived," he spat.

This finally changed her expression. "You— what did you— why would you say that? Are you mad? I don't care how much you want me to suffer, if we don't have children, our legacy dies. Everything *both* of us were. Is this your spite talking? So much for—"

"Do you honestly think the child would have made it past the age of ten with *you* as their mother? Look at you, how you are, how you behave. You don't connect to *anyone,* you plan to murder your brother with the same expression you'd cook eggs, you— you *killed* Waldon, let's not play images and illusions here, you're abusive to everyone who speaks to you. How could you believe you *wouldn't* have beaten our heir to death before they had a chance to grow up?"

Razarkha took the verbal battering, then stood, her makeup running. "You act like I have no sense of restraint. I— I would have kept him alive, I would have groomed him to be brilliant, just like me!"

"Then they were spared a fate worse than death."

Rakh hissed in pain as his sister-wife slapped him across the face.

"Shut up! You never tried to befriend me, you never tried to care! You wrote me off as a monster the day I pushed you down the stairs when we were children!" Razarkha screamed.

Rakh's voice deepened in exasperation. "Oh, *fuck off*, Razarkha, here I am sticking my neck out for you, trying to convince the people to accept your survival, but you're going to act like I'm this vile creature for hating the most despicable woman in existence. I shouldn't be sparing you, I know I shouldn't, but I can't bring myself to throw my own flesh and blood into a crowd of rightly enraged citizens."

"Don't act like you're high and mighty for not being a kinslayer."

"It's better than being an attempted one!" Rakh yelled. "What do you have to say for yourself? Do you feel *anything* in that twisted little heart of yours besides self-pity and savagery?"

"You— you—"

"I give up. I don't know what I thought I could say to you. Stupidly, I thought I could part with my attempted murderer on cordial terms. Am I mad, Razarkha?"

"You're a sneak. You're a cheater. You knew what I'd do, you knew I would disgrace myself, you set something up with Tei and manufactured all of this, up to this sorry attempt to be the 'bigger man'."

"Are you joking? You attempt to kill me and you're going on about— wait, what was that about Tei?"

Razarkha scoffed. "Oh, don't pretend you don't know about her. You felt a third illusionist in the area, and she was there with that fat pig of a royal advisor. Who else would be the height of a seer with a spellbinder's tail?"

"A spellbinder child?"

"Shut up," Razarkha snapped.

"You need to stop resorting to those two words. When you're away God-knows-where, the people won't be as forgiving as me."

Razarkha folded her arms. "If you're genuinely this dense, perhaps you *didn't* know that Tei was there. Go on, then, how did you defeat me? I'm never going to believe that it was a true duel."

Rakh sighed. "I don't owe you an explanation but why not play along? Living with an egotist could twist anyone. After a while you want nothing more than to rant about *your* superiority for once. And guess what? It all relied on you being an *idiot.* Not thinking things through, pouncing too early. You're right, I expected you to try and kill me. I couldn't have possibly anticipated how angry you managed to make the crowd afterwards."

"But you— you supported me, that fake version of you *supported* me! I stabbed him, and yes, the knife went in and out too easily, but he spoke properly—"

"Because I can manipulate sound, unlike you."

"Shut up, I know about your stupid sound manipulation, but you couldn't possibly support me with illusionism."

"No. That was me, but not the image leaning over you. I was knelt behind you, and I pushed you up with one arm. It wasn't a perfect trick, of course. If you noticed that any other point of contact was false you would have figured it out and I'd have needed to switch strategy. Thankfully you're as stupid as you are unpleasant," Rakh said, his breath growing shaky.

"I don't think I want to hear anything more from you," Razarkha mumbled.

"That makes two of us."

Rakh trembled, then walked towards the room's door. "If you try *anything* funny, if anyone breathes a word about you, I won't hesitate to take any kind words I tell the people back. I'll let them tear you apart. Am I clear?"

"Fine. I won't move until you say so."

With that, Rakh made to leave, only for Razarkha to speak once more.

"Rakh."

"What?"

"Don't you have anything to say? About how you'll miss all this conflict, how I've been a good rival? Aren't you going to ask where I'm going?"

"No."

* * *

Royal Advisor Quira Abraxas stood behind the crowd of rowdy peasants, listening closely to their northern-accented remarks. Dark elves whispered about all the ways they'd snap Razarkha's twiggy body, spellbinders and necromancers called her a disgrace to magic users, and even the guards joined in, calling for the death of a woman that, from the phrases Quira picked up, was elitist, racist, and despicable in every way.

She knew that it was unwise to be so close to what was likely to devolve into a full-scale riot, yet her need to have a story for when she returned to Deathsport compelled her to stay. She'd urged the majority of her servants to hide out at the inn they were staying at; with her daemonic bards, Quira was untouchable.

The trio surrounded her, no longer playing their instruments, all human-like women with identical bodies and features, with only their clothing and 'hair' differing, as though they were a collection of living dolls. Occasionally their hair writhed to reveal sucker-pads, and each of their tops were backless, just in case they needed to step into action.

Quira received information from the Royal Looking Glass that Rakh Fel'thuz intended to address the people personally after he hurriedly took Razarkha in. Unless the announcement involved the scheduling of an execution, King Landon would consider it a perversion of justice, but so long as he remained on his throne in Deathsport and let his advisor visit cities on his behalf, he couldn't force anybody's hand.

She wasn't wearing clothes appropriate for the weather; her blue, branch-embroidered kimono was deliberately a size too small and worn off-shoulder. As such, she fiddled with her umbrella as the snows worsened, and by the time she was done opening it, Rakh Fel'thuz had projected himself as a massive, translucent image, holding a letter in his left hand. She extended her hand to the bard in black with the blonde 'hair', prompting the daemon to pass her a bhang-weed pipe and matchbox. She rested her umbrella on her shoulder, lit up, and listened.

"People of Moonstone," he began. "I'm well aware of the outrage surrounding the duel between Razarkha and I. I'm not going to pretend what she did was right or even understandable. She's not welcome in this city, and I'll see to it that she's not welcome anywhere else in the kingdom. I will not deliver her to you, however.

"Why? Because I'm not going to commit the crime you're so outraged at Razarkha for attempting. I'm holding back with every bone in my body. Believe me, I'm as angry with myself as you are. It's easy to think that because a victim had it coming, murder is acceptable. However, if I throw her to you, if you rip her apart, no matter how you see it, vengeance, 'justice', or something else, ultimately I'd be throwing my sister to her death knowingly. I am not the kinslayer she wishes she could be. Worry not. You will never see her again. I'm not even going to let her contaminate the dungeons. She's not worthy of Arkheran freedoms and so she will be stripped of them."

He lifted his left hand. "This is a document for the consideration of Royal Advisor Quira Abraxas. If she is honourable and does her duty, then it should reach the King. This is a request for a kingdom-wide exile of my former spouse, Razarkha Fel'thuz. She is to be stripped of her titles, her access to Moonstone coffers, every honour afforded to her by birthright. Perhaps in sparing her, we have allowed her to suffer to the extent she deserves. She will be gone by tomorrow's morning light, that I can guarantee."

Quira felt a finger tap her back, and she jumped, then noticed, flickering in and out of vision, a letter with a white wax seal. She unsurely took it, causing the letter to solidify in her hand, and with that, all traces of Rakh Fel'thuz vanished, projected and otherwise.

The response of the crowd was split between disappointment and unadulterated frustration. At the back, people disbanded and ranted to each other on their way home, but the front swiftly devolved into madness. Peasants banded together to scale the gates of Castle Selenia, while musketeers positioned in the castle grounds shot to disarm. Unfortunately, with the accuracy musket rifles afforded, this often didn't go to plan. Quira backed from the situation and hid the letter in her top, then nodded to her bards.

"Riversongs, reveal combat tentacles."

The daemons' backs split open, revealing red, many-eyed tentacles, which unnerved the commoners enough that they gave them a wide berth. From there, she rushed through the city, leaving the built-up, ilmenite-guarded metropolis that directly surrounded Castle Selenia and entering the industrial district, where the *Moon's Vein Free House* stood amidst the snow.

Outside the building, a grim human with a shaggy beard shovelled snow beneath a swaying board that depicted a silvery full moon with noticeable red veins shooting through it. Quira handed the daemon with blue 'hair' and a pink outfit her pipe, which they quickly blew out.

"Here we are. Retract your tentacles and have fun for the rest of the night."

The bards slipped their tentacles back into their bodies and gave her three identical glassy-eyed smiles. In unison, they spoke.

"We suppose you mean non-fatal fun?"

"Yes, of course I mean non-fatal fun. Why not give the punters a free show? I could do with the distraction."

With that, the bards plunged their hands into their strange, spongy torsos and retrieved instruments; one had a viol, another a crumhorn, and the third an accordion. The snow-shoveller looked up from his work for a moment, then continued without a word.

The four entered the *Moon's Vein* to be greeted with a notably underpopulated, but warm building, serenaded by the crackling of a log-burning hearth. A plump dark elf with an old man's jowls manned the bar, while a set of bearded humans played cards with each other in the corner. Quira chuckled to herself as the Riversongs dispersed and announced their presence with unrequested music. In typical daemonic fashion, they failed to understand why deafening the residents of a landlocked city with sea shanties was inappropriate. Quira sat at the bar, taking the stool directly opposite the tender.

"Please may I have my evening meal? I'm staying in room twenty-one," she half-shouted.

"Oh, twenty-one, yes, the other girls under your payment have already claimed their meals. Wise girls if you ask me, staying out of that riot waiting to happen," the keep mouthed. "Come to think of it, one of 'em hasn't ate yet, I think she's upstairs."

"She'll come down now that I'm here."

"Do your bards want anything? I don't know what things like them enjoy."

Quira's brow furrowed. "While they're certainly not like we mortals, it isn't fair to call them 'things', especially peaceful daemons like the Riversongs. They'll go hungry for now, but be assured, I keep them well-fed."

The barkeep's eyes widened. "That's— well, I'll tell the girls to plate out two servings of mince and dumplings. Where are you sitting?"

"I'm sure your waitresses will figure it out, given there's only me and the gamblers over there. Thank you."

With that, she walked over to a nearby shelf stocked with board games, found a set of *Wraiths and Wyverns*, then sat alone at a table, setting the eight-by-eight board up while her daemons sang of falling in love with a lordling who thought they were a dead woman. While one of the singers kept a playful tone throughout, the blonde one regularly cracked her voice in what may have been genuine emotion.

Eventually, one of Quira's servants, a girl in a black, hooded cloak, headed down from the residential section of the inn and sat opposite her mistress. She had dark hair, mismatched eyes of teal and purple, a rippling illusion over the lower half of her face depicting a stereotypically attractive human's, and stubby arms that didn't match her torso's size.

"Nicely done, Quira. Hand over that letter, I need to see it."

"Come now, Looking Glass, if my bards weren't going at it, you'd have given yourself away to anybody with ears. There's a reason I told you not to come out of hiding."

"This event was personal," the Royal Looking Glass said. "I was so frightened when Rakh feigned his death. I told him forever ago that the only way we'd be free is if Razarkha died, but he's too sentimental."

Quira rubbed her chin and put a zombie from each side of the board into her hands, then mixed them about behind her back. "I wouldn't say he was sentimental when he made that speech. He openly stated that he despised himself for his decision. Still, I can appreciate it."

"You've been in a similar situation," the Royal Looking Glass remarked as she picked the hand with a black zombie in it. "I suppose your Uncle Saruin was let off because of your mercy?"

"No, I'm sad to say. I wanted him castrated and flung into the dungeons to be miserable forever. Then he disappeared within his cell, without a sign of breaking out. Rakh is the kind of strong I wish I could be."

The Royal Looking Glass unsealed the letter and looked it over. "Exile. Of course. I exile myself because of Razarkha's madness, but when she finally expresses it for all to see, she gets the same."

"Do you know the best part about self-imposed exile?" Quira said with a smile, pushing a zombie forward.

"Go ahead, Abraxas."

"You can change the terms at any time. Once Razarkha's gone, what's stopping you?"

The short woman paused, then moved a zombie to meet Quira's in the open. "You wouldn't believe me even if I told you. For now, I just hope Rakh knows Razarkha as I do."

"What do you mean?"

Tei Fel'thuz met Quira's gaze with her true eyes. "Razarkha never lets go of a grudge. She never accepts humiliation. She's eternally vengeful, even if it means failing again and again. I know that, and I hope the man who's shared her bed for the past decade understands the same."

Redemption

The recently liberated Rakh Fel'thuz lay alone in his double bed, staring at the ceiling. To his left was his wardrobe, to the right an empty, unmarked one. Razarkha had taken her portrait with her, as expected, along with every other personal effect she had. It would all be ash or scrap otherwise, so it was just as well.

Normally, Rakh would have woken up in some inn, or a woman's house; there was once a marriage to escape. Now there was no reason not to sleep behind metal gates under the watchful eyes of underpaid Selenia guardsmen. He blinked slowly, then sat up and leaned towards his bedside table. He struck a match, lit his paraffin lamp, and checked his clock. It was already noon.

Rakh grumbled and left his bed, opening his window to see that beyond the gates, a small group of protestors remained. He squinted and used his illusionism to magnify his view of one of the commoners' signs. It read *'Wun rool fur us, anuvver fur nubbilitee!'* and depicted Razarkha delightfully skipping town as a man in rags hanged.

He put on a dressing gown and little else, then slinked down the many flights of stairs to the dining room, a banner-filled hall large enough for a noble family that hadn't exiled all its members. Kagura Selenia was at the head of the sixteen-seater table, eating lunch with Erwyn and talking about whatever Kaguras talked about.

"If Razarkha is gone forever, why are there still protesters? Didn't they get what they wanted? If we hanged her she would go to the moon and instead we're letting her choose where she wants to go. That's the only difference, isn't it?"

Erwyn's eyes creased. "It's as you say, my lady. There's no way for them to get what they want anymore. They'll stop soon enough."

Rakh sat a healthy distance from the pair and looked over the platters. There was too much food for three people, though an extra spellbinder could have easily devoured the surplus. Rabbit stew, game soup, roasted vegetables, mashed yams, numerous pastries filled with Madaki-spiced meats of ambiguous origin, and Jaranese-style duck rolls lay before him, but Rakh's stomach refused to crave anything.

He took a duck roll in silence, and Kagura was quick to speak. "Oh, Count Fel'thuz, you're finally awake. I was getting worried, because my father slept a lot before he decided to join mother on the moon. Just remember that Razarkha isn't on the moon, she's somewhere here on the ground."

"I'm fine," Rakh muttered. "The last thing I want is to see her again."

Erwyn put down his fork "You've been sleeping in for the last week. It's all right if you're upset. Would you like to talk?"

"I would like to eat," Rakh snapped, eating half a duck roll in a single bite.

Erwyn eyes met Rakh's. "Denying your pain doesn't make you strong."

"I'm not in pain over *her.*"

"Then what *are* you in pain over?"

Kagura jumped in. "Oh, oh, I know! He's in pain because of the heirs he can't have! How are you going to have heirs, Count Fel'thuz? Are you going to marry your other sister? Where is she, anyway?"

Rakh stuffed the last of his duck roll in his mouth and left the table. He strode through the castle, upping his pace as the ever-predictable clacking of Erwyn's hard-soled boots pursued him.

"Go away, Erwyn."

"I'm not letting you lock this up within you," the wisdom said, his voice close enough to pique one ear over another.

Count Fel'thuz gave up, standing in the middle of a hallway, staring at the ground as servants glanced, then quickly moved on. "What's the point in telling you? What can you do about this?"

"Advise you," Erwyn said as he finally caught up. "Rakh, you're obviously troubled by Razarkha's absence. I'm not going to act like that's rational, but our feelings rarely are. You may think I'm unfeeling, but I'm in constant conflict with myself. We all have these moments; you're just more swept up in it than usual. There's research that suggests spellbinders are more likely to have mood swings beyond adolescence as a means of amplifying their magical potential—"

"Shut up, Erwyn!" Rakh shouted, turning around and looming over the elf. "Stop thinking you can fix everything with your oh-so-rational advice. When I see you giving Lady Selenia platitudes, do you think I see you as a truthful person? Do you think I'll see your advice as anything more than empty comfort?"

"Lady Selenia is a different person to you. She's a child in a woman's body, but you're a man I trust. I wish you could return it," Erwyn said, his voice cracking, his eyes fixed on his count's face.

Rakh winced, his eyes leaking. "I hate it so much, Erwyn. Knowing she's out there, alive. I shouldn't have given her a chance. You were right. I should have had her executed. It was only fair, even to her. What's she going to do without us? She's only good at complaining, she doesn't have an innovative bone in her body. She's going to die alone and in pain, so what did my decision bring? Misery for everyone. I'm a failure, Erwyn. I wish Tei was here. She would have known what to do."

"You did what you thought was right," Erwyn said, offering an embrace. "I may not have agreed with your decision, but you followed your convictions. That has my undying respect."

Rakh turned away from the wisdom. "You're lying. You think I'm a moping layabout who couldn't kill the woman who tried to kill him. Don't act like you respect me. I know a failure when I see one."

"A mirror never offers a proper perspective. Even the smoothest, cleanest silver will flip the image. As an illusionist, you know that better than anyone," Erwyn said. "Please listen to me."

"What else is there to say?"

"You need to find another purpose," Erwyn said. "Let's talk in my laboratory."

Rakh begrudgingly followed the wisdom to his spire. Erwyn led him to a door marked with a red and blue flame, and behind it lay countless desks and shelves, most containing flasks of chemicals or recipe books. Taxidermised reptiles native to Jaranar and Elarond stood as statues within in glass boxes, and amidst it all lay a single chair, tucked behind the only desk that had an inkpot and notepad.

"Do you remember thirteen years ago?"

Rakh's cheeks tingled. "Of course I remember."

"We agreed it would be best if you didn't know where young Rarakhi went," Erwyn said. "However, I always checked up on him. Once a year, I would give him a naming day gift on your behalf. He always asked after you, but of course, I could only say that you hoped to meet him someday."

"What were you thinking?" Rakh asked, his tone sharpening. "Why get the boy's hopes up? Erwyn, I know you have a hard time telling difficult truths, but this is *wrong.*"

Erwyn sat on his laboratory's only chair and opened a desk drawer. "You still don't understand what this means, do you?"

Rakh tried to rest against a free wall, but his back remained straight, and his voice shook. "Are you suggesting I reconnect with him now that Razarkha's gone?"

"That's exactly what I'm suggesting," he said, taking out a piece of paper. "Here is the orphanage I sent him to. He was there to receive my gift last year, though I shall admit he was a lot angrier at you than I'd hoped."

"Angrier than you'd hoped?" Rakh said, his voice's pitch rising. "I don't know what you can expect of a boy who's been told that their father loves them without any evidence. Gifts don't replace company."

"Yes, but he was so eager to meet you before. In his twelfth year, he's grown impatient. He told me that he's 'done waiting'. I think that makes Razarkha's exile quite fortuitous, wouldn't you say?"

"At least I can finally put an end to his wait," Rakh remarked, and moved to take the piece of paper. "Let's see where he is."

The note claimed he was at *Defiance Against Acedia* orphanage, a building he'd passed without thought multiple times during his cavorting with the lower class. He squeezed the slip in his hands.

"Did Tei know about this?"

Erwyn paused and focused on his inkpot. "Yes."

"Has she visited him, or is she a ghost even to you?"

"I don't know where Tei is," Erwyn said. "Perhaps she's visited him, perhaps she hasn't."

"I thought I saw her in Moonstone on the day of the fight," Rakh said. "If it was her, she was serving Quira Abraxas."

"I can't confirm or deny that. What I do know is where your estranged bastard lives. Please, take that information and do what you need to. Razarkha can't stop you anymore."

Rakh's voice shook. "Why did you trust Tei with this but not me?"

"Because you have a heart that's too open for its own good. Tei feared Razarkha appropriately, you didn't."

"Thank you for giving this to me now," Count Fel'thuz snapped. "You were only eleven years too late."

Before Erwyn could reply, Rakh strode to his room. He washed himself briskly, put a thick, fluffy hooded cloak on, and donned an amulet with an aquamarine cabochon in the centre. After that, he rushed back through the halls of Castle Selenia, practically stumbled down each overly smooth staircase and charged out of the castle grounds.

"Count Fel'thuz! Why won't you listen to us?" a protestor yelled upon his exit. Rakh responded by vanishing, then generating two false images for the people to chase.

Slowed only by the possibility of slipping on Moonstone's icy cobblestone paths, Rakh ran from the central district and south, away from the veneer of class and refinement the elite indulged in. Here, the people smelled of musk, not perfume, and all struggled to make ends meet.

Southern Moonstone's infrastructure was lacking, with the Order of the Shade's lodge being the only remotely well-maintained building. It was a bold presence amidst the deprived district, standing tall, with an octagram hanging above a double door and braziers burning around the entrance in eight different colours. If Rarakhi had truly tired of waiting, it wasn't out of the question for the Order to approach him. As a potentially powerful mage in a grim situation, he was an ideal recruit.

The southern district's snow was especially thick. The industrial roads got a smattering of salted grit, but the area's relatively low-class inns and orphanages weren't deemed essential to Moonstone's economy, hence their roads were neglected by the council. By the time Rakh was past the Order's lodge, the snow had come up to his shins.

He could understand Erwyn's choice of orphanage. There was absolutely no way Razarkha would consider this a worthy place for a boy of Fel'thuz blood to be raised, even if he was illegitimate. If the boy ever stood out with his magical power in a way that could attract his aunt's attention, the Order of the Shade would have already whisked him off to relative safety to be inducted into their mage supremacist cult.

Rakh found the *Defiance Against Acedia* orphanage standing between two ramshackle terraces. Most of the build's windows were broken, one sill being so structurally compromised that a goblinese child was perched upon it, looking over the streets with wide, ice-blue eyes. A faded picture of a hand reaching to a smaller hand could be seen upon its entrance in flaking paint. Rakh shook his head and closed his eyes.

This moment had plagued him since he'd learnt of Rarakhi's conception. He knew he couldn't connect with the boy while Razarkha shared the castle with him, but a decade of gnawing pain had subsided into a dull ache. Now that he was mere steps from the door, the pangs returned in full force, holding his arms hostage as he lingered without so much as breathing.

He finally rapped his knuckles against the door and in moments, it moved, stopped by a latch chain. A buggy eye, a large nose, and a scratchy beard could be seen through the small opening provided.

"Who are you? You a fost— er, Count Fel'thuz, what a pleasant surprise! Looking to open your heart to an orphan? Don't feel bad about your mercy on that bitch sister of yours, I know how it is—"

"I know Rarakhi's here."

The man swallowed, and suddenly shut the door again. "Sorry, I don't know what you're talking about!"

"Erwyn told me Rarakhi was here. Razarkha is exiled, so there's no need to hide. I want to see him *now.*"

The man incomprehensibly gibbered from the other side of the door and could be heard rushing from the entrance to yell about something. The walls were so thin that his stamps could be tracked up the stairs, and at one point he opened the window where the goblin boy was perched.

"Oi, Skarzag, I told you to *stop perching so high,* you wanna get killed?"

"Better than living here."

"Just get in here and help me find Rarakhi!"

"But he left—"

"He might be hiding out here, look, his count father's outside and if I don't have him, I'm fucked!"

The goblinese child almost lost his grip. "His father's a bloody count?"

"Yes, and I can't afford to piss him off!"

Rakh glared upwards at the hairy human. "I can hear you."

"Shit!"

The sound of stamping tracked downwards, and the door opened fully. "Come in, I'll explain. This ain't my fault. I can't control someone like young Rarakhi."

Rakh frowned. "What do you mean by that? You didn't— oh, you *did,* didn't you?"

"He said he was sick of waiting! Then he tells me he's gonna make his own way!" the human said, quavering and holding his hands up. "I tried to tell him that twelve was no age to be acting like a man grown, but he wouldn't have it. He said he'd found a way to support himself and then one day he just disappeared."

"And you didn't look for him?" Rakh exploded.

"He's a bloody vanishing spellbinder like you, how'm I supposed to find someone like that?"

Rakh pulled at his hair. "I can't believe this, I can't believe you'd let this happen. *Erwyn trusted you!"*

"I trusted me too, but the boy can't be stopped! I dunno where he's got to, but I think he's doing something, you know, illicit. Extortion. Just before he left, he'd stolen a book on lending from the local library, and though I got it back for 'em, it was only a week after that he left."

"You're an idiot. I wait all these years with the hope that he's safe and now I'm hearing my son could be trapped in organised crime. I—" Rakh stopped and gathered his wits. "It's fine. It's fine. I know exactly who to consult about this."

"Owt I can help with?" the orphanage owner asked.

"Why would I trust you with liaising with a crime boss when you can't keep track of a child?" Rakh asked.

With that, he left the orphanage with one name on his mind: Plutyn Khanas, the Lost Lord.

* * *

Razarkha sat in the luggage carriage of an eastbound train trundling to Winter Harbour, a port town nestled just beyond the Ashpeaks. She'd kept herself cloaked, sitting in a simple, manoeuvrable nightgown reading more of *The Twisted Past of the Isle of Dreams,* her knife snugly fitting in one of her stockings.

The chapter she was on covered the Plague Emperor's friend, Conditor. While the Plague Emperor was a full-blooded Sulari Galdusian spellbinder, born in the ancient port city of Demidium, Conditor was a lowly human augmentee. In the days of the Golden Galdusian

Empire, spellbinders lorded over all other lowly races, and found humans to have great magical potential that simply needed to be unlocked.

As such, Conditor, and augmentees just like him, were bred by immortal Galdusian ascendants to be submissive, obedient, and receptive to magical interference. While they could never truly ascend as spellbinders and necromancers could, their bodies could be converted to hardy, nerveless rock, their souls bound to the new fleshless vessel. The only remainder of their organic form was their brains' arcana node, the crystal that allowed all humanoids save orcs to access magic.

Made to order as a spineless slave, Conditor served under Demidium's consigliere, Lumus Aurelion, who the Plague Emperor also served as an apparent non-mage worthy of indentured servitude at most. While both were enslaved in some manner, the Plague Emperor had his will, but it took time for Conditor to find his.

It was said that an overseer threatening to disassemble Conditor's stony body was what made the Plague Emperor reveal his chaos-speech to Galdus. He opened a portal, and out lunged a tentacle the size of a Jaranese python. It stopped the overseer and dragged him into wherever the portal led. Upon seeing the outrage of the other overseers, the Plague Emperor pled with Conditor.

The human had the power of geomancy, as was typical of construction augmentees, and surrounding them was stone and mud. All he needed to do was find his anger, to wilfully break his chains and hate the people who rendered him a slave. Somehow, the Plague Emperor got through to Conditor, and together, they tore Consigliere Aurelion's manor to the ground.

Razarkha scoffed. Some of this must have been embellished. The Plague Emperor may have been of such a despised mage caste that he opted to feign powerlessness, but surely he knew he was above Conditor. In addition, how would a creature that had known nothing but submission and acceptance of abuse become enraged by it?

While there was no doubt a person that went by the title of Plague Emperor, and his legacy included modern-day Ilazar, the seven plague obelisks, and the seven soulstealers, the notion that he was some selfless friend to lower humanoids was laughable. Still, the thought intrigued Razarkha. There must have been something to gain from appearing as a friend to the lowly.

He must have known there was potential to topple an empire so reliant on lesser beings accepting their lot in life. Even humans deserved to fight for their freedom, and they inevitably did. The Golden Galdusian Empire had grown complacent. The ascendants grew stagnant while their augmentees underwent continual refinement; why wouldn't the Plague Emperor exploit that? He was a beloved opportunist, nothing more.

As Razarkha pondered over her idol, she came to an uncomfortable realisation: The picture she painted of the Plague Emperor was none other than Rakh's afterimage. He also convinced the lower people that he somehow cared. She shut her book and gritted her teeth. She was the only noble in Moonstone with a mote of honesty, and for her virtue, she was exiled.

The Plague Emperor understood that treating the masses as one easily controlled collective was impossible, and that relying on others was foolish. Hence, he only bettered himself. That was why Ilazari culture was so heavily individualistic. That was why Razarkha didn't need friends.

The train came to a stop at Winter Harbour, and human attendants scurried through the luggage carriage, preparing the bags for first class passengers while second class passengers squeezed past when they could. Razarkha remained invisible, put on her boots, and picked up her luggage.

She hopped out of the back of the carriage between the attendants' collections, taking in the new, fishy air. The buildings here reached two stories at their highest, without any sign of watchtowers, musketeers' posts or protective gates. The guards wore blue and grey, occasionally bearing a gauntlet insignia on their breastplates. They mostly wielded musket rifles and had plump figures even by human standards. Evidently, they did not run about for their earnings.

Almost every lane was gritted, and most of the people were humans in well-worn, but not tattered clothing. More than a few men stank of salt and death as she passed, forcing Razarkha to open her suitcase and retrieve a sachet of fragrant dried flowers to sniff.

All she needed to do was find a boat to Ilazar and sneak aboard. Then she'd be free of Arkhera and its disgusting commoners who drifted listlessly without hopes or dreams. She'd reach the Isle of Dreams, home of the ambitious, where fortunes were made or broken, where the truly worthy rose.

If she couldn't succeed there, then she would accept defeat. But for now, she would prove Rakh wrong. She would prove Arkhera wrong. She drifted to the eastern side of Winter Harbour, where the town's largest house by far overlooked the crashing waves of Accursed Sea. Nearby poles flew dull blue flags with smudged grey gauntlets upon them, the two colours mingling with each other from apparent dye displacement.

The rest of the coast was lined with piers and warehouses, with ships coming in and out of the harbour with surprising frequency. There were considerably more guards here than the rest of town, but as with the men closer to the train station, they had a certain laxness about them. The way they marched was practically carefree, and when people alighted from passenger liners, they gave their paperwork a quick nod before moving them along.

Razarkha frowned as a set of high elven merchants hoisted a box as wide as five men from a cargo ship. Whatever was inside made the crate shake, and there were even breathing holes on its upper side. An Ilazari caravel anchored in a nearby pier, yet something about the situation before Razarkha made her scalp itch.

The dock guard asked the high elves some questions, their leader said something that made the guard laugh, then they were waved off and sent on their way. After that, the elves lifted their cargo and marched it down the pier, as if they were holding some sort of oversized coffin. They headed through an alleyway towards a dingy warehouse whose surface consisted of wood in variable states of rot. Razarkha stopped, looked to the Ilazari caravel, then back at the men with the box. The Plague Emperor would have despised people like this.

Even if there weren't spellbinders in there, humanoids deserved to live and die as their own people. Feral, not enslaved. Everyone deserved to succeed and fail, without help, without hindrance. Razarkha abandoned the caravel and stalked the high elves through the alleys. There wasn't much in the way of cover, but Razarkha didn't expect the guards to grow competence from thin air.

She slipped her dagger out of her stocking and put her suitcase down, then upped her pace so she was directly behind the elven men. Then, she projected Tei's disgusting, deformed image in front of them, who gave them a smile and a wave.

This made them pause long enough for her to drive her dagger into the first elf's back and the resultant shock ensured another couldn't react before his throat was slit. Blood spattered on Razarkha's invisible form, giving her cloaking an undeniable shimmer. The remaining four elves dropped the crate to draw musket pistols and the one at the front yelled in a strongly accented rendition of the Common Tongue.

"Guards! Guards, are there any—"

Another elf broke in. "Are you stupid, you can't let the guards know we're—"

Razarkha took him out before he could finish, and the frontmost elf shifted his head in every conceivable direction.

"Fuck it, the guards aren't coming, men, find whatever it is and *kill it!*"

One of the sharper elves pointed his gun at Razarkha's glistening outline, so she projected a visible rendition of herself while her true self ducked. She couldn't falsify the noise of her own head exploding, but she faked the visuals long enough to buy time. She used her moment to leap forward and stab her would-be killer in the crotch. He screamed as he fell, and last two elves trembled, pointing their guns about. Razarkha remained crouched, ready to lunge, but unfortunately for her, they turned non-existent tail and ran.

Razarkha was ready to abscond, but a woman could be heard within the crate, speaking a language she didn't recognise. Regardless of linguistic nuance, the urgent tone was enough. Razarkha checked for an opening in the crate, and found a panel secured by nails. Her trusty dagger was the solution to most problems that weren't Rakh, so she used it to push up the nails and unmake the box, revealing numerous human women with the brown skin, almond-shaped eyes, and wavy hair typical of the Isle of Malassai's natives.

Razarkha checked that no guards were closing in. When it was revealed the closest patrolmen were occupied chasing the two elven men who'd ran from the alleyway instead of investigating what made them run in the first place, she dropped her illusions and gave the women an unsure smile as they clambered out of their crate.

"You. Speak. Com-mon?"

The closest woman responded by holding Razarkha and rambling in her native tongue, while the others jabbered with wide smiles. The former Fel'thuz felt a warmth grow within her as the foreigners beheld their superior in height and heroism alike, and against all instincts, she returned the embrace.

"You're free."

Moments later, she remembered why she didn't touch people, especially lesser races, and let go.

"All right, er— go on, off with you."

The women didn't understand, and Razarkha retracted from them. They asked her a question in their native tongue, and all the former Fel'thuz could do was wave her arms.

"Me. Not. Friend. You go. You go, now!"

They still didn't understand. Razarkha looked back to the docks, only for her throat to tighten. A spellbinder woman in blue-and-white Ilazari-style clothing was walking with an entourage of similarly tall, tailed individuals towards the anchored caravel from before.

The Plague Emperor must have had a secondary motive after all. Helping lesser beings was a waste of time on its own. She slipped into invisibility once more, rushed from the alley, picked up her suitcase as she ran past it, and in a desperate scramble, snuck aboard her stolen ticket to the Isle of Dreams before its gangplank was lifted.

Tracking

The caravel to Ilazar was known as the *Chernyopal,* Razarkha had discovered. She sat invisibly in the captain's quarters most days, stealing food to maintain her near-permanent magic usage. The white-haired spellbinder Razarkha had followed blamed it on a mystery servant getting greedy, but neglected to punish them then and there, instead promising that her grandfather would hear of it.

Razarkha rested in the shade of the captain's desk, reading *The Twisted Past of the Isle of Dreams* while she waited for the woman to leave her room. According to the exchanges she'd heard, she was Anya Kasparov, a name that placed her as Isleborn Ilazari.

She favoured whites and sky-blues draped upon puffy dresses that served to obscure her sleek, spellbinderly form. Despite her build being idealised perfection for her race, Razarkha had yet to determine what magic she used, if any; perhaps she was simply a careful eater.

Like Razarkha, Kasparov enjoyed reading. Her current book was marked in Isleborn runes that, when translated, read as *Unbreakable Bonds: A Tale of Ropes, Lust, and Hostage Syndrome.* This fact, along with Anya's excited expression whenever she opened the pages, and the bedbound gasps Razarkha overheard when night fell were enough to inform her of the book's contents.

Regarding her own reading material, Razarkha had reached a chapter in her book regarding the desolation of Ante Tertia. It covered the events that changed the Plague Emperor's quest from an expression of hope and liberty into a destructive conquest of his former homeland. So far in their tale, the Plague Emperor had fled to Ilazar and latched to the Isleborn, accompanied by the Sulari Galdusian community that would come to be known as the Plagueborn.

When the Plague Emperor first arrived in Ilazar, it was but an outpost of the Golden Galdusian Empire, but the isle's remoteness allowed it to be swiftly liberated. For a time, the Plague Emperor and his people were content as freedmen upon the Isle of Dreams. If the story ended there, history would have remembered him as little more than a brief, unwelcome plague on a single Galdusian city that vanished without major issue.

Instead, a geomantic spellbinder named Atlas travelled to the Ilazari capital, Zemelnya, and attempted to assassinate the Plague Emperor. They crashed through his most trusted mages, and when the Plague Emperor's most loyal guard, his soul-bound friend, Conditor, moved to match Atlas in geomancy, the spellbinder applied his powers directly to the augmentee's rocky body, shattering him before his emperor's eyes.

The Plague Emperor was said to have impaled his would-be assassin on a thousand pikes throughout Zemelnya, splitting him the same way Conditor was, then rent his clothes in grief for a month. Some sources claimed to find him meditating within the forests north of the city, but none knew to what end. Once he left his depression, he told the people of Ilazar that they would no longer live in fear of the Galdusians, and that his father had provided him with seven great weapons.

The father he referred to was unknown, but if it was truly his blood father, then his lineage had a talent for magical production: The weapons he referred to were the soulstealers, dread items that granted their owners the ability to suck the souls from Ilazar's enemies, and even siphon the acquired souls' energy for themselves.

Leading the charge personally, the Plague Emperor and his seven soulstealer wielders led a campaign against the ascendants of Galdus. City to city, town to town, from the icy peaks of northern Nortez to the chilly ice sheets of southern Sula, no ascendant was safe. His followers stood with him in his vengeance, and none questioned their new emperor's massacres.

Razarkha swooned in wistfulness. If she could murder hundreds and be cheered for it, her dreams would be realised. A sting came to her throat unbidden, and she closed her book with a huff.

Rakh was mocking her again. He sneered that she had no friends, that nobody would ever follow her, that she was the most unlikeable woman in the world, and worst of all, that she'd gone over a week without washing. Nobody would follow her as passionately as the Plagueborn followed their emperor, and worst of all, she had no idea why. How was it that people cared about his pain and anger? What did he do differently to her?

It must have been some clever, Rakh-like plot. Her brother understood the secrets of sound-bending in his illusionism and must have sweetened his words to every peasant he approached. It was all a scheme for him to do as he pleased, to remove his only threat to his succession. For all she knew, Rakh had a bastard heir prepared, sequestered away until he had an excuse to discard his sister-wife.

Razarkha jolted from her navel-gazing when Anya Kasparov approached her desk. She scrambled along the floor and prayed that her shuffling wouldn't be heard over the creaking of the ship, nor her unwashed stench stand out amidst the salt and musk of the sea. When Anya took her seat, she raised an eyebrow, checked her desk for signs of tampering, then unlocked a drawer.

After that, she took out a letter nestled within one of her bodice's straps and compared it to a set of letters from within the drawer. Her blue eyes narrowed, then relaxed. Razarkha stood and snooped on the letters' contents from behind their recipient and noticed they all had a common author: Baron Giles Oswyk, governor of Winter Harbour.

The letters' bodies were of equal sincerity and value. They were flattering attempts at diplomacy, offering

Anya jewels, Arkheran minted coins, antique magitech, and illegally translated Yukishiman books to thank the young woman for her discretion, understanding, and continued patronage of Winter Harbour.

Anya's latest acquisition was an ascension stone made of polished malachite, which she currently wore around her neck. According to the letter, it was so the young woman's mental beauty could persist eternally. It struck Razarkha as odd that a nobleman with such a poorly maintained port city would somehow have the funds to pay an ascensiologist to infuse a semi-precious gem with the right properties to grant a spellbinder immortality.

Kasparov filed her letters away and locked her drawer, then briefly turned to Razarkha's hiding spot. She stared through her clear form, rubbed her chin, then made to prod the invisible woman, who sidestepped, ducked, and scrambled away from the desk. Kasparov frowned and waved at the air in front of her while Razarkha hid underneath her bed, then frowned. From there, she unravelled her clothing, put on some sleek bedclothes, and picked up *Unbreakable Bonds* for another evening of testing the bed's springs.

* * *

Snow crunched beneath Rakh Fel'thuz's feet as he entered the estate of Plutyn Khanas, the Lost Lord of the Flowerfields. Undead, cold-preserved servants silently milled about the gardens, tending to flowerbeds of snowdrops, winter jasmines, crocuses, and irises. Despite his official lack of a title, Plutyn Khanas had black banners throughout his manor grounds, depicting a skull burning a ghostly pale green.

Rakh cringed. It was hardly Plutyn's fault that his ancestors lost the Flowerfields to an upjumped dark elven torturer, but the sense of grandiosity reminded him of

Razarkha. Down the winding, flower-laden path lay the Lost Lord's manor, a straight-edged, rectangular homage to classical necromantic architecture, only allowing for curves in the form of engraved skulls.

It was solid marble save for the doors and windows, likely costing whoever built it a fortune in importation from the Crystal Palace. When Rakh got close, he noticed a pair of large, undead orcs guarding the door, both wielding battle-axes that any other race, living or dead, would be unable to lift at all. He tried to look away from them, but one made a thick, raspy grunt.

"What are you here for? Don't act like we ain't here," he said, somehow wheezing without breathing.

Rakh swiftly inverted his decision and acknowledged the orc. The metal-clad behemoth had one missing tusk, a caved-in eye, and a massive, crushed gash through his breastplate that likely meant he had no choice in wearing it. Straw-like hair crusted with blood hung from every space in his armour, and the only remotely stable part of him appeared to be his legs.

"You're a revenant?"

"We both are, but Notongue over there, well, he ain't got no tongue," the speaking orc said with a dry laugh.

Notongue hissed, adjusted his axe, and turned away. Rakh allowed himself a grim chuckle.

"What's your name, then? One-eye? Nochest? Absolute-bloody-mess?"

"Har!" the orc said. "See, Notongue, people can have a sense of humour about this shit. Naw, my name's Bloodmetal, 'cause blood's stuck this damned breastplate to me."

"Doesn't Khanas maintain you?" Rakh asked.

"Oi, that's *Lord* Khanas to you," the orc corrected. "He maintains as he can, but fuck if he can peel this off. I had a long time dying, so once I was gone my brain was fresher than my blood."

Rakh grimaced. "Don't you ever want to rest?"

"Lord Khanas gives me folks to kill, it ain't too bad. So long as I get to fight and scout out enemies, unlife is still life."

"Not all revenants would agree, but I'm glad you seem to be happy. I booked a meeting with Lord Khanas a couple of days ago."

The orcs looked him over, and Notongue made a few clicking noises, then put two fingers up, behind Rakh's head. It took Bloodmetal a moment to process his colleague's meaning, at which point he spoke up.

"*Oh!* You're Rakh Fel'thuz? Forgive me, I ain't seen you before. I thought your house had blues and whites, not blacks and purples. I heard about your sister trying to kill you. Damned if I understand spellbinders and necromancers. Marrying siblings just gives you mad children, don't you lot know that?"

Rakh hesitated. "It's to keep the blood pure. Apparently."

"Anyway, I'll let you in, jus' be warned, the guards on the inside ain't undead, and they got magitech rifles. Lord Khanas is very particular about he and his daughter's safety."

"I wouldn't expect any less of him."

Notongue opened the door and the first step Rakh took inside he was met with a set of very much alive dark elven guards in black suits, who patted him down on the spot. When the check came up clean, they backed off.

"I'll get Lord Khanas for you right now," the tallest of the group said, flashing Count Fel'thuz a broken-toothed grin.

With that, Rakh hovered in the foyer of the love-letter to ancient Galdusian-Arkheran architecture. The building was uninterested in height, with no staircases being immediately visible. Instead, high ceilings with paintings upon them dominated the upper half of the building, and alabaster statues of ancient necromancers dotted the marble expanse. Metal-meshed braziers burning the same green as Lord Khanas's self-assigned sigil lit areas too far or obscure for the windows' light to reach.

Count Fel'thuz took in the ceiling paintings as he waited. They depicted the founding of the Royal Electorate told from a perspective King Landon Shearwater may have called unpatriotic, if he was feeling merciful. It portrayed the assembled humanoids that weren't spellbinders, necromancers or seers as a mindless, malevolent horde that raided the Plains of Death while civilised necromancers died by the scores.

The Khanases were depicted as fleeing from the Flowerfields in two directions; one group fled south, to a gleaming city that represented the seer-owned Crystal Palace, while the other fled north, towards a silvery-grey city that represented Moonstone. The haughty high elven lord rejected these northern Khanases' pleas to retain their titles, and the next picture depicted these abandoned Khanases adopting business and becoming rich through these means.

"I see you can appreciate the other side of the story," an overly smooth, bass voice said, knocking Rakh out of his thoughts.

Before him was the black-and-green silhouette of an extremely tall, thin man. He wore clothing with simple cuts of cloth that hung off him so much that his arms acted like flagpoles, and a tasselled capelet ensured that his shoulders and back appeared twice as large as they truly were.

"My apologies, Lord Khanas," Rakh said. "I was just appreciating a well-painted ceiling. It must have cost a career's worth to commission it."

"Anything to rebuild our culture," Khanas stated. "Some necromancers played along with the new system, but not my ancestors. Not me. Yet here is someone from the new system, asking me for help."

Rakh decided an awkward silence was better than a misplaced word. "I'm not the person who took the Flowerfields from your ancestors. I just want to trade information, one great mage to another."

"Because one noble to another would be offering me too much respect," the necromancer said, and walked to an archway to the right of the foyer. "With me. Let's discuss information."

He led Rakh into an idyllic marble lounge, artificially heated with a magical boiler and filled with enough flowers to make Rakh sneeze. Tending to one set of potted marigolds was a black-haired girl who shared Plutyn Khanas's pale green eyes, somehow softening the colour with her youthful expression alone. The mood was somewhat undermined by the guards covering every conceivable angle.

Despite this, Plutyn slouched on a velvet settee and allowed his eyes to smile. "This admirable young woman is my daughter, Plutera."

The girl looked up from her marigolds and upon noticing Rakh, blushed enough that she dropped her watering can. She panicked and got to work picking it up, rushing for some towels.

"I'm sorry, father, I'm so clumsy! In front of a guest, too—"

"Don't fret, dear, it's his fault for distracting you," Plutyn claimed. "I understand that you enjoy seducing young women, Count Fel'thuz, but this one is too young for you. Besides, she already has an admirer, don't you, dear?"

Plutera's breathing levelled out, and she finally spoke properly. "My apologies. It's just you look remarkably like my lover."

Rakh and Plutyn glanced to each other, then the former spoke. "Is that so? What's his name?"

Plutera's cheeks filled with red. "Oh, he's— he's too dashing and mysterious to have a name, he goes by the Underground Ghost."

"An illusionist, just like you," Plutyn remarked. "He caused quite a stir and threw some of my operations into disarray, but since catching him he's become quite the asset. Plutera's subsequent joy has only confirmed that I was correct to spare him."

Rakh tensed up. "You're volunteering exactly the information I need. I suppose that means I'm indebted to you."

"You pick things up quickly," Plutyn said. "He's your son, correct? Now that Razarkha's gone, you want to play the attentive father?"

Plutera's expression switched from warm to bemused, and she tried to hide herself in her horticulture. Rakh took a seat by the Lost Lord and exhaled.

"I take it he's uninterested."

"I can't say," Plutyn said. "I'm his employer, not his father. He confides in Plutera, not I, and far be it from me to intrude on my daughter's love life."

"He said that you were a coward," Plutera mumbled. "He stopped waiting for you. He said he's going to find his own way, make his own fortune, and then— then, he's going to pay for a lavish wedding between us and we'll be King and Queen of the Underground."

Rakh groaned. "I thought as much. Lord Khanas, on top of this information, I need to ask another favour of you."

Plutyn took out a sachet of bhang-weed and some rolling paper from his inner pockets. "If you make it worth my while, I'm listening. What do you need?"

"I need to stay in this manor until the next time Rarakhi comes over. I won't do anything but eat, sleep and remain in the shadows. Anything you don't want me to see, I'll ignore. I know how it is, I won't leak anything."

Lord Khanas looked to Plutera, then back to Rakh. "Then it's time for you to pay up. Where is your disgrace of a sister headed? Do you know?"

Rakh swallowed. "I never asked."

"That was stupid of you," Plutyn said as he rolled his smoke. "Always keep track of the people you've made enemies of. It's the first rule of survival. Do you have any hunches?"

"Well, she thinks Ilazar is this great paradise for the independent and strong, which she of course fancies herself as," Rakh remarked. "If she's left the kingdom, Ilazar is a likely destination."

"Ah, I have friends there. Good to know," Plutyn said. "I need more than this hunch, however. Does the House of Selenia have financial issues? I noticed merchant and building taxes have risen this last moon. Why the sudden liquid asset seizure?"

Rakh's throat stung. "I can answer that. The Church of Eternity recently called in House Selenia's outstanding debts due to a... diplomatic breakdown."

Plutyn Khanas's pale green eyes glimmered as he struck a match and lit his smoke. "It sounds like you made a mistake you'd be eager to rectify. I can pull some strings in the Church if I think it's worth it. Some of the things the clergy are embroiled in make me consider cutting ties with them for ethical purposes. I'm a businessman, not a monster."

That was enough to make Rakh regret every donation he'd given out of politeness. "I see. Is there anything else you want from me?"

"I won't ask for anything further until after you and your son meet. To ask what I intend to ask of you before you receive your reward would be remiss, but there are a few problematic entities in the catacombs. Not only are certain trafficking cartels dirtying up my passages, but recently, an entire path has been blocked. I can't say what's responsible, but the runners I sent through this particular route never returned, and the goods never reached their intended recipient."

"I suppose you think I, as a powerful mage, could assist in scouting out and destroying whatever lurks in the catacombs?" Rakh said.

"I'd call you quick on the uptake, but the intent was obvious even to the flowers," Khanas remarked, taking a deep hit of his smoke. "If you can agree to help with these things, then consider your family reunion guaranteed. Plutera, will you help us with this?"

The girl was finally done drying her spillage. "I don't think he would appreciate it. He'd see it as a betrayal."

"Then I shall play the role of the tyrannical father," Plutyn promised with a tone Rakh almost confused for warm. "I'll say that Rakh happened to visit and foist him upon his son, supposedly against your will. You won't have to be the villainess that way."

Plutera's lip quivered, and she rushed around plant pots to hug her father. Plutyn held her in turn, and Rakh stood, tugging at his collar in discomfort. Whatever Rarakhi had to say, it would probably be correct. If a necromantic crime lord was able to be a loving father, what did that make him?

Upheaval

The Underground Ghost was projecting the face of a liquid shade runner for the Liquid Shade Cartel's Moonstone branch. Of course, the Boss had offed the real runner a couple of days earlier, some dark elf by the name of Vyrax. Lord Khanas had Rarakhi look the body over carefully, and only sent him on the mission once his illusion was perfected. After that, he presumed the body became part of the staff or the organ supplies. Even if he was in love with a necromancer, Rarakhi couldn't say he understood their nonchalance around corpses.

The young spellbinder slunk through the sprawling underground catacombs of Moonstone. The dark passageways were dimly lit by braziers that must have been maintained by the odd passer-by, but he couldn't say they belonged to one gang in particular. The Khanas Family, the Liquid Shade Cartel, the Malassaian Traffickers, even the Order of the Shade, all had some stake in these sun-starved, repetitive halls.

As Rarakhi neared a three-way crossroad, he noticed a set of directions splattered upon a wall in white paint. To the left was Fairtree Lane's exit, forward was the Church of Eternity, and to the right was the passage that once led to Icewater Canal's largest wharf, a convenient point for runners hoping to export.

Now it was known as 'the breathing passageway'. Despite knowing the cost of lingering, Rarakhi briefly stopped to hear the odd, wet wind that came from the rightmost path. Within the darkness was the sheen of something distant and slick, accompanied by distortions of the air that couldn't be replicated by illusionists. How any runner persevered along the path long enough to feed it escaped Rarakhi.

He settled for Fairtree Lane's pathway. According to the Boss, the Cartel had been taking the same detour. He scurried along the left path and upon finding a mould-covered stairway barely wide enough to fit his projected form, headed upwards. Sunlight broke into Rarakhi's eyes and briefly disrupted his illusionism, which he regained control of by the time he poked his head above ground level.

Fairtree Lane was connected to a large industrial estate, with factories both active and abandoned. His target was a former wine bottling plant for the Wintervine All-Year Wine Company; clearly attempting to grow evergreen vineyards in the northernmost province of Arkhera didn't work out. Rarakhi may have been twelve, but he knew a lost cause when he saw one.

The bottling plant stood two stories high, with crumbling, disused chimneys and boarded up windows. While the upper floors were grimy and poorly maintained from the outside, the lower half of the building was surprisingly spick and span, the only evidence of decay being a heavily vandalised board that once depicted an anthropomorphised bunch of grapes in winter clothes.

The Underground Ghost had a suitcase full of vials containing purple ink masquerading as liquid shade. Lord Khanas confiscated the true contraband when he had Vyrax killed and told Rarakhi under no circumstances was he to take the stuff, repeating the same to Plutera. He didn't personally see the appeal of liquid shade but given the Cartel and the Order both had a vested interest in it, it had to be good to someone.

In addition to his suitcase of false promises, he'd brought a set of hidden wares in his illusorily obscured woollen coat: A volley of smoke bombs, a dagger, and most importantly, a vial of everflame, an incendiary substance so volatile that sunlight could set it off on a warm day. He walked with certainty into the old factory, moving past a decayed foyer and into the bottling area, where crates of misted bottles were set tidily aside in the corner of the vast room. A few tables sat on their side against the walls, their legs removed and frames largely stripped of wood.

There were multiple exits to this room: The old delivery processing area, the defunct supervisor's office, and quality control. Rarakhi edged towards the latter and upon moving the paint-flaked door, discovered his marks. Sat behind a wide, horizontal desk were thugs of various races.

The apparent leader was a huge, hairy orc with tusks that reached his cheekbones, wearing little more than slack trousers and a metal vest. Beside him was a hard-scaled goblin with a set of circular glasses that made his eyes look massive even by goblinese standards, and surrounding them were elves, humans, and gnomes with various muskets and magitech firearms.

One of the humans, a black-haired, olive-skinned man, had a vial of liquid shade in his left hand, with no apparent weapon in his right. He had a twitch and was the first to speak.

"Lookie here, Vyrax finally made it. I was getting worried you'd been caught by those Khanas punks on the way."

The orc nodded. "It's a growing concern. Khanas has dirt on everyone and controls enough debt that his plants are doing a better job finding us than the Moonstone authorities ever could."

Rarakhi smirked beneath his disguise while 'Vyrax's' expression remained respectful. He put on a deeper voice and did his best impression of Lord Khanas's animation of the true Vyrax's vocal cords.

"I got past 'em without a hitch. Here's the shit, all I want to see is the colour of your coins," the Underground Ghost said, placing the suitcase on the table.

The goblin took the goods and raised a thick black eyebrow. "You seem a little unfriendly today. Something got to you, Vyrax?"

"I'm just eager to be paid," he said. "Nothing wrong with that, right?"

As the goblin opened the suitcase, Rarakhi hastily split his mind. One part of him had 'Vyrax' stand about in anticipation while his true self retrieved a smoke bomb and his everflame vial. By the time the goblin was done checking, he had the former in his left hand and the latter in his right.

"Vyrax, could the supplier have tricked you?" the goblin asked.

"What do you mean, Zik?" the orc said. "Is that even real shade?"

"Doesn't look like it."

The twitchy human hesitated. "Hey, Vyrax, you're smarter than this. You wouldn't have run this all the way from the Sanguinas Territories unless—"

Rarakhi flung his smoke bomb down and shed every form he had, true and false. The orc's voice bellowed amidst the confusion.

"It's that bloody illusionist! What are you idiots waiting for? Fill the air with musket balls, magic, whatever it takes to *kill that fucking Khanas imposter!*"

The Underground Ghost stood a chance of becoming an above-ground ghost. He lowered his stance, rushing out of the room as the air filled with gunpowder explosions and whizzing lead. On escaping quality control, he threw the everflame vial at the exit. The glass tube shattered, allowing red-green flames to bloom and illuminate the smoke cloud he left behind. He scrambled through the old bottling area, looking back at the silhouettes in the glowing fog.

A musket ball whizzed past his head, and another hit the floor inches from his foot. Suddenly, a beam of light powerful enough to scorch anything it contacted blasted through the old building's walls, missing Rarakhi by a wide margin but causing his everflame blaze to explode further, dislodging dust from the higher floors of the factory.

Rarakhi had almost cleared the bottling area when a harsh pain struck his right shoulder blade. He failed to suppress a scream and allowed his cloaking to falter. Driven by pure fear, he sprinted for the foyer, shut the double door on the steadily expanding fire, and reached for his damp, stinging shoulder. He picked out the still-warm musket ball from his flesh and grimaced.

"Shit. Fucking hell, I'm—"

Plutera. She'd fix this, her and the Boss. He steadied his shaking breath, he ignored the burning in his forehead, and he let his mind wander. He was in Plutera's indoor garden, stroking her hair and thinking of all the ways they could get married. Once he found this place, his cloaking behaved itself. The fear-dominated side of his magic wanted to throw every power at the wall until one of them stuck, but with the thought of his Petal in a small, tasteful wedding dress calming him, he kept himself limited to the one power that mattered.

He couldn't cloak his blood trail all the way back to the Khanas manor, so he would have to use the underground passage once again. The rush through the darkness was driven by instinct, the only active thought being to avoid the beast's territory at all costs, especially with a gaping wound. Whatever it was, it could smell blood, and craved warm bodies.

ND path, turn, dark path, turn, on it repeated until Rarakhi was light-headed. He could have been walking for an hour or five, but in the end he emerged from an exit just around the corner from Plutyn Khanas's estate. He staggered onto the grounds, dropped his cloak, and without warning, the dams holding his panic back burst. He scrambled to the door guards and screamed at the one that could speak.

"Bloodmetal! Help me!"

"Oh shit, what happened to you?"

"Isn't it obvious? I was shot!"

"Fuck, let's get you in."

* * *

Plutyn Khanas sat alone in his office, his thin nose wedged within a tome covered in Old Galdusian runes. It was a lounge-like setting, strong with the scent of bhang-weed and rotten books. He was attempting to make sense of a passage that claimed with enough arcana, revenancy could be achieved on a corpse that had been dead for more than three days. His concentration was ripped from him abruptly, however, as one of his orcish thralls shoved his door open. Plutyn sharply inhaled, then stood.

"Bloodmetal, don't make me regret giving you autono— Rarakhi!"

The boy lay limp within the revenant's arms, his teal eyes just barely open. Plutyn gritted his teeth, then pointed towards the hallway.

"To the operating room! Lower him carefully face-down onto the operating table, then keep him company until Plutera and I arrive."

"Petal…" Rarakhi mumbled.

"Don't fret, boy. Plutera will be with you shortly," Plutyn promised, and with that, his orcish thrall left with the boy in his arms.

Plutyn's throat tightened. With Fel'thuz lurking in the shadows, he couldn't afford for the boy to be in such a state. Plutera didn't deserve the panic, but two necromancers were always better than one when it came to stabilising the injured. He headed into Plutera's personal garden, where she was tending to the marigolds Rarakhi had given her.

"Father!" Plutera said, approaching for a hug. "You're done with work earlier than expected. I thought the Deathsport informant was coming this afternoon, did something happen?"

The girl's smile died once her eyes met his. Plutyn took a deep inward breath, then spoke.

"It's Rarakhi. He's alive, but it looks like he's been shot. We need to work on him together. He asked for you personally—"

Plutera pushed past her father before he could finish and rushed upstairs without a word, filling the Lost Lord with bittersweetness. He soon caught up to his daughter and together they made their way to the operating room, a minimalistic affair with naught but a set of drawers and a marble slab lined with a duvet and pillows, the sun shining from a singular window.

Rarakhi was still conscious, somehow, breathing slowly and shallowly against his pillow. His top was already removed by Bloodmetal, leaving his torn-up shoulder exposed. Plutera took the boy's hand and spoke in a soft voice.

"We're here, Rarakhi. My strong, scary ghost."

"I'm not so strong right now, Petal," he replied in a wispy voice. "When I was hurt, when I needed to focus my powers no matter what, I thought of you."

"The moment father told me you were hurt I rushed over. I'll keep you breathing no matter what, you know I will."

"Yeah," the boy said. "Hey, Boss, you probably want a report, right? The operation went well, 'sides from this."

Plutyn frowned. "You need to save your energy. Sleep for now. I promise you won't be made into a revenant. Certain associates are very invested in your life."

"What he means is he wants me to be happy, isn't that right, father?" Plutera interjected.

"Of course. Stay strong, Rarakhi. Plutera, can you handle matters alone for a moment? Prepare the scalpels and, if you can, perform *narcos* on Rarakhi."

"I don't want to be asleep for the operation," the boy claimed. "I'm strong enough to be there for Plutera."

Plutera stroked the boy's tangled black hair and smiled. "I won't think any less of you for sleeping. Goodbye for now, father. Return soon."

"I shall."

Lord Khanas left the operating room, and rushed through the marbled halls of his manor, heading to the guest rooms. He knocked on a door with a sapphire skull upon its knocker, which marked the residence of his recently acquired new system noble.

"Count Fel'thuz? Are you there?"

There was no answer. Khanas groaned and turned around. "Show yourself."

The spellbinder faded into view, his irises appearing redder than usual. "Did you think I *wouldn't* investigate the panic? My son is injured because of you!"

"Injured because of the Liquid Shade Cartel," Khanas corrected. "He willingly took part in this disruption operation knowing the risks, and from what I can gather, it was a success."

"You call him getting shot a success?"

"He's not fatally injured. Plutera and I are preparing to work on him. What I need *you* to do is stay out of the way until we're ready to share you with him."

Fel'thuz's brow wrinkled. "He hates me that much?"

"We cannot unload your newfound desire to be a father on him along with this trauma. He has his own life, his own commitments. You are nothing but unwelcome change for him. Wait for him to recover, and then, I promise, you shall have your reunion. Are you still willing to solve our little beast problem?"

"Provided I have backup, absolutely."

"Good. Rest assured, Count Fel'thuz. He'll see his father, even if he doesn't want to. His lord demands it."

* * *

The salty air of Zemelnya filled a small bedroom, flushing out the scent of soiled bedding and fragrant oils. Lying bedridden was Ivan, a spellbinder whose chaos-speech was once so effective that he'd taken to teaching others. Now he was a pale-haired, paler-skinned husk of his former self, his orange eyes scanning the area for something familiar.

Sitting by him was a young man, brown-haired and as soft-faced as a spellbinder could be. He had his share of Ilazari accessories, but in this moment, he wore a simple dressing gown of red and black. Like his father, he was a chaos-speaker, but even he couldn't make sense of the things Ivan said anymore.

"Weil," the middle-aged man said in slurred Isleborn Ilazari. *"The doctor's oils hurt my skin. They give me rashes. I think she's with them."*

"With whom?" the young man asked.

"The timekeepers. They're always watching from beyond this realm. They're here to punish me for my transgressions."

The man started to convulse, and Weil hastily checked through a collection of fragrant oils on the bedside table, each vial labelled in Plagueborn runes. By this point, he had an approximation of the routine. He took out the chamomile to calm his father's seizure, and prepared oil of bergamot to wake him up once he was in an appropriate state. Yet when Weil attempted wafting the chamomile beneath his father's nose, the convulsions continued.

Weil's face twisted with frustration. *"By the Plague Emperor— Vi'khash, get in here, quickly!"*

The door opened, and a satisfied Plagueborn woman wandered into the room with the urgency of a slug. Her clothing was rich; her shoulders were replete with feathery accoutrements, her neck and ears were accentuated by the nacreous inner lining of an abalone shell, and her purple dress had glittering sequins along its length.

"Whatever is the matter— oh, your father is seizing! What did I tell you, Weil? This is why you mustn't be alone with him. I need to be here to administer the essential oils."

"Administer them, then! I don't know what to do, I'm sorry, just help him!"

The woman rubbed her chin, then swiped the chamomile and bergamot from Weil's hands. *"It's a tricky business. That's why I strongly advise you pay for another month of in-house monitoring. I'm as concerned about your father as you are."*

Vi'khash rubbed the chamomile into his father's neck and upper lip, then made motions above his shaking body, while Weil's eyes narrowed.

"You said he'd be cured last month."

"And he has unexpectedly deteriorated."

"You said your oils were better and cheaper than any Yukishiman doctor," Weil said, his voice straining.

"And they are. It's not my fault you cannot properly administer them. If I didn't have to be here, monitoring the situation, then you wouldn't have to pay me for anything more than the supplies," the woman said, her tail perking up as the seizing finally stopped. *"You're good for another month, yes?"*

Weil looked at his heavily breathing, sleeping father, then at the woman applying bergamot oil to his nose. Perfumed misery filled Weil's lungs, and finally he answered.

"Fine. I'll find another three thousand credits."
"I thought you would."

Weil covered his face, and without thinking, opened a portal beneath himself. It was a great purple-red fissure in the floor, and though Weil fell into it as befitted the rules of the world, once within the portal's realm, he couldn't fall at all.

It was a deep, abiding void wherein naught lay but the many eyes and fleshy tendrils of the Great Rakh'vash, God of Chaos, or at least, one of its many manifestations. It didn't truly lie before Weil, rather it permeated everything he floated within; no matter where he turned, the many-eyed tentacles and numerous fleshy maws could always be seen within the unnerving expanse.

Weil closed the portal he entered from and curled until his knees were in front of his face. Eventually, he found the will to speak, shifting his tongue to that of his god.

"Great Rakh'vash, I don't know who to turn to. I don't know what I can do."

The mouths of every direction spoke in return. **"We are not one of our Rakh'nas. To confuse us for a companion is folly. Your father wrangled us well, but it is his time to decay, as must happen for all mortals. All must tend towards the disorganised. Your attempts to restructure his death will fail."**

"You can't be sure!" Weil screamed.

"This part of us is not omniscient. No god need be. But your father is subject to the laws of the mortal realm. He shall not ascend without blasphemous, orderly trinkets. If he did, we would sabotage his ascension ourselves."

"I consider ascension to be abominable, just as you do!" Weil protested. *"I don't intend to cheat death, I just need him back as he was, as the man I loved. I need him to say goodbye as himself."*

Tentacles slipped out of the darkness, surrounding Weil's body while making wet, fleshy squelches. *"Mortal minds are meat, imprinted upon by experience. It must warp and decay as all matter shall."*

"*That's not true!*" Weil yelled, and with that, he opened another portal, hoping that the Chaotic Realm's whims still placed him in walking distance of his home.

"Ah, you wish to avoid the truth? How predictable of you. What a shame that your blood puts you in contact with us. You have much more in common with the Rakh'norv."

Weil said no more and swam into the portal. The world's rules suddenly and brutally reapplied themselves, making him drop into the streets of Zemelnya, just outside his house. It was part of a large, blue-painted terrace close to Torgovyla Shipyard, and while it didn't stand out to most Ilazari, it did to a certain passer-by in blue and white.

A pit formed in Weil's stomach as the all-too-familiar woman approached. Captain Anya Kasparov was surrounded by mages whose powers couldn't be ascertained by looks alone, though at least one of them had killed on the way here, as a distinct scent of blood and sweat followed the perfumed woman.

"*Ah, Weil, good of you to drop in,*" Anya said in Isleborn, before tittering to herself. "*Get it, drop in? I was hoping to visit you* after *reporting to my grandfather, but your timing couldn't have been more convenient. Would you invite me in?*"

"*Yes, of course,*" Weil said, standing himself up. "*This way.*"

He opened the door marked with the number seventy, and soon enough, his front room was filled with Anya Kasparov and her entourage, along with the ghastly stench. Unpainted rectangles dotted the walls, a single couch lay in a space large enough for several armchairs, and a shelf stood, mostly devoid of books, instead containing a safe.

Weil offered his guest the couch. *"Would you like a drink, Captain Anya?"*

"I don't drink essential oils, I spray them onto my clothes and sachets like an ordinary person," Anya said. *"I'd like to discuss your loan. Provided you have the monthly repayment funds at hand, this visit will be short."*

"I understand," Weil said, and with that, he headed to the safe.

He lingered momentarily before turning the appropriate combination, revealing ten white golden rectangles with Plagueborn runes etched into them. They were marks, each worth five hundred credits. He handed the lot to Anya, who in return gave him a smirk.

"Very encouraging," she said. *"If we had more debtors like you, we wouldn't need to break kneecaps. Very good, Weil, very good indeed."*

Weil sighed with relief, and for a moment noticed something rippling by the window. He blinked, twitched away his tension, and concluded it must have been a trick of the eye. He found his words and addressed Anya.

"Captain Kasparov, your kindness and understanding is always appreciated. As I can trust you with such a request, may I extend the loan? I would like three thousand credits— no, no, four thousand, if that is acceptable."

Anya covered her mouth. *"Oh, Weil, you're so reliable. Of course you can. Just be sure to pay us five thousand five hundred over the next ten months."*

"Without question, Captain."

With that, the young woman returned eight of the five-hundred-credit marks, clicked her fingers and left the room, her guards swiftly following suit, yet the scent of death lingered. Once the sound of his front door shutting was heard, Weil drew his front room's curtain, breathed with an audible quaver, and wept into his hands.

His breakdown was interrupted when a woman abruptly came into being in the corner of the room. Her black hair was sparsely covered in faded purple dye, while her lithe body was barely covered by blood-covered bedclothes and a pair of stockings.

"Who the fuck are you—"

"I can't take it anymore!" she screamed in the Common Tongue. "I can't, I can't, I can't! *Give me a bath and perfumes and food, now!"*

Weil hesitated. "I do not speak Common Tongue well, you in Ilazar, you stay calm, you speak our tongue, yes?"

"Just run a bath for me before I kill you!"

Before Weil could answer, the woman hyperventilated herself into a state of faintness, and collapsed face-first onto his bare floor. As her magic failed around her, Weil soon discovered a suitcase, a book, and a suspiciously clean knife she'd smuggled with her.

She wasn't the worst person he'd let into his house. For the time being, he'd lend her his bed; it was the Isleborn way to show hospitality to foreigners.

Connection

A sharp, zesty scent permeated Razarkha's perception while the rest of her senses restored themselves. Upon function returning to her ears, she heard foreign mutterings from an unknown woman, and her view shifted from black to blurry. The aroma that masked the stench of sweat and blood was likely oil of bergamot; the pungency and proximity made Razarkha sneeze the moment she got a proper snort of the stuff.

As she scratched a rash the oil had given her, the room became fully clear. There were dirty men's clothes all over the floor, most some variant on red and black. While the outfits were rich, the fool who owned them clearly had no sense of pride. The lucky few articles that were hung up lay in a wide-open wardrobe deprived of mothballs.

The only part of the room one could remotely call tidy was the desk. Books were arranged across it according to the runic alphabet of the Isleborn, and a small square was left free for any letter-writing the room's owner had. There was one book missing, as it was in the hands of the room's only other occupant, a feathery-shouldered, purple-clad spellbinder with a self-satisfied edge to her smile.

"You," Razarkha snapped in the Common Tongue. "You're the one who put this awful, irritating oil on my face, aren't you? Get it off me now, give me a bath, or so help me I'll—"

"*Ah, stupid Arkheran brown-neck. The fool doesn't even realise she's in Ilazar. Hey, Arkheran pig! You speak Ilazari in Ilazar! Imbecile,*" the doctor jeered, her dialect a harsh, Plagueborn-accented rendition of Isleborn.

"*Perhaps Arkheran pigs have the capacity to learn Ilazari,*" Razarkha responded in proper Isleborn. "*You're in Zemelnya, speak like you're Isleborn, you uncultured swine.*"

"Oh! My apologies, I assumed with your repeated Common Tongue demands that you didn't know either Ilazari tongue."

Razarkha sat up. *"Ah, so if I didn't speak Isleborn, you'd be justified in mocking me? You have no idea who you're talking to, do you?"*

The feathered Plagueborn scoffed. *"If you're somebody in Arkhera, go back to Arkhera. You are nobody in Ilazar."*

This was enough to restore strength to Razarkha's legs. She stalked up to the woman despite lacking her favoured dagger. The purple woman stood her ground, her teal eyes meeting Razarkha's fuchsia.

"Are you going to hurt me? Try it. You're some brown-neck in her undergarments while I'm a cryomancer," the Plagueborn woman said, opening her hand in front of Razarkha. In a crackling flash, she formed a frosty gauntlet with an icicle bayonet stretching up from the wrist.

"Anything to shut cretins like you up," Razarkha replied, leaving a still rendition of herself while her true self vanished and took a step back.

Suddenly, a slimy, purple-red tentacle pushed the door open, causing Razarkha to jump and scramble behind the bed, making her projection vanish. The great tendril retracted, and in walked the physically withdrawn, pudgy boy who first saw her. What was it Razarkha had done? It was a blur to her; she likely threatened him, then he must have done something to make her feel faint.

Yet if he was truly that powerful, why did he tremble so? Why was his gait comparable to a worrisome teenage boy? His voice, meek and mild, only added to the incongruence.

"What is this, Vi'khash? I told you to make sure she wakes up, now you're preparing to skewer her?"

"She provoked me, young Weil. I assure you, a healer's duty is to protect. However, for the sake of my other patients, I must protect myself."

Weil voice deepened but remained shaky. "Leave us."

"You don't blame me for—"

"*I said* leave us, Vi'khash!" he said with a cracking voice.

"She'll just try to kill you too," Vi'khash said with a shrug. "*If you want to die, so be it. You've already paid me, and I'm only tasked with saving your father.*"

"Tend to him, then. Leave her to me."

The cryomancer let her gauntlet melt, and sauntered off with a dripping hand, shutting the door behind her. The young man walked around the bed and looked down on Razarkha with creased eyes.

"Don't you dare pity me!" Razarkha snapped.

"Sorry, I know little Common Tongue," Weil responded, his Isleborn accent thick. "I learn in book, but only small part. Great apology."

"*I told you not to pity me,*" she clarified, taking a stand. "*You will bathe me, you will remove this worthless oil from my face, and you will feed me.*"

Weil bit his lower lip, his orange-brown eyes shifting about. "*You can bathe yourself. I'll show you the bathroom, but I am not— I have not seen a woman nude, and it would not be right for me to see a stranger in that way.*"

Razarkha raised an eyebrow, then scoffed. "*As you wish, boy. When I'm done, I expect your servants to have prepared me a feast.*"

"I don't have— I had to lay the servants off— they're— I'm sorry, if you want food, I'll have to make it myself."

"Then do that, you lazy cretin! What are you waiting for, why haven't you led me to the bathroom?"

Weil's shoulders slackened. *"Oh, I'm sorry. This way."*

He opened the door with his own hand this time, though a small portal formed above his head. He gazed into it, smiled desperately, then closed it again. Without explanation, he beckoned and led Razarkha out of the room.

The upper floor's landing was simple and wooden, the walls' paint having numerous rectangular blank spots. Some of the bannisters were fashioned into the shape of tentacles, and occasionally, slabs of nasite could be seen resting on tables, sucking the daylight out of the surroundings.

Weil opened a door to reveal the bathroom. The only surfaces that weren't covered in dust were the sink, toilet, and bath; two taps were at one end, along with a bottle of shimmering, artificially coloured oil. Razarkha folded her arms as he ran both the taps, plugged the bath, and poured some oil into the steadily-building pool.

What was the boy doing? Why wasn't he protesting? Insulting her for her weakness? Rakh would have mocked her for her idiocy five times by now. His constant shakiness made her itch more than the oil on her face. The boy was no peasant, he didn't need to tolerate her, yet he did.

She rolled her eyes. *"I will take it from here. I can bathe myself."*

"Of course," Weil mumbled. *"I'll make you some kasha. You must be starving."*

Razarkha slumped as the boy left her alone with her thoughts and the noise of running water. While disrobing, she pondered over his behaviour, his swift acquiescing to her demands, his nervous tone, and all at once, her chest fluttered.

"Weil!" she called. *"Weil, come back, I need you!"*

The sound of footsteps swept back upstairs, and the bathroom door opened once again.

"*What is it, guest*— by the Plague Emperor's many daemons!"

Weil covered his eyes and turned his head at the same time, as though doubling his efforts would somehow double his chivalry. Razarkha smirked and turned off each tap without regard for her nudity, then slipped into the fragrant water.

"*It's all right,*" she assured him. "*You can look.*"

Her heart raced. Someone had finally noticed her beauty for what it was, even while she was a dishevelled mess. Yes, he was likely desperate, but this level of terror inspired by her attractiveness alone was exactly what she expected of Rakh on her wedding day. Instead, her dear husband was dispassionate as ever, never suffering a moment's doubt or attraction. It was quiet, miserable, and dutiful. This foreign stranger had taste. Better yet, he despised himself for it. Razarkha basked in the joy of being appreciated throughout his apparent struggle to remove his hands from his eyes, and when he finally looked, she spoke again.

"*See? You don't need to be ashamed. I know I'm perfect, but that's why you must look.*"

Weil awkwardly shut the bathroom door. "*What are you doing? I don't know you, you don't know me, showing me your body is folly!*"

"*Yet it's on show. I think you're a very good listener. You can cook me dinner later and make something better than kasha. I'm an Arkheran noblewoman, after all, I expect you to at least put in some effort. For now, I want you to listen to my story.*"

Weil folded his legs and sat on the floor, his back leaning against the bath. "*As you wish, but looking at your body makes me uncomfortable.*"

"*Why? Am I ugly?*"

"*No,*" he confirmed.

"*Then I'll assume I'm the most beautiful spellbinder in the world,*" Razarkha said with a snorting laugh. "*You want to know who I am, don't you? It's every man's dream to take in a beautiful, mysterious woman and find out what led her to his residence, is it not?*"

"*I don't know about that—*"

"*I'm Razarkha Fel'thuz,*" she offered as an answer to an unasked question. "*Though I suppose I don't get to wield the Fel'thuz name anymore. I was exiled, you see. Even though I'm the eldest child, and even though I show more initiative and desire for productive change to Moonstone, I wasn't allowed to inherit my family's position as advisor to the Selenia family.*

"*Instead, my younger brother got the position, just for being a man. He's a wishy-washy lickspittle who lets the common people walk all over him, and one day I tired of him being a disgrace to the family name. I challenged him to an honour duel, I even made it non-fatal for his sake! And despite that, he still cheated, he sabotaged the duel and got people to believe I tried to kill him. After that, he used the peasants' outrage as leverage to exile his own sister like the coward he is.*

"*After that, stripped of family name and holdings, I had no choice but to find my fortune in Ilazar. I was following that woman, Anya, and unfortunately, I couldn't hold my powers any longer. Thank every god there is that you took me in. Even if you're a babbler, you can at least appreciate a woman of refinement.*"

Weil paused. "*I'm sorry to hear you're a displaced noblewoman. I'm in a similar position myself—*"

"*Oh, it's awful, isn't it? Worst of all, my parents forced me to marry him, but we never had children together because he hated me so much. Instead he made love to every woman but me. He's pure evil.*"

"He sounds terrible," Weil said in a quiet, defeated tone. "Did you ever try to love him?"

"All the time," she said. "But he never gave me a chance. He wouldn't stop taunting me, either. Once, he even said he was happy all my children were miscarried or stillborn, just to see me suffer. What kind of monster does that?"

"A monstrous one, to be sure."

"You wouldn't ever do something like that, would you?"

"Wouldn't ever do something like what?" Weil asked.

"Mock me for stillbirths or call me unlikeable or frame me for attempted murder."

The boy's voice grew shaky. "Absolutely not, nobody's that heartless."

"Tell that to my brother," Razarkha said in a bitter tone. "Still, I'm glad there's at least one man in the world with taste."

Weil laughed shyly. "Oh, you're too kind. I'm a fool, truly. My father has fallen deathly ill as of late, and I've given up so much just to keep him healthy. I don't like Vi'khash, but she's the only person keeping him in one piece. She's a miracle worker, using her cryomancy and oil displacement, she's able to make her fragrant oils bestow healing properties. She'll restore my father to his lucid self soon enough."

"Fascinating," Razarkha mumbled, slipping her ears into the bathwater.

"I borrowed money from the Kasparov Family to pay for Vi'khash's services. Duke Mayenev may be the one Yukishimans and Nortezians negotiate with, but if it's connected to Zemelnya, only two people matter: Elki Kasparov and War'mal, the two biggest crime lords of the city.

"Anya, his granddaughter, is more understanding than I expected, but I'm always selling heirlooms at a loss and capsizing ships just to find the credits to meet her monthly demands. I'm not foolish enough to arouse the Kasparovs' anger. There's a reason Elki Kasparov is bigger than War'mal, and it's not his personal strength. It's said that every debtor to the Kasparovs is warned with a kneecapping, but after that, they're taken to Elki personally. Then he uses his ultimate weapon: The Soulstealer of Craving. He takes his debtors' souls and uses them to power schemes only the gods know of—"

"Wait," Razarkha snapped in the Common Tongue, sitting up with enough speed that she splashed Weil's bathroom walls. She shifted her tongue back to Isleborn and continued. *"What did you just say? Something about soulstealers?"*

"Yes, that's right. Elki Kasparov is so powerful in Zemelnya because he keeps everyone in line with the Soulstealer of Craving."

Razarkha's eyes lit up. The orcish collector known as Antique had laid claim to the Soulstealers of Obsession, Emptiness, and Vanity, but that left four unaccounted for. While a hairy, magic-challenged brute like Antique couldn't do a thing with his three soulstealers, Razarkha only needed one to challenge a polluted population like Arkhera.

She leaned over the side of the bath, allowing her chest to linger above her host. *"It's your lucky day, Weil of Zemelnya."*

The boy panicked and moved away from the bath once again, covering his eyes. *"Please don't do that, I'm not sure how to behave in front of a beautiful woman."*

"I'm not just beautiful," she said, climbing out of the bath and covering the floor with water. *"I'm going to free you of your financial bondage. All I need is your help getting to know Zemelnya."*

"*What do you mean?*" the self-blinded spellbinder said.

Razarkha's eyes danced over his tail, causing her face to pull into a smile. "*What I mean, dear Weil, is that you and I are going to change Ilazar together.*"

* * *

Rarakhi's shoulder stung the moment Plutera's sleeping spell wore off. She was the only girl her age he knew that could perform spellwork, and it seemed she did it well enough to save his life. The Underground Ghost remained a mere moniker for another day; his lungs filled with and expelled air, pain remained part of his existence, and the left side of his chest was beating as he'd hoped.

"Still a warmbody," he rasped, opening his eyes. "Plutera? Where are you?"

He didn't need to scan the entire room; sat alone, with a pair of knitting pins and a spool of wool she was forming a coat from, was his underground princess. She was lost in her efforts, her pale green eyes fixated upon every crochet. Rarakhi allowed himself a moment to watch her strange, wonderful expressions, then finally sat up and spoke.

"I'm back, Petal."

The girl was swift to put her work in progress down to rush up to the bed. "*Rarakhi!* My strong, scary, ghost, you're all right, you're all right now. Father and I did everything we could. He says that you shouldn't try to lift your arm and that it needs to be in a sling to keep it from dangling. You'll be out of work for at least six weeks."

Rarakhi's throat stung. "Six weeks. Shit, how am I gonna get by?"

Plutera's expression approached disgust. "Rara, how can you ask that? I'm going to take you in and look after you, do you think I'd leave you alone after you got shot?"

"Well, it's just I'm supposed to make my own money, get my own food, stay at my own inns, all that stuff. I'm a man, not some boy."

Plutera took him into her arms. "Of course you are. But men who get hurt need time to recover. I won't think you're weak. I think you're brave for taking on those cartel fools!"

Rarakhi smiled despite the pain. "They knew something was up, but by that point they'd already let me in. My only regret is I didn't get to take Vyrax's payment before running. Their checker was too sharp, I needed to smash and run as quick as possible. Their fucking lumomancer, though. He treated me like an old friend, but when I was revealed, completely missed his big ray. Just made the everflame worse."

"It sounds like you really scattered their plans," Plutera said, stroking his tangled black hair.

"It's a shame, I only saw one captain, one advisor, one mage, and a few soldiers. I expected more, but I guess it was only a standard shade runner payment."

"For what the mission was, you did well. Even if you failed, I'd still love you," Petal assured him. "My big, scary ghost."

Rarakhi couldn't hold himself back. He kissed his girlfriend, in the passion forgetting that his right arm was all manner of defunct. The aching and nausea killed his joy mid-kiss, forcing him to pull back and see that the operating room's door was open. The Boss stood in the doorway, his silhouette oppressive as always.

"You're finally awake," Plutyn Khanas said. "Plutera, why haven't you put a sling on him? Don't tell me you've been too busy kissing him."

The mobster princess reddened. "I was going to; he's only just got up."

"A likely story," he said, his eyes glimmering for inscrutable reasons. "Go on, Plutera, prepare a sling."

Plutera rushed to the drawers, while the Boss neared his secret weapon.

"How did the mission go?"

"I told Plutera already, but here goes," Rarakhi said, muting his excitement. "I didn't stick around to confirm the kills 'cause it was too dangerous, but I think I got Captain Metalchest and Advisor Zik. Also killed a human lumomancer under the cartel, and a few soldiers, probably high-level given they were guarding a captain. I couldn't get the payment intended for Vyrax, it's probably all melted gold and silver now. The lumomancer made the fires even worse, and though a couple were still shooting, they stopped not long after I got hit."

"Their lumomancer, did he have a twitch?"

"Yeah, why?"

Plutyn came disturbingly close to smiling. "Rarakhi, my dear boy. If he's dead, you just eliminated Edmond. He was a thorn in the side to both our family *and* the cartel. His liquid shade addiction made his magic powerful, but unwieldy as a hiltless sword. If he's gone, good work. The fool should have joined the Order of the Shade when he had the chance."

Rarakhi allowed a shaky laugh. "Yeah, glad to have helped eliminate a threat."

"Illusionists are generally perceived as weak compared to flashier mages like pyromancers and cryomancers, but you've proven your worth," Lord Khanas said. "When Plutera is done with the sling, I have a surprise for you. I can't say you'll enjoy it, but it's something you need to see nonetheless."

Plutera, as if on cue, returned from the drawers and began work on the sling. Her expression was sullen, and her eyes didn't meet Rarakhi's. Lord Khanas was similarly pensive, forcing Rarakhi to fill the silence.

"What do you mean by a 'surprise'? This isn't about my recovery time, is it? Are you going to put me down like an injured horse?"

Plutyn shook his head. "I would never hurt Plutera like that. Why would we spend all this time healing you just to kill you?"

"Then why are you afraid? What's the surprise? If it's harmless, you can just tell me, right?"

"No," the Boss insisted.

"Plutera, you'll tell me, won't you?"

"I'm sorry, I don't know what it is, just that it's coming," Plutera said in a flat voice.

Rarakhi narrowed his eyes. "Don't lie to me, Petal. I'm not some stupid kid."

"I'm not allowed to tell you," she admitted.

"Oh, fuck it, I can't refuse the Boss's orders anyway. Why bother being upset at all?" he said with a bitter edge to his voice.

"I'm glad you understand the situation," Lord Khanas stated. "When Plutera is done, you'll accompany me to the lounge, no questions asked. Am I clear?"

"Yes, Boss."

Plutera finished her work, then took Rarakhi's hand. "I'll be with you, I promise. I'll be on your side no matter what."

Rarakhi paused. She'd lied to him moments before, there was every chance she'd lie again. He was a fool to think the daughter of a mob boss could ever love someone like him. He wasn't big, or scary, or a man. He was just some spooky child, and a crippled one at that.

"If you say so," he mumbled, then stood, yanking his hand out of hers.

Plutyn glared at Rarakhi, then turned to his daughter. "Plutera, don't follow him. He doesn't deserve your support if he's going to be ungrateful. He'll apologise later, I promise."

"You mean you'll force him to apologise?" Plutera asked.

"No. He'll see the error of his ways. With me, *boy.*"

Rarakhi slipped off his operating table and followed the Boss to the doorway. Before he left, he turned back to Plutera. "Thanks for saving my life."

"Just go, Rarakhi, I don't want to speak to you until you're done," the girl mumbled.

Rarakhi's ache worsened as Lord Khanas led him through his marble masterpiece of a home in silence. Together, they reached the lounge that functioned as an indoor garden of Plutera's. Sweet, guilt-tainted aromas swept out the room the moment its entrance opened.

"You enter first," he commanded.

When Rarakhi obeyed, he instinctively scanned the area. For the most part, couches and flowers posing as potential carriers of allergens were the only threats present, however, part of one settee was too smooth compared to the rest of the depressed cushion. He knew exactly what this meant; he'd made similar mistakes himself.

He panicked and turned back for the door, only for the Boss to shut it on his face. Behind him, a tall, adult spellbinder with minimal makeup despite his fancy, expensive clothes faded onto the couch, his face a replica of Rarakhi's, save the deep eyebags, blood-red eyes, and laughter lines.

Rarakhi banged on the door as his seed-sower left his comfy seat to approach him. *"How the fuck did you let my father in? I told you before, I told you that I never wanted to see that worthless coward or his stupid bookworm lackey! Boss, you're not inept enough to let this fuckhead make demands! What's going on, Boss? Tell me!"*

"Believe me, he's paid his fair share to allow this meeting to happen," Lord Khanas said from the other side of the door.

"Don't tell him," Rakh said, having reached his son. "He doesn't need the pressure. All you need to know is I'm here, Rarakhi, as I always wanted to be."

The bastard boy turned and attempted to backhand his father, but was easily caught by the wrist.

"It's all right. I know you're angry," Rakh said in a shaky voice. "Please, hear me out."

"*No!* You threw me into Falmon's place, where I had no future!" Rarakhi yelled. "You never visited, you just sent that elven cunt with the stupid eyeglass to give me gifts you obviously never picked yourself. Erwyn gave more fucks about me than you ever did, and even he never rescued me."

"*I didn't know where you were!*" Rakh yelled in return. "Your mother knew where you were, Erwyn knew where you were, everyone knew but me!"

"Why the fuck would I believe that? Why would anyone hide me from my own father?"

"Because—" Rakh took a step back, then found his words. "Because they didn't trust me. They thought I'd follow my heart and visit you. To their credit, they were right. If I knew where you were, I'd have visited you in a heartbeat. If that happened, there wouldn't be *any* future for you."

The boy pushed his father away, then slipped into invisibility. Rakh opened his hands, made a short pulling motion, and to Rarakhi's shock, his cloak was seized from him as if physically dragged away.

"You're self-taught. It's obvious from how you hide yourself," Rakh stated. "As long as Lord Khanas is out there, you and I are stuck together, so let's talk. Do you know who your Aunt Razarkha is?"

"Some crazy bitch who spent all her time cooped up in the castle until she tried to kill you."

"She's murdered before," Rakh said. "The wisdom before Erwyn, Waldon, never got to train his own novice.

He'd failed to keep her pregnancies viable, and the last one, where our child was carried to term, it…"

Rakh covered his mouth, forcing Rarakhi to finish his tale off.

"I never got a trueborn half-brother. Yeah, I get it."

"The poor boy came out with his umbilical cord around his neck. He'd been strangled on the way out. Razarkha blamed Waldon, and one day, he was found as a red puddle in the courtyard. He'd fallen from the window, and while nothing was proven, we all knew the culprit. What do you think a woman like that would do to her husband's illegitimate son?"

"You could have visited me in secret. You could have done *something.*"

"If I knew where you were, I would have done, you must believe me," Rakh said, his voice cracking and his eyes welling.

Rarakhi looked away from his father. "What's this about, then? Now that mad Aunt Razarkha's gone, you're just going on a rotation through all your bastards, trying to act like you're a good dad? Is that it?"

"No. If I have other bastards, their mothers haven't told me about them. They would have grown up with at least one parent. You're a special case, Rarakhi. There's a reason your mother left you too. She couldn't stay beneath Razarkha's notice the same way a peasant could."

"And you're just gonna stay vague about all these reasons, aren't you? If you're really an idiot who never knew where I was, then I should really hate my mother. She *knew* where I was but couldn't care less that I didn't have someone looking out for me," Rarakhi said, his speech degrading into sob-tainted noises.

Rakh took his son into his arms. "She left you because she cared for you. She kept your location secret from me because she wanted you to be safe. Even Erwyn wanted to let you know that you were loved, even if he couldn't tell me what he was doing. We didn't leave you in the best conditions. We wanted you to be somewhere Razarkha wouldn't dream of exploring. If you proved to be gifted, we hoped the Order would take you in and—"

Rarakhi wriggled out of Rakh's embrace and shoved him away again. *"Shut up!* You don't know me; how could you possibly love me?"

For once, the count didn't have a platitude. His lips quivered and his knees became weak, but the sorry display couldn't stop his son's charge towards the exit. Rarakhi banged the door once more.

"Boss, I've done everything I can. Send me to kill more cartel goons, I can't stand missions like this. Let me out."

Plutyn allowed silence to linger for a moment. "On one condition."

"Whatever you ask, Boss."

"I'm going to tell you what your father agreed to. He's tattled numerous secrets about the nobility and is set to be deployed to the catacombs. He's going to unblock the passageway to Icewater Canal."

Rarakhi turned back to the broken man upon the floor, and after a moment's thought, knocked the door again.

"I still want out."

"If you feel that way, there's nothing I can do for him. Thank you for tolerating this."

The door opened, and Plutyn Khanas offered his soldier an embrace. Rarakhi held his employer and breathed heavily.

"Sorry, Boss. I know it's just business."

Lord Khanas put his hand on the young man's intact shoulder. "You spoke your mind. Though Plutera knew what I planned, know that she was opposed from the beginning. She knew you disliked your father, and said you'd consider it a betrayal. She never stopped showing concern for you."

Rarakhi's throat stung more than ever. "Petal…"

With that, the young illusionist cloaked himself and dashed through the manor, leaving the Boss to deal with his father's pathetic display upon the floor. He owed Plutera every apology and kiss he could muster.

Investigation

The notes left by Khanas's men left much to be desired. They were scrawled, misspelled, and even after transcription, the content's vagueness was practically deceptive. Still, Rakh Fel'thuz worked with what he had, and found multiple common threads regarding the Beast of the Catacombs.

It was consistently mentioned to have long, slick arms, squishy when struck but sharp as a knife when striking. Several accounts mentioned it having eyes on the underside of tentacles in place of sucker pads, and some mentioned seeing beaks upon its appendages. It was clear that the monster was some sort of daemon, same as the Royal Advisor's bards, writ large. All daemons, no matter how humanoid they chose to be, retained some level of familiarity with octopods. Rakh didn't understand what limited their shifting forms, but he was grateful for the tells.

The count rubbed his eyes with one hand and propped his head up with the other. His room in Plutyn's manor had devolved into a pile of scrawled notes surrounding a desk and a badly made bed, but thankfully it was time to leave the devastation and share his findings with Lord Khanas. When he opened his door, he heard steps to his left, but nothing visible to match the sound.

"When you're ready to talk, do so without hiding," Rakh said. "I'm sorry for pushing myself on you. That's why you need to make the first move."

His vanished son refused to answer. He'd been playing this game with him for over a week, and wasn't about to give in. If Rakh tried too hard, the boy would pull away. He had to treat him as he treated all family: As an opponent in a game.

He headed to Plutyn Khanas's office, locatable by the constantly emitted aroma of bhang-weed. Despite how much he smoked, Lord Khanas never seemed to mellow out from the stuff, to Rakh's chagrin. He used the skull-shaped knocker and waited.

"Who is it?"

"Rakh. I wanted to give you a progress report."

The necromancer paused. "Then by all means, come in."

Rakh entered to find Plutyn Khanas reading a book, glancing at the pale corpse of a high elf he'd made stand, then checking back with the book, a simple paper smoke sticking out the side of his mouth. Laid next to the book on his desk was a vial of inky purple fluid and numerous scalpels.

"Well? Make it quick."

"What are you working on?" Rakh asked. "If my suspicions are correct, undead soldiers could be rather useful in removing the Beast of the Catacombs."

"You don't need to know what *I'm* working on. In our arrangement, you report to me. Get reporting, I'm in the middle of something."

Rakh glanced at the swaying, gaping high elf, then snapped back to attention. "Of course, my apologies, Lord Khanas. The Beast of the Catacombs is likely a daemon. Given their appetite for humanoid flesh, providing it with corpses should be ample distraction."

"A distraction while you do what, exactly?" Khanas asked. "The reports have it at the size of a small house. It's difficult to keep a daemon the size of a human down, how can we hope take advantage of a distraction?"

"This is where my being a 'new system' noble could help. I could go back to the castle and ask Erwyn what he knows. Admittedly, he's a biologist, not a daemonologist, but surely he—"

"No," Khanas said. "If you were to ask about these matters, how would Erwyn respond? What is it wisdoms are best known for?"

"Learning," Rakh said in a flat tone. "I understand you don't want him asking questions, but don't you think that the time I've spent away from the castle would already attract suspicion? I have to return to the castle at some point."

"Yes, you do," Plutyn replied, raising his left hand, then using his right to pick up a scalpel and cut open the wrist of his corpse once it presented it to him. "However, I'd prefer it if you returned saying 'I had a wonderful break with my son' instead of 'I'm helping an organised criminal clear a smuggling passage, could you offer me advice on how to do that?'."

"I wouldn't word it like that!"

"The last thing we want is to reignite official interest in the catacombs after they've enjoyed such a long tenure of neglect from the new system," Khanas explained, rubbing the purple liquid into the gash. "I suggest you find another way to research daemonic weaknesses."

"But I have no leads on daemons—"

Rakh stopped himself and formulated a question. There was a slim chance of it yielding anything worthwhile, but with Khanas remaining obstinate, there was no other choice.

"Lord Khanas, were you watching when Razarkha and I duelled, by any chance?"

"Of course," he said, jumping as the zombie's eyes began to glow brighter than usual. "Oh, that's a good indicator. You, can you speak?"

"Can... speak..." the zombie droned.

Rakh tried to get a word in edgewise, but Khanas was first to speak. "Five days dead and you're able to speak. Your soul must have returned, this cannot be your brain alone. Fascinating. I wonder what other applications—"

The zombie felt its own face and screamed. "No! Put me back, put me back, *put me back!*"

Khanas lowered his hands and let the body slump once more. "Back to planning. Sorry, what were you saying?"

"You were watching the day of my duel. Did you by chance have a man following Royal Advisor Quira Abraxas?"

"Not closely. With her daemons around, one can't push their luck."

Rakh shrugged. "That's fine. All I need to know is the inn she stayed at."

Plutyn frowned and checked his desk, giving Rakh a moment to glance at the fallen body. It was still twitching from whatever arcane energies Lord Khanas had applied, thankfully without a word to say. The body may have once been a gangster, but gangsters had parents too. The thought of Rarakhi becoming another canvas for his lord to practice upon made Rakh shudder.

"Here," Khanas said, jolting Rakh into the room. "The inn she stayed at was the *Moon's Vein Free House,* within the industrial district. If you intend to visit, stay away from the Fairtree Lane Industrial Estate. Our men are currently conducting reclamation operations enabled by your son's work."

Rakh hesitated. "Lord Khanas, may I ask you a question?"

"Ask, but I'm not obligated to answer truthfully."

"What do you think of Rarakhi? I've noticed you two are close. Do you truly want him to reconcile with me?"

Plutyn sucked the last of his smoke's fumes. "I fully expect to be his father by law. Plutera and he are inseparable, so I imagine it'll happen the moment he turns sixteen. Most men have a father and a father by law at some point. And most fathers worth a fig aren't threatened by their legal equivalent."

"As you say," Rakh muttered. "Do you think Rarakhi will ever love me?"

"I can't say. I'm a necromancer, not a telepath," Plutyn said, his tone shortening.

"Thank you for the information," Rakh concluded, leaving the necromancer to his corpse.

With that, he headed into the industrial district, where the snow was shovelled into regular piles due to all the grit-salt being saved for the central district. There was a team of orcish builders working hard on the Fairtree Lane Industrial Estate, renovating a burnt-out wine bottling plant of some sort, and just past said estate lay the Industrial Crawl, as Rakh called it.

It was a set of taverns and inns used by factory workers celebrating their imminent days off, an area that was simultaneously homely and deeply unsafe. A few homeless people haunted the crawl, sleeping in the day and begging uninhibited drunkards for coppers at night. The third pub along the crawl was the *Moon's Vein Free House.* While it was no good for women or music, it had a set of board games for the inebriated to attempt, and cards for the gamblers of Moonstone.

Rakh entered to the warmth of a crackling hearth and the smiles of the regulars. A weak-chinned dark elf in his twenties approached him from the bar with a wide smile.

"Holy shit, Rakh, buddy, it's been too long! I heard rumours you ain't been seen in the castle. People think you're dead. What's the story?"

"Hey, Jakhal," Rakh said. "I'm sorry I haven't been around. You haven't been visiting every night hoping I'd be here to play *Wraiths and Wyverns* with you, I hope."

"I— 'course not, buddy, I'm not that desperate!" he claimed.

"Well, I can't stay long, I'm actually doing a bit of snooping," Rakh said, heading to the bar. "Sontaro, two Summertree Reds!"

The dark elf at the bar was an older man who'd spent too many days eating dumplings without walking them off. He gave Rakh a smile and filled two wine glasses.

"Nice to see you, Count Fel'thuz," he said.

"Please, call me Rakh," he said, taking the glass while handing the other to Jakhal. "Were you here on the day I beat Razarkha?"

"'course! I needed to celebrate that bitch finally being put in her place!" the young man said with a forced chuckle. "Remembering it makes me laugh. You just appeared behind her and *thwack,* the fight was over. You had me going, though, I was ready to kill that bitch myself when you pretended to die."

Rakh's throat tightened. "I'm sorry I did that. I had to lull Razarkha into a state of pride and security. When the people became enraged, I had to exploit her panic instead. Seeing everyone's anger humbled me."

"You're a good guy," Jakhal said. "Pretty much the only politician I can think of who isn't a corrupt, incestuous fuck. Well, I guess you married your sister but that wasn't your choice, was it?"

The world darkened for Rakh. Memories of Rarakhi's conception, the deal he had with Plutyn Khanas, and his failure to look out for the people against the Church of Eternity danced before him as refutations to the elf's bold claims.

"Thank you for your kindness," Rakh said. "Anyway, I'm snooping, as I said. Did anything interesting happen here while you were celebrating?"

"'course! You know how there were a bunch of snooty nobles who came to watch your fight? Turns out one of them ain't so snooty after all. 'twas a spellbinder, well, maybe a spellbinder. Not built like one at all. Tits you could bury your face in, and I don't recall seeing any tail, but what else 'sides from orcs are that tall?"

"Necromancers share our height but have shorter tails, though if I recall correctly, the Royal Advisor's family has a tradition of docking their tails," Rakh replied. "Was she with three daemons by any chance?"

"Yup, you got it!" Jakhal said. "They were quite nice actually, brought this place to life for the night, even if they sang about the sea and lords I ain't even heard of. They all spoke as one too, utterly strange women. Still, if one of them offered to kiss me, I wouldn't say nay."

"Good to know," Rakh said with a smirk. "Don't worry, your secret's safe with me."

The dark elf's voice tightened. "What secret? I know you like your women too, and those daemons were pretty, I swear it. I'm not the only one who's into 'em, I can't be."

"Of course," Rakh replied. "Was there any point where the daemons seemed afraid or panicked? Perhaps uneasy about something?"

"Come to think of it, there *was* something like that," Jakhal remarked. "Later on, this tall, blonde-haired, blue-eyed human, probably Yookie or something came into the pub. The daemon bards all screamed, fused together into one big woman and hid in the corner away from the man. I tried to comfort 'em, but they kept babbling about knotweed or something. Anyway, the noblewoman with the tits didn't like me helping and told me to stay clear while she tended to 'em."

"To be fair to her, in your mind 'comforting' women means tricking them into going home with you," Rakh pointed out.

"How else am I supposed to get laid?"

"Be honest. Women like lovemaking too, that's what you're forgetting. You don't need to pull any tricks or illusions, just see if they want it as much as you. Don't try to lower their guard while they're vulnerable, it's scummy," Rakh advised.

The elf's tone grew defensive. "Scummy? You saying I'm scummy?"

"I'm saying you're better than this," Rakh said. "Let's change the topic. So, the Yookie came into the bar and the daemons panicked and talked about knotweed. Did they say anything else?"

Jakhal squinted as he recalled. "Something about mortals betraying existence? Really weird shit."

Rakh frowned. "Well, it's a terrible lead, but it's the only one I have."

"What you talking about?"

Count Fel'thuz stood, downed his wine, then patted Jakhal on the back. "Don't be down-hearted just because I pointed out your gauche behaviour. Why not try to find women who enjoy board games like you? Are there any women at the musket factory?"

"Nope."

"You'll get there, Jakhal. I've got to get going. See you around!" Rakh said, then swiftly dashed from the *Moon's Vein*.

His next destination was the Yookietown of Moonstone. Yukishimans were an odd bunch; their home nation had very few settlements, but those few were massive city-states the size of kingdoms. They lacked magic as Arkherans knew it but had wrought a comparable replacement: Advanced technology.

It was through their scientific prowess that Rakh figured out how to apply his magic to sound as well as light, but much of Yukishiman culture was a mystery to him. If the tales were true, they had vehicles that acted as horseless carriages, rifles that could shoot in bursts when the trigger was held, and bombs that rendered their lack of magic irrelevant.

Despite this, some Yukishimans chose to live in Arkhera over their homeland. They brought fragments of their technology with them, leading to prosperous, yet segregated areas known as Yookietowns. The humans that lived in these districts tended to be pale skinned, blonde, blue-eyed and freckled. Their elves, meanwhile, were generally light-haired with pale red eyes; Lady Kagura's bloodline likely received a dash of Yukishiman at some point. Perhaps it was their anti-magical nature that frightened Quira's bards. Arcane magic and the magic of the Rakh'vash were cousins at best, but it was the best hypothesis Rakh had.

Moonstone's Yookietown was gritted efficiently, the immigrant population taking it upon themselves to do what city taxes couldn't. Their buildings were mostly multi-story terraces, though there were manors with sprawling winter gardens dotted amidst the urbanity. A large hall marked with a wide, curved roof stood as a landmark, with a statue of a tall, beautiful woman standing vigil by the doorway. If Rakh recalled correctly, this was a temple to the favoured goddess of the Yukishimans, the Mother. There was a second god in their pantheon, but its name escaped Rakh.

Walking through the Yookietown's streets netted him glances from numerous humans in dinner suits and Wrenfall kimonos. While there was no *physical* barrier between Moonstone and its Yookietown, but there was a reason he didn't frequent most of its bars. Xenophobia notwithstanding, the price of Yookie commodities were downright extortionate.

Rakh picked a Yookie pub at random, finding himself at the *Sovereign's Shade*. When he entered, he was surprised to find that much like any Arkheran establishment, the primary aromas were burning wood, sweat, and alcohol on men's lips. There were tables with booths, and a square-shaped bar in the centre where people sat about with their tipples. Along the back were strange machines with single levers and rolling wheels depicting three symbols in a row.

The count slunk up to the bar, sticking out like a snake in a mouse enclosure. The bar chairs were as accommodating for his tail as he could hope, and he sat by a woman with long ginger hair and freckles. She wore dark dress trousers and a buttoned-up shirt, along with bright red lipstick and dark eyeshadow.

"Got bored of prowling the Arkheran establishments, then?" she asked.

"Oh, you know who I am?" Rakh replied.

"No, you could be *any* black-and-purple spellbinder with a proclivity for bar crawling," she replied with a sly grin.

"Unfortunately, I can't say the same for you," Rakh replied. "What's your name?"

The woman brushed her hair back. "I'm Heeyun. I'm surprised I haven't seen you here sooner, the Yookie bar scene is far better than the brown-necker one. The only reason a Yookie would go to your side of the city is to save money. I suppose there's more variety for conquests if you're that way inclined."

"Believe me, you haven't lived until you've made love to a seer. They challenge you like nothing else because they've already anticipated so much," Rakh said with a laugh. "Well, as much as I'd love to sit and chat, I'm actually here on business."

"Oh, what a shame, I won't get to be ravished by a scary-looking snake man," Heeyun scoffed. "What's your oh-so-important business?"

"I was wondering if there's anyone in this side of the city that knows why daemons fear Yukishimans so much."

Heeyun gave Rakh a blank stare, then burst into laughter so loud that she attracted confused gazes. "You're joking, right? You think it's that big of a secret? This is why we call you Arkherans brown-neckers. Heads firmly stuck up their asses."

Rakh felt blood rushing to his face. "It might be obvious to you, but we Arkherans can't learn unless we ask."

"Of course. The big secret of Yukishima that isn't exactly a secret is the Thread. It's some strange golden stuff that eats magic. Some people can get so much of it that it turns their eyes gold. Those folks are called kogane. Anyway, thread eats magic, makes us resistant to the cold, and sometimes we stick it in engines so they run with arcane fuel. If I recall correctly, it kills all immortals. Daemons, angels, whatever the other two sorts are called, kills them dead."

Rakh cringed as he weighed his words. "And if I wanted to acquire some loose thread, how would I go about this?"

"Hold it, I thought you *weren't* being lady-killer tonight!" she jested. "The Thread sticks to vital organs. Either you buy it for a lifetime of debt, or you kill a Yukishiman and take their guts out. I don't know how you brown-neckers do justice, but over here, you don't get away with murder."

Rakh stammered. "I just wanted to know how to acquire it, I don't intend to murder anyone."

"Of course, of course. I must say, for a famed womaniser you're pretty terrible with women. Then again I don't imagine you're pumping your usual conquests for information."

"If I'm interrogating them it's for facts of a much more personal nature," Rakh replied.

"My vital organs are about as personal as it gets!" Heeyun said with a chuckle. "So, what's the deal? You looking to kill a daemon?"

"Something like that, yes."

"Best of luck. In Yukishima our leaders stick to leading. They leave the fighting to the people who can afford to die."

Rakh declined to ask her why she was in Arkhera if Yukishima was so superior, opting instead to make his way back to Plutyn's manor. If the young woman said anything else, he didn't hear it. Through the city he travelled, past the shambling gardeners and guards alike, until finally, he reached the manor, where Lord Khanas was already waiting in the foyer, poised as the alabaster statues surrounding him.

"You were gone a while, Fel'thuz. I feared you'd lost your nerve and requested help from your wisdom friend. You didn't do that, of course."

"Not at all," Rakh stammered. "I've discovered a weakness all daemons share: The Thread. I don't know the full details, but it resides in the vital organs of Yukishimans. If you have a body of a Yukishiman spare—"

"Why in the world would I have such a thing?" Khanas asked.

Rakh's temples flared. "What do you *mean?* You're a necromancer, retaining the corpses of your enemies and using them is what you do!"

The boss clicked his fingers and a set of dark elven guards flowed into the room. "Revaluate your tone, Fel'thuz. If you allow me to explain, this will be easier for both of us. Easier for Rarakhi too if he's remotely fond of you."

As the threat forced pause upon him, Rakh realised the issue. The Thread ate magic; it only followed that Khanas's necromancy wouldn't animate a Yukishiman corpse. The brain and spinal cord would be the most affected organs of all.

"Do you understand?" Khanas asked. "All one needs to do is to think for a moment. If the same force that inhibits my necromancy inhibits daemonic life, then it seems we need some Yukishiman organs."

"How can I do that when you haven't retained any bodies?"

Khanas shrugged and maintained his flat expression. "You're in charge of this operation. It's up to you to create some bodies of your own."

* * *

Over the last two weeks, Razarkha had been flitting between resting in Weil's home, arguing with Vi'khash, listening to the fevered rants of the boy's father, and touring the city of Zemelnya with her new pet boy.

On the first tour he'd shown her the Credit Bank of Zemelnya, owned by a spellbinder so monochromatic that his skin appeared to be pure white. Nobody attempted bank robbery, so it was safe to assume he was impossibly powerful.

The second served as an introduction to the various establishments owned by the Kasparov Family: The Kasparov Pearl and Nacre Evaluation Centre, Kasparov Financial Solutions Limited, and the Kasparov House of Chance and Dreams.

The third was a trip to businesses owned by the rival family of the Kasparovs, a Plagueborn faction known as the War'mal Group. There was the Zemelnya Academy of Higher Magical Learning, the Plague Emperor School of the Healing Arts, and several train companies controlling routes to nasite mines on the Isle.

The current tour was in theory much duller, yet it was the one Razarkha had been waiting for. Nestled within the brightly coloured central district of Zemelnya, a large building with twisting, ornate, tentacle-like spires lined with ruby and amethyst stood amidst the terraces. To look at its entrance one had to face north, forcing them to behold the sky-piercing Plague Obelisk of Ilazar beyond it.

Razarkha grinned at Weil. *"Are you trying to make me fall for you? I love this already."*

Weil had an insular posture, as per usual. *"I'm sorry, Razarkha, I don't know what you mean, it's just the Central Library."*

"The Central Library of Zemelnya, home of the Plague Emperor and all his secrets. Don't you understand? In Arkhera, libraries contained all manner of banal nonsense. But here, magical secrets abound!" Razarkha called with a grandiose gesture, drawing bemused glances from passing spellbinders.

Weil hesitated. *"Actually, the predominant form of literature here is fiction. There are many classical Ilazari authors you might like. We are famously apt poets, with our ability to incorporate Isleborn with Plagueborn along with mocking use of Old Galdusian—"*

"Yes, yes, wonderful, but I want the forbidden texts," Razarkha said, shoving the boy aside and heading into the library.

The interior was enough to force stillness upon Razarkha. Rows upon rows of shelves lay before her, regimented and stinking of an acrid, alcohol-like preservative. Spellbinders sat in stoic silence as they read, with the occasional strangely pale, but otherwise Jaranese-looking human taking books out. At the desk, a smoky cloud with glowing orange embers floating within hovered, a set of deconstructed armour giving it some semblance of form; this was a Galdusian ascendant, somehow tolerated within the home of their ancient enemies.

Isleborn numbers marked various areas, likely representing the Ilazari Numeric Knowledge System. The first group of hundred was general, the second group philosophy, third matters of the gods, fourth objective studies, and on it went. All numbers beyond five hundred were on the first floor, so Razarkha made to climb the stairs, but a hand grabbed hers.

"*Please don't leave me behind,*" Weil said. "*If you were to get lost or anger the wrong man and I wasn't there to protect you, I'd never forgive myself.*"

Razarkha made to reply, but the ascendant at the desk shifted its luminous orange glare towards Weil, then spoke in an echoing tone that appeared to come from the surroundings, rather than the cloud itself.

"*Be quiet. This is a library.*"

Razarkha hoped to goad Weil, but the boy was already shrunken in shame. Teasing him was nothing like teasing Rakh; he never fought back and always gave up too easily. With a single huff, she took him by the wrist and dragged him towards the stairs.

"*Where are we going?*" Weil asked.

"*To the nine hundreds, history and geography. The Plague Emperor must have left memoirs of his—*"

Upon reaching the first floor, a notable aggression permeated the air, cutting her words short. Clad in blue and white were numerous cryomancers, armoured in ice atop fluffy coats and balaclavas, prowling the upper floors' corridors. Weil lowered his voice to a whisper before he explained the situation.

"*One of the sections is under heavy guard, but I don't know why.*"

Razarkha led him through the six hundreds and seven hundreds. "*Let me guess, it's the section I want.*"

"*I don't know, I haven't checked out that many books.*"

"*And here I thought hiring Vi'khash was the sign of an educated man,*" Razarkha remarked.

"*Really?*" Weil said, his voice containing a mote of hope.

"*No, you imbecile.*"

"I don't know why you have such a problem with her," Weil said, his voice shaking.

"Because she's scamming you, Weil. She's the worst kind of worm. The strong and capable are supposed to flourish, but instead people like her create a facsimile of service and drain money from hard workers like you. She's a tumour upon the Isle of Dreams," Razarkha muttered, but her agitation earned the attention of section eight hundred's guards.

"That's not true!" Weil sputtered without regard for his surroundings. "She's healing my father! She's providing me with medicine! She's capable, that's why she's flourishing."

"If she was healing your father he'd be up and about, speaking full sentences."

"You're going too far!" Weil stammered. "She's doing me a favour and that's that!"

The cryomancers had the pair surrounded in no time, one having already formed an icicle in his hand. He spoke a rough variant on Isleborn, muffled through his balaclava.

"If you two want to make a commotion, make it downstairs."

"What's all this in aid of? Why so many guards?" Razarkha asked, glancing at section nine hundred.

It was completely sealed off, with the bulk of the guards congregating near the only entrance remaining. On top of cryomancers, lumomancers with refractive armguards and pyromancers with black, body-covering suits were also part of the troops.

"Don't stare too long, little woman," the nearby guard said. "Turn your troublemaking selves around and don't breathe a word on this floor again."

Weil swallowed and lowered his head. "Yes, of course. Razarkha will leave too, won't you?"

Razarkha paused. "Yes."

The guards laughed to each other, then shoved Weil away, leaving Razarkha out of the physical altercation. Almost offended, she opened her arms.

"Why didn't you shove me too?"

"You're some idiot foreigner. You're no threat to us."

Razarkha simmered over this, then offered her hand to Weil. "Come. I've lost my appetite for reading."

Weil nodded, and the pair left while the guards jeered about brown-necked swine. Razarkha stormed all the way through the building, dragging her tour guide behind her until finally, they were out into the salty-aired streets of Zemelnya.

"I'm sorry the trip didn't end so well," Weil said.

"No, no, I think I've learnt something interesting," Razarkha said. "The blue-white colour, that's the mark of the Kasparovs, correct?"

"Yes, those men are likely part of their protection racket. The library owes many things to the Kasparovs, least of all the librarian's ability to operate as a heathen ascendant on the grounds of our hallowed Plague Emperor," Weil ranted. "I hate those abominations."

"As a chaos-speaker, that's natural," Razarkha said, poking his pudgy cheek. "There's nothing more blasphemous than removing your soul from a body that rots over time and replacing it with one that's eternally still and orderly."

"Exactly! Sorry, I'm angry with how they treated us. I just wish I had the power to—"

Razarkha put a hand on his shoulder. "One day, you will. Come, let's finish this tour. What's left? You said you wanted to show me something else tonight, didn't you?"

"Yes. Apologies in advance. I'm going to show you how I find money for the Kasparovs."

Justification

Salty waves crashed against the Sudovykly cliffs of Zemelnya's south-east coast, a name that roughly translated to 'the Shipbreakers'. Despite the precipice's height, sea spray leapt at Razarkha and Weil's faces as they watched ships pass them by on the Accursed Sea. Weil stood in a soaked white tunic, having lent Razarkha his red-black overcoat, but this wasn't enough to stop the former countess from shivering in the near-horizontal rain.

"You'd best make a fortune from these horrible cliffs, otherwise I'm going back to your house," she said with a huff.

"It varies from haul to haul. First, I look for ships with black sails," Weil said.

"Why black?"

"Aren't they the sails of pirates?"

Razarkha put a finger to her chin. *"Not in Arkhera. There are two piratical groups in the Sea of Wor'ghan that have sapphire blue sails and multicoloured sails, respectively. Why would pirates unanimously decide to give themselves away? What would happen in a fight between two pirate fleets?"*

Weil bunched up in humiliation. *"All the novels I read had pirates donning black sails, sometimes with skulls."*

"Novels are stupid. A true scholar reads history."

"Of course," the boy mumbled.

Razarkha huddled within Weil's coat and stewed amidst the whipping winds. Rakh was probably laughing at her, fucking peasants in their marriage bed, telling everyone how stupid she was. She couldn't argue with him anymore, or stop him falling for short, fat humans, or siring every kind of bastard under the sun.

"There! I'll take that one!" Weil shouted, pointing to a ship the size of a galleon with great black-and-white sails. *"Even if my thoughts on piracy were wrong, this should be fine. It doesn't have Kasparov or War'mal colours, so it won't come back to haunt me. Also, it's a warship, so the people on it are probably ready to die."*

Razarkha scoffed. *"Are you trying to convince yourself you're not about to murder these people? If I were you, I'd relish the moment."*

Weil's expression flattened. *"Perhaps I'm not strong enough to enjoy it. I know as an Ilazari citizen, it is my prerogative to be self-serving and powerful, yet killing brings me no satisfaction. At least I serve the God of the Plague Emperor."*

He made a staccato, terrifying noise that almost resembled pure Plagueborn. Despite Razarkha's familiarity as a Plagueborn-Arkheran, she still couldn't process his words, or even repeat the articulation he somehow managed. There was a brief stillness, before a great tear in the fabric of the sky opened above the ship, a rift of red, purple, and black, with myriad eyes within staring at the unfortunate sailors beneath.

As if pulling it further apart, a set of tentacles grabbed the edges of the rift, then, upon eight wrapping into reality, the rest of the great daemon's body slipped out. Razarkha had seen humanoid daemons in Arkhera; they were unnerving, socially awkward freaks that kept to their side of the Kingdom unless they were hungry. This monster was something else.

It was a falling, shapeless lump of flesh, tentacles, eyeballs, beaks, mouths, and hands, and the moment it crashed into the ship it bisected it with its weight alone. Its subsequent rampage was surprisingly fluid, especially within the water. It effortlessly swam through the restless tide and picked scrambling survivors out, throwing them into one of its many orifices.

Once the sea was thoroughly chummed with the blood of unsuspecting sailors, Weil waited for the pieces of the ship to drift to the foot of the cliffs, then opened another rift for the monster to climb into. Once the great daemon was safely back within the Chaotic Realm, Weil turned to Razarkha. She was frozen in place, a smile shining through her running makeup.

"You're perfect," she said breathlessly.

"I am?"

The woman shifted her tone in no time. *"You're perfect until you open that doubtful little mouth of yours. Why can't you be this great destroyer of ships all the time?"*

"I'm only doing this to pay my debts."

"Stupid."

Weil said nothing, and instead took to clambering down the nearest cliffside. Razarkha slowly made her way to the edge, fixating on the sea-sharpened rocks below.

"What are you doing? Why don't you portal your way down?"

"I am not on good enough terms with the Rakh'vash to do so reliably. Summoning a daemon that obeys only its stomach is simple, chaotic, easy to convince the Rakh'vash to allow. Forming portals that fit an agenda from one side to another is not the way of the Living Entropy."

Razarkha swallowed. *"I can't climb down there, I'll fall!"*

"That's fine, I'll do it alone."

"No, you'll open a portal for us both and save everyone some effort!"

Weil slipped his foot on a wet foothold and clung for dear life with every other appendage, then found his tongue. *"Unless you want to find yourself dropping into Nortez, Azraiyen, Jaranar, or Arkhera as the Rakh'vash wills, I suggest you follow me, or stay up there."*

Razarkha found herself smiling despite her frustration. *"You— you're— all right, I'm climbing down with you."*

"I'll meet you at the bottom."

Razarkha removed her shoes and clambered down the cliffside, with Weil several yards beneath her. On the way down, she regularly came close to losing her footing, but the threat of a sheer drop into gut-splaying jags kept her slow and steady enough to recover. She glanced downwards to find Weil already at the bottom, using his long legs to stride between the wave-stricken intertidal rocks and reach the gutted aft of the ship he'd sunk. She upped her pace, but in the process let both her feet slip on the slick footholds beneath her. With one hand desperately gripping a jutting piece of rock, she screamed in the Common Tongue.

"Weil, Weil, help, please, help me, help, I promise to be good!"

Despite the linguistic barrier, distress was a universal expression. Weil opened a portal beneath Razarkha, and as she fell, a tentacle reached out and caught her, wrapping itself around her body and covering her borrowed overcoat in inky black goo.

The tentacle lowered and gently placed its passenger on a rock close to its wielder. After releasing Razarkha, it slipped back into the rift, which closed shortly after. Weil gave her a shaky smile through his mop of sodden brown hair, and a pair of words broke through Razarkha's lips.

"Thank you."

"I'm just glad the Rakh'vash likes you," Weil said. *"He said he would only do it because of your unstable nature."*

"Tell your chaos god he doesn't know what he's talking about."

Weil didn't even attempt to chaos-speak to appease her, instead heading to the nearby shipwreck. There was an entrance already formed from where the hull had splintered against the cliffside, but the downside was that the potential treasure trove was steadily sinking.

"Four hands are better than two," Weil said. *"Come, let us plunder while we can."*

Together, the pair of spellbinders snuck into the partially submerged ship. The room they entered appeared to be an office. Old tapestries flowed into the water, losing their value with every drop of seawater absorbed, a desk bobbed with the tide. Razarkha raided it to find numerous gemstones and arcane crystals, while Weil rescued numerous oil paintings of the sea, fishermen, and war galleys from nearly-sunken walls.

Other treasures flowed from the ship's massive wound, and their way in was quickly descending. There was no more time to forage; the wading pair rushed out of the wreckage as quickly as their soaked clothes allowed, and once they escaped, watched the thwarted remains of some shipwright's vision slip into the ocean's unforgiving depths.

Weil opened a portal. *"Place all the treasures in here, we need to keep them safe from damage on the way back."*

"If you're able to reliably store treasures in your little rifts, why can't you transport yourself?"

"It's easy to open a portal to the Chaotic Realm," Weil explained as he sequestered the paintings into his tear in reality. *"It's not hard to find an object within it given my space is rather small. However, if we were to enter the Chaotic Realm together, any new portal I form from within could take us to anywhere this side of reality."*

"That sounds like an excuse to me," Razarkha said, passing him her plunder regardless.

"Next time you negotiate with a god, let me know."

"Shut up."

Disappointing as always, Weil obeyed, hopping from rock to rock in silence before starting his ascent up the Sudovykly cliffs. Razarkha tugged at her hair and followed, though not before imagining pulling him off mid-climb. The daydream ended when she remembered his weight would pull her down too. Climbing upwards, despite being defiance against all things' tendency to fall, was somehow safer than descending. It appeared that relying on nature as an ally was even less reliable than opposing it.

Once they made it to the top, the beaten-up pair of spellbinders returned to Weil's home. In Ivan's room, Vi'khash was rubbing oil on the old man's chest and face, making ludicrous mimes that Weil somehow took seriously. Razarkha stared at the sick chaos-speaker from a safe distance while his sea-soaked son staggered towards him.

"It's going to be all right, father. I've been working extra hard. I'll keep treating you until you can properly bid farewell."

"There's no time," Ivan said in slurred Isleborn. *"No time. The great darkness comes for us all. It comes for the very cosmos. I see stars wasting away, I see great dark spheres consuming their corpses and taking their place. My time is nothing to the infinite beyond. The timekeepers are coming for me."*

Weil's shoulders slumped, and Vi'khash spoke her rough dialect. *"He's delirious. He can be rescued; you know that as well as I."*

"I know, but it's hard to see things that way when he seems to have accepted his fate."

"How can a madman possibly accept anything rationally?" Vi'khash asked. *"I promise, this month you'll see improvement."*

Razarkha couldn't help but break in. *"What happens when the next month comes and he's still there, suffering? What about the month after that? How long are you going to lead this boy on?"*

"He is free to send me away as he wishes, aren't you, Weil?" Vi'khash claimed.

"Yes," Weil stammered. *"Razarkha, let's get changed and sell what we've found. I don't need you two arguing on top of everything else."*

Razarkha's frustration wrangled her tongue. *"I don't mind murder, or even twisting the knife. I'm all for usurping and taking what is yours, but* Vi'khash *is a wretch!"*

"Wretch? Look in the mirror, brown-neck," Vi'khash retorted. *"Your pretty face is streaked with rain-ruined makeup and you're wearing a man's cloak because you're too weak to wear your own clothes in such weather."*

"At least I go outside."

"Unlike some, I have healing duties that keep me indoors."

Weil was facing the floor, gripping his head. Without warning, he unleashed an anguished scream, opening a portal by the wall that thrust a tentacle straight through it.

"Both of you will be quiet! Vi'khash, return to your duties. Razarkha, get changed and go with me. Am I understood?"

The women stared at the damaged, writhing appendage oozing a thick, black liquid that seemed to be reattaching to its own droplets and, as a pair, let their argument lie. Weil retracted the tentacle, closed the portal, and let his body go limp.

"Now I have to fix the fucking wall too."

Razarkha backed out of Ivan's room and went into Weil's, where she currently kept her clothes. She flung off

Weil's coat and put it where he put all his others: On the floor. After that, she swapped out her slit dress for a slightly warmer, but still form-fitting dress with hardened spines about her shoulders and hips. She reapplied her makeup and stewed upon the situation.

Weil wasn't waking up. She'd told him blatantly, she'd confronted Vi'khash directly, what more could she do? She could just leave him to waste his money, but that would allow the cryomantic charlatan to succeed. She painted three trailing black spikes beneath her eyes, as if extending her magic usage eyebags. Not long after, Weil joined her, unbuttoning his sodden undershirt with defeat in his eyes.

"Are you going to apologise?" Razarkha asked. *"You destroyed a wall and frightened me for no good reason."*

"I'm sorry," the boy said monotonously. *"We have to go to the pawn shop, and I'm not trusting you alone with Vi'khash."*

"I'm not a monster. Do you think I'd try to kill her? I'm an illusionist, how could I possibly overpower a cryomancer?"

"Illusionists never overpower fellow spellbinders; they outwit them."

Razarkha faltered. *"Well, it's a good thing I'm stupid, isn't it?"*

"Let's get going," Weil said, throwing on another set of trousers, another undershirt, and another overcoat. *"I'm not in the mood to be strong."*

He walked out, and while Razarkha contemplated staying behind, it would be obvious if Vi'khash turned up dead on his return. Weil was the only person who let her stay with him of his own free will. His disapproval was her probable death.

She slunk behind Weil as they headed into the western shopping district of Zemelnya, home of the

Kasparov Pearl and Nacre Evaluation Centre and Kasparov Financial Solutions Limited. Their destination was a pawnbrokers a couple of streets away from the latter, a shop with window frames covered by reinforced metal and several scorch marks marring its stone-bricked exterior. Swarming outside were mages in similar uniforms to the library guards of Zemelnya Central, a sight that slowed Weil's pace.

"*Shit.*"

"*What's wrong?*" Razarkha asked. "*Are you still upset about that argument?*"

"*This isn't about you. It's probably nothing,*" the boy said, edging into the building with Razarkha in tow.

Various wares were hidden behind what could have been yards of glass, and the payment desk was as heavily reinforced as the building's windows, with a small opening where the cashier could be seen. Weil approached without looking, opened a portal, and dragged the treasures from his bizarre realm. When he looked back, he found a beautiful, pale-haired woman with cyan eyeshadow, a black-and-green malachite necklace, and an upturned white collar returning his gaze. He jumped and very nearly dropped his paintings.

"*Captain Anya, what a pleasant surprise!*" Weil spluttered. "*I didn't think you'd be extending your business into pawnbroking.*"

The young woman narrowed her eyes at Razarkha, then gave Weil a soft smile. "*I see you have a new lover. A tad old for you, but at least she could provide financially. Does she know about your problems?*"

"*I know,*" Razarkha snapped.

"*Oh, and she's Arkheran too. The accent's subtle, but it's there,*" she said. "*I'm so sorry, but as of today, the Yahontov Goods Depot has been seized by the Kasparov Family. I'm sad to say this, but old Yahontov broke my heart.*"

"What did he do?" Weil asked, trembling.

"Sold information to the War'mals for credits he hoped to pay us back with. I can't understand why friends must betray friends. You'd never do that, would you?"

"No," Weil said.

Anya's gaze became sultry. "Well then, you'd best find a new pawnbroker to sell to, but I hope you find one. After all, I'm always happy with how regular and painless your payments are. Don't break my heart as well, dearest Weil."

"Never. I'll leave you to it."

"I'm sure you will. And you, Arkheran woman!" Anya called out.

"My name is Razarkha Fel'thuz."

"Fel'thuz, how interesting. I thought I recognised your looks," she said, then looked away from her opening to stamp on something soft and wet. "You and I ought to have a cup of tea sometimes. Perhaps Yukishiman-style hot chocolate? Provided you have the money to afford chocolate, of course."

"Weil provides for me currently, but that won't always be the case."

"Of course not. Please be on your way, we wouldn't want any collateral damage."

"Yes, Captain Anya," Weil replied, and with that, he dragged Razarkha out of the pawnbrokers.

Once far enough down the streets to escape the Kasparov guards' earshot, Razarkha raised her voice. "What was that?"

"What do you mean?"

"Can't you stand up for yourself? You should have asked where your stupid pawnbroker was and demanded that a sale be allowed! Challenge that girl instead of just simpering to her!" Razarkha ranted.

"You're welcome to attempt it, but I won't save you from her."

Razarkha smirked. *"You should be grateful you have me. You may have to settle for cowardice now, but after seeing your work today, I have a plan on how to escape this rut."*

Weil's voice filled with dread. *"This isn't going to involve releasing a great daemon upon the city, is it?"*

"Nothing of the sort. Come, let's go home, then we'll figure this out. I think I should apologise while we're there. I feel simply dreadful for the way I treated Vi'khash."

* * *

Night had fallen on Moonstone, and Rakh was stalking the Yookietown, ostensibly looking for a good time. With him were a portion of Khanas's muscle, all high elves to fit the Yukishiman scene. Rakh was bad enough, the last thing he needed was a set of dark elves and orcs to act as ink blots within clam chowder.

Bright lights marked the richest bars, dyeing the snow with each flicker, and while there were still Yookies in three-piece suits and impractical dresses, the time of night had caused a clear switch from dining attire to dancewear. Rakh's first destination was a club on the very outskirts, the only Yookietown establishment he regularly appreciated: *Kirito's Coffee Shop.*

"So, who's the guy?" a lean elf with prominent cheekbones asked.

"It's not decided yet," Rakh replied.

"You're joking, you got Lord Khanas to make us follow you like you're a damn captain, but you ain't even figured out who we're liquidating?"

"That's right," Rakh said. "If we head out and directly take down a target, it'll be obvious what's gone on. We're going to act like drinking buddies on a pub crawl, discovering the expensive Yookietown life together."

"Yeah, this is a waste of the lord's resources," a shorter elf said. "We got our mission; we should just do it. You're an illusionist, it shouldn't be hard."

Rakh raised a finger. "There's a lot about Yukishimans we don't know. I'm going to test a few things before we get to work. I'll also be able to decide on a deserving recipient."

The group unleashed an array of sounds ranging from scoffs to laughter, and the short elf spoke again. "None of this is about who deserves what. It's about business."

"Businesses don't have to be unethical. I'm sure Lord Khanas will agree with me on that," Rakh bluffed.

Kirito's was a jazz bar with a stage open to all acts, as was heavily advertised on the boards outside. However, the regulars knew that the stage was generally populated by the same troupe of musicians in dark suits and dark glasses: A jazz band known as the Park Pals. Tobacco smoke filled the air and casually-dressed Yukishimans filled the seats. The fashion of the day was little black dresses for the women and white trousers with half-buttoned shirts for the men.

A fat, bearded Yookie in a white suit sat at the bar, watching the jazz musicians play, chomping on a thick Na'liman cigar as they completed another song to thunderous applause. Rakh recognised him as Park Jon-Seong, the manager of the band. Rakh paused, then addressed his men.

"Go off, do as you wish, but when I leave, you come with."

"Fine," the short one said. "But I ain't wasting money on overpriced Yookie swill."

"Try to enjoy yourselves," Rakh said, then shimmied next to Jon-Seong.

"Ah, it's ol' Fel'thuz. It's strange, I heard rumours you'd vanished since that duel with your sister. The girls here were starting to get worried," the Yookie said with a hearty laugh. "A shame, too, the boys loved the act you put on, even if they only see half the picture."

Rakh seized his opportunity. "I've always wondered what Yookies see when I work my illusions. Were they as convinced as the rest of Moonstone?"

"Not really," Park said. "What they saw was lots of flickering lights, your sister stabbing thin air with the conviction of three men, and you, behind her, putting on a great dramatic show like you were about to die. They stopped playin', as you asked, 'course, and then your sister went on with her big speech. After that, you walked right on up with your plank and *smack,* goodnight twisted sister!"

"I see. So, illusions rarely if ever work on Yukishimans?"

"Not sure, we certainly saw some strange lights, but nothing that'd trick us. Seems like if your arcane magic directly messes with folks' bodies, it won't work on us, but say a pyromancer set our clothes on fire, we'd probably still get a mean burn!"

Rakh frowned. He'd have to work this out like a regular street thug. It was little wonder Plutyn Khanas had crossed off the entire Yookietown from his viable territory if they were this immune to magic. Still, there were catacombs entrances throughout Moonstone, even beyond the city walls. He could work something out.

"You Yookies seem to have it all. You're even more orderly than we Arkherans. A side-effect of coming from an imperial nation, I imagine."

"Like feudalism's much different," Park said with chomp of his cigar. "Naw, there's plenty of troublemakers in Yukishima, they just get treated like shit, an' rightly so. Then again, the worst of us don't stick 'round Wrenfall, so maybe I'm not the best man to say whether someone's a troublemaker or not."

"You hardly seem like the worst man in the world," Rakh said. "Maybe the worst in Wrenfall, but certainly not here."

"*Ha!* Believe me, I've had my share of hedonism. No man gets to my size by showin' restraint!" the manager said, patting his belly. "Tell you what, though, there's a man 'round these parts so bad only one bar here'll take him. Even we expatriates gotta have standards."

Rakh leaned forward. "Oh? What got him thrown out from the others?"

"Harassing women, starting fights, talking shit to the owners, you know, general shithead. I think he's the son of some big businessman, living off daddy's money in an Arkheran holiday home, you know the sort."

"I do," Rakh muttered, the face of his eldest sister wavering in front of him as though a lingering remnant of her magic. "What barkeep would be mad enough to keep him around?"

"They guy who runs that shithole, *Bryson's*. Even new-rich brown-neck—er, Arkherans know to stay away from there. Sovereign's sins, there's only two sorts of people there, bitter old men who hate their wives and shitheads who got kicked out of everywhere else."

"Hopefully he gets what's coming to him."

Jon-Seong downed his mead. "I'll drink to that."

Such a person would be easily noticed. If there was one thing living with Razarkha had taught him, it was that unpleasantness choked a room and made its source impossible to ignore. Perhaps, deep down, that was his sister-wife's desire all along. If that was the case, her wish had briefly been granted by her attempted kinslaying, before being yanked away.

He had everything he needed. As such, he spent the next two hours listening to the jazz show, drinking enough to be convincingly jovial and not a droplet more. When the performance was over, he gave a wholehearted clap, a respectful nod to the band members, and downed the remainder of his wine. After that, he clicked his hands as he jived out of alleged coffee shop, then waited for the others to join him. Sure enough, his goon squad arrived in a staggered manner, with the gaunt elf speaking first.

"You learned anythin' helpful? I feel worthless right now."

"Your time hasn't been wasted," Rakh assured him. "We're going to a place called *'Bryson's'*, apparently it has a young man who's so unpleasant, nobody would miss him."

One of the high elves in the squad, silent until this point, spoke up. "Hey, so Fel'thuz, I think I know the guy you're talking about. If the rumours are right, the Malassaian Traffickers run girls to the basement at *Bryson's*. It's close to an entrance to the catacombs. Sadly for the girls, the path ain't blocked by the beast."

"That's convenient," Rakh said in an uneasy tone. "Perhaps we could— no, I'll leave that decision to Lord Khanas."

"Believe me, nobody likes those trafficker fucks," the short elf said. "Still, we can't afford to make waves in the Yookietown."

"I understand. For now, let's find our target," Rakh said, turning to the quiet one that knew of the catacombs entrance. "Can you lead us to *Bryson's* and secure the entrance?"

"Sure. Name's Malyn, so you know."

"The rest of you, hide out in the alleyway closest to the entrance. Leave the rest up to me," Rakh commanded.

The elves nodded to each other, finally content with Rakh's leadership. Malyn pointed out the entrance to the catacombs, a small hole in an abandoned, overgrown winter grove. There was an alleyway connecting it to the back side of *Bryson's,* which Rakh approached once ensuring his men were in position.

The only thing Yukishiman about the bar was its location. It looked like it was built by Arkherans, for Arkherans, a business decision so inept that it felt intentional. Despite this, the prices advertised outside were only slightly less expensive than the other bars in the area, and no regular Arkheran could afford to drink there.

While the building was heated evenly and the bar was glossily clean, a certain dinginess clung to the air. A red-haired human with one eye washed a glass, and a bodyguard stood at a door by the toilets, protecting something a nearby sign claimed was the 'VIP Lounge'. Rakh ordered a mead and kept his eyes peeled.

In no time, his target became apparent: A human with long, scraggly blonde hair that verged on brown. He was chatting with an uneasy, chubby man about his age, which wouldn't have been inherently troublesome if not for the fact everyone else could hear it. All Rakh had to do was linger at the bar and bide his time.

"Seriously, you ought to try the lounge sometime. The girls they got there are way prettier than any brown-necker, even if they don't speak Common. Think they're from some island in the middle of the Eastern Seas, Mally Lally Island, something stupid like that."

His portly friend replied in an unsure tone. "You mean Malassai? Johansen, not to be a downer, but there's only one way Malassaian women get to Arkhera without learning Common, and isn't a way I'm comfortable with."

"Oh, *lighten up,* Jensen, what's the problem? You can't even tell if they're saying no!"

The young man hooted with laughter at his own joke, causing the barkeep to call out. "Oi, Johansen, keep it down, will you?"

"It's not my fault this place is so dead you can all hear me!" he responded. "You should be grateful I'm here, funding your little lounge. Nobody else likes this place. Look, it's so shitty even one of those brown-necker snakes has stumbled in here. Hey! Hey, shitface! I'm talking to you!"

Rakh rose with the leisure of a cat. "You're talking to me?"

"Yeah," he said, standing up and holding his arms out. "You know that all those stupid feathers and long coats don't make you look any less weedy, right? The only thing you got on your side is that you're tall. Magic ain't worth shit on a Yookie with a gun. What else has a snake like you got? Being ugly? Disgusting rat tails?"

This was almost too easy. "I'm sorry, did I do anything to offend you?"

Jensen stood to take his 'friend' by the shoulder. "Hey, Johansen, I think that guy's—"

"Yeah, he's probably that Fel'thuz guy," Johansen said. "So what? He's just another snake here. You like duels, 'zari boy? Let's see you win a duel without illusions on your side."

Rakh smirked. "You want to do this the Ilazari way? To the death?"

The long-haired Yookie's assured expression faltered. "Not to the death, just— I'm a merciful guy, I'll beat you *mostly* to death!"

"And who here wants to watch that?" Rakh asked, looking to the other punters, all six of them, dead-eyed and uncaring. "I think they'd be grateful for the peace and quiet."

"Jensen's got my back," Johansen said, putting his arm around his social punching bag. "Ain't that right?"

"Look, you can get yourself killed all you want," the overweight Yookie said. "Your father's going to kill you anyway when he finds out what you're doing in that lounge."

"Oh, you have a spine now, huh?" he said. "You wouldn't stick up for me when I crashed dad's car, but now you're sticking up *to* me? Fuck you, Jensen. When I get back from beating this flimsy little snake into the ground, you're next."

Jensen fell silent and sat down, while Rakh folded his arms. "It looks like it's just you and me. Bryson, is it?"

The barkeep looked up from his latest glass-cleaning project. "What?"

"Don't worry yourself. I'll take this outside."

"Thanks," he said. "So long as it doesn't come back to me."

With that, Rakh led his target outside, and the moment he was beyond the premises, the fool swung a dreadful, overcommitted hook. Rakh stepped backwards and tripped him up, then put his plan into motion. He ran down the street while Johansen was busy picking himself up and darted into the alleyway that led behind *Bryson's*. As he'd hoped, four of his five men were waiting, knuckle-dusters at the ready. When Johansen inevitably came charging after Rakh, the illusionist tripped him up one last time.

"Stop doing that, you son of a bitch!" he screamed from the floor, apparently unaware of his situation.

"I'd apologise, but that'd be offering you too much respect," Rakh said, backing from the downed Yookie and clicking his fingers. "Liquidate away, men."

Johansen couldn't get up in time. The elves left the shadows and surrounded him, thwarting every attempt at retaliation he made. As he was kicked and stamped upon, as partial sentences were cut off time and time again, Rakh found himself smiling. In that moment, he knew what it meant to be Razarkha.

Execution

The scent of perfumed death consumed Plutyn Khanas's operating room. The Lost Lord and his daughter were experimenting with the thread-covered guts of Johansen with multiple non-Yukishiman corpses laid out nearby, while Rakh and Rarakhi stood in the corner, of little use to anyone. Plutyn took a piece of the cretin's liver, whose lobes were lined with shimmering golden strands, and placed it in Plutera's gloved hands.

"Apply this piece of liver to Marix's, then attempt to raise him," Plutyn commanded.

Plutera nodded, and as she cut open the body, Rakh finally engaged with the situation.

"I see what you're trying," he said. "If we can transfer some of the thread into a body without fully compromising it, we may be able to send undead into the catacombs to deal with the daemon, correct?"

Plutyn frowned. "Please refrain from statements of the obvious. I'm an artist, not a butcher, and my craft requires concentration."

"Yeah, be quiet, he'll talk to you when he's free," Rarakhi added. "You're not a captain, just some upper-class consultant."

Rakh groaned. Here he was, reunited with his son, but the boy could only muster disparagement for his father. He could hardly blame young Rarakhi; even now, the boy was a stranger to him. It didn't help that so far, the only thing they had in common was the work they'd done for a necromantic monster.

"As of late, the men I've worked with see me as a captain," Rakh pointed out.

Rarakhi folded his arms. "I didn't think you had it in you. Erwyn always acted like you were the kindest man in the world, but from what the boys have been saying, you were one cold son-of-a-bitch to that Yookie on the slab."

"I did what I had to," Rakh said in an undertone. "All for an opportunity to connect with you."

"Yeah, yeah, and Petal keeps going on about how I should give you a chance and all that, but I dunno," he said. "I don't know you. I had this image of you in my head, this great man who loved too hard and had to give me up for my own safety, but then the thoughts came."

"The thoughts?"

"You know. Little voices that tell you hard truths. They told me that Erwyn was lying, that you never cared, that you were just like my mother."

Rakh's tone grew dire. "Your mother loves you just as much as I do."

"Why should I believe that?"

"That's a fair question," Rakh admitted. "All you have is my word, but perhaps if I can get into Lord Khanas's good graces, we can—"

"It's working!" Plutera called out, drawing the Fel'thuz duo's gaze to a slowly rising zombie. "Father, you're a genius! It should take *ages* for that thread stuff to spread to the spine—"

Abruptly, the zombie flopped to the floor, and Plutera jumped back so the rictus-grinning dark elf didn't fall on her. Plutyn ensured his daughter was safe, then voiced his conclusion.

"The Thread must spread faster than is practical. Open the back, Plutera."

She took a scalpel and got to work. In moments, she had something to remark upon.

"Well, there's one benefit to this; any bodies we're willing to sacrifice will be efficient thread farms."

Plutyn face tightened in a way that caused Rakh's bones to shake. "Clever girl. Did you hear that, Fel'thuz?"

"Yes, I know, you and your daughter have a loving relationship. If I'm honest, it's irritating," Rakh remarked.

"Not that, fool. We may not be able to deploy thread-tainted zombies into the catacombs, but if we have spare bodies, using Johansen, production is practically free. How fast would you say it took to consume Marix's body, Plutera?"

"Less than two minutes," Plutera said. "We'd need more bodies than we currently go through to take full advantage."

"We've already got the organ market cornered, adding thread-consumed organs to our stocks would be lucrative," Plutyn said, his pale eyes glimmering with avarice. "You're a worthy successor, Plutera."

Rarakhi whispered to his father. "If I'm honest, I don't like Plutera when she's got her work head on. She's kind of scary."

"Being casual about death is just a side effect of being a necromancer. It doesn't mean she'd grieve you any less if you were—"

"You two, stop whispering. Count Fel'thuz, the solution lies before you. I need you to get to the catacombs as soon as possible," Lord Khanas commanded.

"What do you mean?"

"I'll get to work infesting these corpses. You summon Malyn and the others. After your work in the Yookietown, they're quite fond of you," Plutyn claimed.

"Really? They complained all the way up to the— the critical moment—"

"The moment you killed this Yukishiman," Plutyn said, casually extracting a piece of lung encrusted in odd golden moss and handing it to Plutera. "Their biggest qualm was your inability to accept the act. I will agree, however, that if people need to die, it is better that innocents are left out of it. Why do you think my main source of income is blackmail? Good people don't need to worry about blackmailers."

"Johansen had it coming," Rakh insisted. "He bragged about using trafficked Malassaians. Speaking of which, I think that you should—"

"Don't fret. Once we secure the catacombs again, this city shall see *change*. Scum like the Malassaian Traffickers will be rightly afraid to walk the streets at night. For now, the passageways must be cleared. Summon your men."

Rakh nodded, and headed into the manor's downstairs lounge, where the 'staff' resided, playing cards, joking, and training their bodies through weights or scrapping. A few spellbinders had their small noses in books pertaining to their natural magic, and the air was filled with bhang-weed smoke.

"Malyn, Azrael, Kareon, Vledyn and Joon, Lord Khanas wants you all," Rakh said with a beckon.

"We working under you again?" Azrael, the gaunt one, asked. "Are we clearing out the catacombs this time?"

"That's right," Rakh said. "We can't use undead on this one, unfortunately, so I'll be leading you there personally."

"Remember, even if you're a count out there, in the underground you're the disposable one," Malyn said with a grin. "Right, let's see what Lord Khanas wants."

They headed towards the operating room, where self-proclaimed nobleman stood outside its door. He'd traded his rolled-up sleeves and gloves for his usual flowing attire. At his feet was a sack with a meaty, bloody stench to it.

"What's in the bag, milord?" Joon, the short elf, asked.

"Thread-infested viscera. Hopefully they'll be indistinguishable from regular guts to the catacombs daemon," Plutyn explained. "Throw them to it like it's an offering. The Wor'ghanese offer their weak and stillborn to their daemon king, and this should be similar. Once it partakes in the offering, it'll be poisoned."

"That don't sound like a five-man job," Azrael remarked.

"That's 'cause there's a lot of 'shoulds' and 'hopefullys', idiot," Malyn pointed out.

Plutyn nodded. "Just so, Malyn. Fel'thuz shall carry the last resort."

The Lost Lord put his hand in his inner pocket and produced a glass tube filled with glittering golden grey matter. "This is concentrated thread I extracted from your contribution's brain. If the daemon rejects the offerings, then somebody needs to find a way to apply this directly to it. As you are a guest with illusionism on their side, I have taken the liberty of volunteering you ahead of time."

"I'm honoured," Rakh said with an edge to his tone, taking the vial with some hesitance.

"If any of you need to bid farewell, now is the time. Meet each other at the manor's catacombs entrance, and remember I have eyes everywhere. If any of you try to abandon the mission, I'll know, and you'll wish you risked your life fighting a daemon," Plutyn promised.

The elves nodded and made mutters of general acceptance, then headed their own ways. Rakh, however, stayed by Lord Khanas.

"May I talk to my son alone? If this really is my last day alive, there's something he needs to know."

"I see no reason to stop you. Best of luck in both your endeavours," the Lost Lord said, then stuck his head into the operating room. "Rarakhi, you and Plutera have had enough time together. Your father wishes to speak to you before he possibly dies. Unlike your aunt, the creature he faces stands a chance, so I command you to speak to him."

"Of course, my lord," Rarakhi said before stepping out of the operating room.

"Is there somewhere you go when you want solitude, Rarakhi?" Rakh asked.

"Why do you care about that?"

"I want to know before it's over. I need to tell you who you are, and I'd rather do it in private. If you have anywhere you've claimed as your own, please let me know," Rakh begged.

Rarakhi voice tightened. "No. We're not going there. You'd just tarnish the memories."

Rakh's entire upper body ached. "So be it. Let's go to my room."

Even though he was fulfilling his boss's commands, Rarakhi was, as always, reluctant to follow Rakh. As he walked through the never-ending, Khanas-aggrandising marble hallways, the weight of Rakh's secrets pushed his shoulders down. He opened his door and offered a pitiful conversation starter.

"I'm sorry I failed you."

"It's too late," Rarakhi said, following his father in and shutting the door. "You've sacrificed a lot to try and talk to me and stuff, but I just don't know you."

"I was hoping I could tell you a little about myself. If you're willing, I'd like to learn about you too," Rakh said, sitting on his bed. "How about it? Let's just talk about us. Not our anger at being abandoned, not our regrets, simply the men we've become. Do you like jazz?"

"I think it's pretentious crap."

Rakh's inner fire was rekindled. "See? We're learning about each other. If this is my last day alive, I want to spend it doing this. Can you spare the time for a dying man?"

"You're not dying, but yeah, let's talk. What did you want to tell me?"

"It's about your mother. If I don't return from this mission, you need to ask Lord Khanas about the whereabouts of your Aunt Tei."

* * *

Weil's game room was as bare as the rest of his house, with various unpainted rectangles on the walls and the only remaining games being damaged or incomplete sets that couldn't be sold. Thankfully, there were a few fixtures that remained: A table, a lamp, numerous rolls of parchment, and ink pots of variable fullness.

Razarkha had apologised to Vi'khash, ensuring the gutter-tongue was relaxed enough to continue her charade of nursing Ivan to 'health', leaving her occupied upstairs. This allowed Razarkha and Weil to use the dysfunctional game room as their plotting chamber undisturbed.

"So, what's your plan to liberate me?" Weil asked as Razarkha scribbled on a piece of paper.

"If we remove the Kasparovs, we remove your debt, and thankfully, they've given their weaknesses away," Razarkha explained, revealing a doodle of Anya Kasparov pointing at her guards around Zemelnya Central Library.

"What do you mean?"

Razarkha covered her face with her palm, then immediately regretted it due to the makeup she smudged. *"What I mean, Weil, is that there's a reason the Kasparovs have the history and biography section of the library on lockdown. Arkhera is by no means perfect, but the King has no need to hide history books despite being some overweight teetotalling imbecile with no personal power. To him, the truth is not a threat. By contrast, these people, allegedly in possession of a soulstealer and with numerous mages under their employ, are terrified of whatever histories lie within this section. That means we need to raid the library and find their weaknesses."*

Weil started his usual nervous babbling. *"It's a fine idea, it truly is, but I don't know how we can possibly heist the library as a pair."*

"Who said we're alone?" Razarkha asked. *"You could unleash that daemonic monster of yours upon the library and take the spoils while they're busy recovering!"*

"Do you realise how rare chaos-speakers are? If they figure out a chaos-speaker was behind the attack, Anya Kasparov would trace it back to me and my father immediately!"

Razarkha put a hand between her and Weil. *"Come to think of it, your daemon-releasing idea simply won't work. It's too loud and suspicious, and besides, they'd probably destroy the books in their rampage, which is exactly what the Kasparovs want."*

"How about we use your illusion powers to—"

"Quiet, Weil, can't you see I'm thinking? I can't use my illusion powers to slip past the guards, they probably have other means of detection at the entrance to the nine hundreds section. Therefore, entering from the library interior is off limits."

Weil made his annoying mouth-noises once again. *"Yes, but what if we were to hide ourselves with your powers outside the library—"*

"I have it!" Razarkha declared, holding a finger up. *"Instead of using my powers where they'd expect it, I'll use my illusionism* outside *the library, cloaking us while you use a portal to bring relevant books into the Chaotic Realm for later retrieval."*

Weil sighed and put his head on the desk. *"Brilliant plan, Razarkha."*

"I know," she said with a wide smile. *"Don't tell me there are problems, this plan is flawless. If the only oddities they find are a few missing books, nothing can come back to us!"*

"Any books we don't keep should be sold—"

"*Absolutely not,*" Razarkha said. "*If any missing books re-enter circulation they can be traced back to us. Soon, you won't need to reflexively sell everything you steal. You'll be able to keep the spoils of your glorious conquests. You'll be your own man, and I will share in your victories. We'll ravage this isle together.*"

Weil allowed himself a wholehearted smile. "*Thank you for giving me hope. Why are you so invested in my freedom?*"

Razarkha almost said 'the Soulstealer of Craving', but something stopped her. Without a moment's thought, genuine words spilled from her mouth instead.

"*You showed me kindness and put a roof over my head. You see me for the magnificent person I am. And I see you as a magnificent person in the making that needs a Plague Empress to show him the way.*"

Weil became shy. "*Do you consider me your Plague Emperor?*"

"*Not yet. But one day, you will be.*"

* * *

Rakh had told his son what he needed to hear. Whatever reservations the boy had were left unresolved. With a vial of thread in his inner pocket and sacks of organs in the capable hands of his muscle, Count Fel'thuz strode through the catacombs of Moonstone. While the underground was largely dank, dimly lit and monotonous, signs were consistently present at branching paths, so finding the crossroads that led to Icewater Canal was simple enough.

"Here we are," Malyn said as they reached the correct crossroads.

The right path was full of wet, warm wind, and even the darkness was distorted by otherworldliness. The mould-covered walls took on a glistening, slick appearance the further down the path one looked. Rakh shook, but took the lead regardless.

"All right, men, we have our plan. Leave the body parts for the daemon and wait to see what happens."

The men all had sacks in one hand and Na'liman machetes in the other, while Rakh only had throwing knives and a dagger. Kareon, a slope-shouldered young man, was the first brave volunteer, heading into the mist of distortion and flinging a disembodied torso into the unknown. The view became a little clearer as Rakh used his powers to illuminate the way, but strangely, he couldn't scrub the air clean of the blots this creature's presence brought.

The rocky floor of the catacombs splintered as a large tentacle with an eyestalk at its tip ejected itself. It wrapped itself around the body part and stared, with Kareon backing off slowly. Its eye scanned the piece, and after a pause, it stretched its tentacular form to smother the offering.

As the odd, filled tentacle pulsated, Rakh sighed with relief. "It looks like this will be easy after all—"

A deafening screech invalidated his conclusion in swift order as the tentacle detached from the floor and degenerated into an inky-black, tar-like substance. The gang covered their ears as the catacombs rumbled, and against all comprehension, the beast spoke the Common Tongue, albeit a broken, antiquated rendition.

"Didst thou truly consider me foolish and death-seeking?"

Kareon somehow found words for the creature. "Well, shit, we thought you'd at least try it—"

"Die for thy trespassing, become one with my perfect form!"

The walls flaked away, and at a deceptively close range, tentacles erupted from the shambles that were once considered to be catacombs. Rakh pulled back to the crossroads, as did most of his muscle, but Kareon was too far down the path. As he turned around to run in earnest, a tentacle erupted from the ground in front of him, bearing an eyestalk like all the others. He sliced it away with a machete, but in staying still to do so, allowed several more tentacles to emerge around him.

"*Help! Somebody, help!*"

The muscle's response was complete disarray; Malyn outright fled the scene, Joon and Vledyn jabbered to each other, and Azrael breathed heavily before calling to Rakh.

"The fuck do we do, we can't just leave him to die!"

Rakh had no time to ponder. He flung three of his throwing knives towards the eyes upon the tentacles, and when one hit, a screech rang out again.

"Thy hopes to blind me are futile, for my eyes are legion."

Despite the beast's bold claims, enough tentacles retracted to allow Kareon to break free. While Rakh hoped he'd regroup with the others by the crossroads, the elf instead ran straight past, calling out a desperate apology as he charged for any destination beyond the catacombs. They were down to four men, and the guts weren't of use. The distortions along the path steadily neared the junction, and Azrael dropped his body parts to grip his machete with both hands.

"What now, smart-arse? It's coming for us!"

Joon shook. "It can't have unlimited arms; it has to end somewhere!"

Vledyn turned to Rakh, whose face creased as he searched for an answer. He felt the vial in his pocket and knew what needed to be done.

"Men, I'm going into the beast, but I need you lot to help that happen."

Vledyn's voice sharpened. "You mad? You expect us to cut down all those fucking tentacles?"

"Not all of them. Enough to distract it and clear the way."

"Thou art naught but arrogant beasts, here for us to consume," the beast mocked.

"And where will you be while we're cutting?" Vledyn asked.

"Gone," Rakh said, and with that, he clicked his fingers and applied a cloak to himself. He spoke one last time as a word upon the wind. "Keep it occupied for as long as possible, and you will be relieved eventually."

The last three members of the muscle hyperventilated, hugged one another, and finally, charged at the creature with machetes in hand. They hacked, they slashed, they stabbed, but for every tentacle they cut down, the walls birthed three more. As they worked, Rakh slipped through the corridor. First, the way was dusty, a mockery of the integrity the catacomb walls once had, but as he continued, the walls gave way to flesh. Eyeballs no longer lined tendrils, but the walls themselves.

His invisibility and muting bought him time as he headed closer to the source of the humid furnace winds, but unfortunately for him, he stepped on a sucker-pad. This caused the slime-covered surroundings to pulsate and contract, and a roar of pure hatred pierced Rakh's ears. Beaks sprouted from every part of the fleshy expanse and yelled the creature's verse in unison.

"Vicious, monstrous mortals! What unique crime doth I commit?"

Rakh looked back at his men, wrapped in tentacles and hacking where they could. If they weren't relieved soon, they would be killed, and if Plutyn was as protective as he claimed he was, he'd die if he survived without them. There was no time for further deliberation. The amalgam of rock and pulsating gore closed in on him, beaks gnawing at the air. Rakh pulled out his vial of thread, and thrust his hand at one of the beaks, screaming as the razor-sharp construct dug into his wrist. His cloaking failed, and he felt his right hand slip through pain, agony, then nothing at all.

"Thou art foolish as thou art capable of death. Perish."

Rakh backed from the beak that took his hand, vomiting as he listened to glass and bone grind apart, and suddenly, the warm wind quickened.

"Impossible! Knotweed hidden within a living mage?"

The flesh around him swiftly became veined with golden strands, then devolved into black sludge.

"No, you're just stupid," Rakh said, laughing through his agony.

The beast's final words were laced with a spite Rakh didn't know immortals possessed. *"This is not how my long life ends, I'll kill thee and thy friends!"*

Rakh sighed with relief as he saw the three men kicking off the inky goo surrounding them, and Azrael shouted to his temporary captain.

"We did it, boss, we— *boss!*"

For a moment, Rakh didn't understand. Clarity came in the form of the rising, collapsing tentacle above him. He tried to run but slipped on the liquid-covered floor. He had no choice but to lie down as a collapsing, inky tendril the weight of a small tree fell upon him.

* * *

Under her cloak, Razarkha and Weil were behind Zemelnya Central Library, with a perfect view of the great nasite obelisk of the Isle of Dreams. From a brief scouting run, they knew which wall had to be bypassed to access the nine-hundreds section, all they needed was to pull it off.

They were sat on a tentacle that extended upwards from a portal in the ground, looking through the window at people entering and exiting the history section. Though these guests were few and far between, it wasn't worth the risk of detection to leap between visits. Eventually, the ascendant librarian headed into the section, gathered the remaining readers, and herded them out.

Once the section was empty, Weil looked to his foreign associate. *"How long should we wait?"*

"Half an hour should do it. The guards will remain, but I can't see them going beyond their door duty."

"That's a big assumption."

"It's the only chance we have," Razarkha claimed. *"What would you suggest, we spend years getting cosy with the Kasparovs, wait for them to trust us and then make our move? That seems like something Anya would do, but I'm Razarkha Fel'thuz. I crush my enemies, I don't stab them in the back."*

Weil neglected to mention that according to her own tales, she'd only experienced minor victories against unarmed malpracticing doctors and failed at any remotely challenging fights. He didn't want to lose the only friend he'd made in the last five years.

"All right. I'll start negotiations with the Rakh'vash ahead of time."

Razarkha patted his head. *"That's what I like to hear. Just tell it to open a portal within the library, take as many books as possible, and leave them in the Chaotic Realm to pick out later."*

"I'll try."

Razarkha put on a mocking voice. "I'll try, look at me, I'm Weil, I don't have a spine, *just be assertive with your god. The Plague Emperor wielded the Rakh'vash with impunity, and you should be able to as well."*

"Thank you for your faith in me."

Weil opened a rift in front of his face, and a glittering eye with a square pupil stared out from the other side. After a pause, the fleshy 'orbit' of the eye pulsed as its many-layered voice whispered forth from the void.

"We see that your friend has a grand plan for the upheaval of Zemelnya. We are willing to assist, but only according to our will."

"Of course, Great Rakh'vash," Weil said in Chaostongue. *"What we need is for you to take books that are significant to the Kasparovs from the library section up there in about half an hour."*

"We shall decide the appropriate time and place. The Living Entropy does not adhere to a schedule."

"So you'll extract them over time?"

"No," the Rakh'vash answered. *"All at once, some time this night, and only We shall decide what books to take."*

Weil's voice tightened. *"No, no, you don't understand, we need to have books significant to the Kasparovs, that's how we'll start the chaos you so deeply desire!"*

"We created daemons so they may understand mortals in our stead. Do you think We know anything of these Kasparov mortals' desires or wants? We shall decide as We wish, and you shall accept the plunder We retrieve."

"Living Entropy, why are you like this? Why aren't you cooperating? I thought you liked Razarkha! It's her plan, don't you want to help her?"

"We are in a bad mood. A great part of our soul has been lost to the knotweed, taken before they could regroup within us and reincarnate. Millennia of experience pointlessly destroyed. The culprit was kin to your friend, fittingly named 'kin' himself."

Weil grimaced. 'Kin' in Chaostongue could be closely approximated in mortal languages as the sound 'rakh'. The same Rakh Razarkha ranted about non-stop had somehow slain an ancient daemon. Weil gritted his teeth, then switched his tongue to Isleborn.

"I'm sorry, Razarkha. If you can believe it, your brother is sabotaging you even now."

Razarkha's body tightened in a way Weil had never seen before and she started to rant in the Common Tongue. "How is that no-good peasant-fucking brawn-muscled unfairly-handsome falsely-kind bastard-siring monster ruining my plans *now?*"

"I didn't understand half the words you said, but it's because he killed a daemon. The Great Rakh'vash is not appreciative of your kin in this moment."

"Tell your stupid chaos god that Rakh and I are enemies! *I never asked him to kill a daemon!*"

Weil shrugged. "The Living Entropy has made his decision. We can go home."

"You want us to go home empty-handed?"

He shook his head. "No. I will check the Chaotic Realm in the morning. Whatever books the Great Rakh'vash chooses, we shall receive."

Razarkha paused, then pushed Weil off the tentacle. He was quick to open another portal, allowing a tentacle from within to catch him. After that, he lowered both tentacles, allowing Razarkha and himself to dismount.

"Let's go home," he said with dissonant serenity.

Razarkha brushed herself off. *"I try to kill you and that's all you have to say?"*

"You'll have to try harder than that," Weil said. "I don't think you'd try to kill me in earnest."

"Of course not," Razarkha muttered. "I suppose we're stuck playing Yukishiman chess until your stupid chaos god decides I'm not responsible for my brother's actions. Perhaps it can provide the missing knights and bishops."

Despite the pain that gnawed at his temples, Weil was warm. It may have been perverse, but since his father's fall into delirium, this woman was the brightest light in his world.

Duplicity

The morning sun travelled through a window and forced Razarkha's eyelids apart. She rolled off Weil's couch and scrambled along the floor like a Madaki desert lizard before standing up and rushing to Weil's room. Somehow, the boy was still sleeping when she burst through his door, so Razarkha leaned over him, grabbed his shoulders, and shook.

"Weil, get up, we need to check our plunder!"

"Why so early? Day has barely broken," he grumbled.

"Aren't you excited? Where's your drive? Let's see them sooner, rather than later!"

Weil rubbed his eyes. *"I had a dream that my father died while I was sleeping—"*

"That's wonderful," Razarkha said, physically dragging him upright. *"Just open one of your rifts and retrieve the books, I don't even need you after that."*

"Fine," Weil muttered, and opened a portal above the foot of his bed.

A set of books dropped out, many with covers depicting spellbinders in various states of undress wielding ropes or being bound by them. Razarkha's teeth ground as she sorted through the titles until the floodgates of her mouth burst open.

"What is this? His Secrets Unravelled, A Guide to Taming Lovers, Ropes and Romance, *is your chaos god mocking me?"* Razarkha spluttered as she flung each sultry fiction to the floor. *"Nothing but erotica, erotica, erotica, erotica! I don't even know what that bitch sees in ropes, what's the appeal of waiving control when love-making, it makes no sense!"*

Weil yawned. *"I don't know, I think I'd like to be tied up."*

"*You would,*" Razarkha snapped as she threw *Her Secrets Bound* over her shoulder. "*Tell your chaos god that he should kill himself and throw this world into eternal stillness, he's been completely—*"

Weil cocked his head. "*Aren't you supposed to say something derogatory? Are you looking for the word 'useless'?*"

"*Shut up, I've found something,*" Razarkha said.

In her hands were two potentially useful documents: A scroll that when unravelled revealed the Kasparov family tree, and a small book titled *Founding the Family: Kaspar of Ilazar's Thirtieth Journal*. Beneath another smattering of smut was an additional scroll whose presence darkened its surroundings.

Weil immediately perked up. "*Oh, look, that one's written with nasite ink.*"

"*People use nasite as ink? Whatever for?*" Razarkha asked.

"*It is simply the way with Godspeakers of Darkness,*" Weil said. "*It enables them to write in godly tongues, the dark ones at least. Let me look at it.*"

He unravelled the scroll while Razarkha checked the Kasparov family tree for any anomalies, and immediately a matter piqued her attention. At the very top, above Kaspar himself, were his parents: Fel'thuz of the Plagueborn and Darya of the Isleborn. Razarkha frowned and checked Fel'thuz's other side to see a second marriage to Rina of Arkhera.

There were unusual markings beside each name; Fel'thuz was marked with a starburst, Darya with a similar starburst, and Rina with a skull. The family tree from Rina's side was familiar to Razarkha; they were her kin, ancestors both great and disappointing, all marked with a symbol that resembled a silhouette.

Kaspar, meanwhile, had children with Cythria of Nortez, also marked with a skull, following which his children and their children's children were marked with the same silhouette as the Fel'thuzes. Razarkha had her suspicions as to what this meant but would need to check the journal to see if there was any information to confirm or refute her hypothesis.

"*Any progress on your god-tongue scroll?*"

Weil paused. "*Don't get too excited, but I managed to read the title, and it's written by the Plague Emperor himself.*"

Razarkha swiftly put her journal aside and attempted to read over Weil's shoulder. Unfortunately for her, the symbols constantly shifted, and were nothing like runes written by mortals. She squinted, she changed her angle of gaze, she craned her face close to the scroll, but nothing made the writing more legible.

"*What are you waiting for? I can't read this on my own, you'll have to read it for me!*"

Weil's face reddened. "*With time! This isn't just written in Chaostongue, there are passages which are in the tongue of the god known to Isleborn as 'the Bold Individualist'.*"

"*What in the world is the Bold Individualist?*" Razarkha asked. "*That doesn't sound like a god, it sounds like an adventuring explorer!*"

"*The youngest of the Dark Four,*" Weil explained. "*My father knew many things about every god, light and dark, but I'm only truly knowledgeable about the Great Rakh'vash. What I do know is there are eight true gods. Four light, four dark, paired into opposites. On the dark side, there's the Primordial Darkness, the Living Entropy, Mortality's End, and finally, the Bold Individualist.*"

Razarkha groaned. "*The Plague Emperor must have obfuscated some of his texts behind this Bold Individualist tongue using broader knowledge of the dark gods. Does your father have any books that could be helpful?*"

"I've probably sold them if they're of interest to people," Weil admitted.

Razarkha slapped his face. *"Then what are you waiting for? You'll have to get the information directly from your father."*

"But he's ill! Delusional!"

"Believe in him," Razarkha commanded. *"He's likely more lucid than you think. I watched my mother die too, and she was a font of useful knowledge to the very end."*

Weil shifted, then got out of bed. *"I suppose I should spend some time with him without Vi'khash while I can."*

"Exactly, and if there's a part of his old self remaining, wouldn't he be proud of his boy trying to learn broader godly magic?"

"I suppose he would," Weil said. *"Good luck with your reading, I hope you find something of value. The Great Rakh'vash will help us find a way out of our bondage, just as he did with the Plagueborn."*

The two spellbinders shared a prolonged gaze, then locked their hands together. After that, they nodded and let go. Weil left the room and Razarkha got comfortable on his bed. She wrapped herself in his musky duvet and opened Kaspar's thirtieth journal.

The founder of the Kasparovs was the lumomantic son of Fel'thuz, just as the family tree implied. According to the journal, he'd resented his father for abandoning his Isleborn mother, leaving her at a time when the weaker Isleborn mages needed a Plagueborn to vouch for them. A split-cultured person like Kaspar belonged nowhere in Ilazar, so he started a journey to Arkhera to find his father and kill him. By the time he found him, he saw that he was with a necromantic woman, Rina Khanas of Moonstone.

The revelation made Razarkha's heart sink. She'd always wondered if Rina was truly a commoner, and now the reason her family name was censored was clear. Starburst was lumomancer, skull was necromancer, which made Fel'thuz and Rina's children half-breeds. Kaspar noted the same, writing that illusionism seemed to arise from weak lumomancy and weak mental magic mingling.

Razarkha scratched at her cheeks. This was why the Fel'thuzes needed to stay pure; they were an easily disrupted mix of necromancer and spellbinder. Apparently Kaspar considered this a good thing, as his next quest took him across the world, to Galdus, in search of pure-blooded possessor necromancers to breed with.

Sula, Galdus's southern continent, didn't yield results due to the prevalence of ascendants; most Sulari were already ascended by twenty, and those that weren't were already paired off as dutiful breeders. Meanwhile Nortez, the northern continent, proved fruitful; the old imperial state had somewhat caught up to Ilazar in tolerating the fleshly, so unpaired, unascended folk were much more common.

There he met Cythria, and though he approached her with heredity in mind, he soon fell for her as a person. Razarkha scoffed and put the book down. She didn't need to read the story of the first Kasparovs' conception to make her conclusion. The Kasparovs were illusionists, just like her, all of them were apparently biracial, and yet they maintained control of pure-blooded, objectively stronger spellbinders. Even the low-ranking guards of the library would be able to kill an illusionist with ease.

Razarkha let her self-hatred flow from her throat to her chest. Weaklings like her and the Kasparovs only had the Soulstealer of Craving as leverage. In Ilazar, the strong deserved to dominate. If they'd managed to keep their weakling heritage a secret for so long, what else about their strength was an illusion? She rushed to Ivan's bedroom, where Weil sat beside his father. The twisted scroll was rolled up in the boy's hands, prompting Razarkha's ire.

"You're joking. You did nothing but comfort your father? Why haven't you pumped him for information? We don't know how long he'll linger! You need to use his knowledge while you can!" she ranted.

"He translated it for me already, but you're not going to like what it says," Weil claimed.

"What joy, that I get to read the Plague Emperor's greatest secret before the end," Ivan said. "Thank you, timekeepers, for slowing your approach."

Razarkha's chest began to flutter. "I don't care if it's bad news. What did the Plague Emperor say?"

Weil looked to his father, then Razarkha. "According to my father's translation, the soulstealers were the product of a deal with the Bold Individualist, or as the god calls himself, the Sovereign. The Plague Emperor, as well as being a chaos-speaker, was one of the Sovereign's representatives on this world, the Sinchild of Wrath, whose divine duty was to drive others to murderous rage.

"When Conditor died, his rage became contagious, but the people's will to fight exceeded their ability to take on the ascendants of Sula. Fortunately, the Plague Emperor's spiritual father, the Sovereign, also disliked ascendants. In his eyes, they attempted to violate the cycle of death and decay that all dark gods hold sacred.

"Therefore, the Sovereign created weapons that would be nigh-unstoppable, themed after his seven sins just like his children. They were made to punish ascendants' arrogance by turning their souls magical fuel, denied an afterlife once consumed. However, the Sovereign limited them so that mortals would not have their souls annihilated as collateral damage."

"What do you mean, limited them?" Razarkha asked, her voice shaking.

"I'm so sorry, but the Soulstealer of Craving Elki Kasparov has won't work on mortals. It'll sap the souls of *the recently deceased and ascendants. Even if we kill him, we won't be able to seize—"*

Razarkha cut Weil off with a wholehearted kiss to the lips, mingling her tongue with his in an aggressive attempt to reward him.

When the ordeal ended, Weil asked, *"Why did you do that? Isn't this terrible news?"*

"Not at all, it's the best news I've heard since arriving here!" Razarkha declared. *"I've just found out the Kasparovs are illusionists! They're as weak as I am! And if their soulstealer is feigned power, then I have a plan to seize Zemelnya, and it doesn't require excessive death!"*

Weil laughed awkwardly. *"That's a good thing, I suppose."*

"I need you to take me to the leader of the War'mal Group. We're going to make some friends."

* * *

Rakh could only experience dampness and pain. He could breathe without issue, but whenever he moved his limbs, a nausea-inducing ache followed. When he pawed at the ground, slime clung to his palm, making him slip whenever he tried to get up. Eventually, his eyes opened, revealing naught but a small light at the end of an extremely dark tunnel.

He tried to check his stump, but darkness obscured the bloody details. Erwyn would have told him not to touch anything unclean with his handless wrist, but after lying unconscious for God knows how long in the catacombs, precautions were likely meaningless. He used his remaining hand to push himself up, but when he tried to stand, a pain shot through his leg.

His second attempt yielded further pain but successfully put him on his feet, though limping was the best locomotion he could manage. He hobbled through the tunnel, reaching the light and exiting the catacombs to find himself in a bustling industrial area, illuminated by the white of the snow. A canal was nearby, and a barge upon it was being filled with goods.

Rakh almost laughed with joy, but soon noticed the people around him. He was too weak to cloak himself throughout his subterranean limp, yet he'd still acted like he was invisible. The commoners stared at his crippled, bloody, goo-covered ugliness, murmuring amidst themselves.

The crowd began to part and distant upper-class yelling could be heard. The people cleared for this disembodied voice, until its possessor broke through the closest peasants to reveal himself. It was a familiar high elf with silver hair, a ruffled cravat, and a monocle, straight-backed as always. Rakh's eyes welled and his throat hurt.

"Erwyn."

"By the Ghosts, Rakh, what happened to you?" Erwyn asked. "That entrance to the catacombs is off limits, surely you knew that. There's a— oh, forget that, let's take you in."

Rakh's heart thrummed against his ribs. "No, don't, please, if you take me in then—"

"Rakh, you've been away for *over a month*. I thought you'd taken some time off to see Rarakhi, and some of guards spotted you at a bar, but I can't ignore this."

"You have to, *please,* for your own sake, for my sake, for *Rarakhi's* sake!" Rakh gibbered, his breath increasing speed.

Erwyn filled his voice with an affected gentleness. "Will you at least let me treat your stump? I know you must be traumatised—"

"Stop!"

Rakh shoved the wisdom away, then promptly tripped over his own crippled leg. His lungs may have been working, but in his panic, they overworked, and steadily, the downed spellbinder's vision blurred, leaving only noise to inform him of his surroundings.

"Go on, away with you, on with your day," he heard Erwyn yell, before his tone became commanding. "I need two guards over here!"

From there, consciousness fled from Rakh entirely. Despite his mind's void being dreamless and free of stimuli, time was somehow still perceptible. Nausea and a harsh sting returned ahead of his senses, and when he spoke, his throat's dryness blunted his words.

"Erwyn..." Rakh mumbled, his back and eyes informing him that he was lying on Erwyn's operating table.

"Ghosts, Rakh, you're awake!" Erwyn said, jumping from a chair to loom over him. "I'm sorry, I'm going to have to put you to sleep again soon, but first I need to talk to you."

Rakh's lucidity rushed towards him in a wave, and he forced urgency from his parched throat. "Erwyn, I can't tell you what's happened. He'll kill us both. Perhaps Rarakhi too."

"You've already given something away," Erwyn said. "You said 'he'. Who is 'he'?"

"The person who has custody over Rarakhi. He stopped waiting, Erwyn. He wasn't at the orphanage, and when I said I needed to sort out some papers, I was actually visiting Plutyn Khanas for information on the underground."

"Plutyn Khanas? Oh, heavens, no, you didn't get involved with him, did you?"

"I had no choice. Rarakhi's working under him," Rakh said, his voice cracking. "I'm sorry, Erwyn. I've doomed us both, we're going to die and it's my fault."

Erwyn paused, then prepared a bone saw and poppy milk. "You've made it this far without him killing you."

"Rarakhi doesn't even like me," Rakh blubbered. "I'm a terrible father. I should have asked to see Rarakhi sooner, I failed him, I've failed you, I've failed Tei, I've failed *everyone*. I killed a man just to reconnect with him. I can't go back—"

Wisdom Erwyn put his hands above Rakh's face and unleashed a single deafening clap. "Rakh."

"What?"

"I won't have you give up like this. Plutyn Khanas is a powerful blackmailer, correct?"

"Yes, and that's why we're dead!"

"Not true," Erwyn insisted. "Blackmailers crave information, and what is it I, a wisdom, have in abundance?"

Rakh's breathing slowed and shuddered. "Information."

"Then Khanas and I will have much to discuss. Perhaps if I make a particularly good deal, I can get a few thorns in House Selenia's side taken care of in the process."

"You're not angry with me? I'm a murderer, Erwyn. Why aren't you looking at me differently?" Rakh asked.

Erwyn's voice lowered. "I've cut open enough bodies on the slab, commanded enough deaths, helped the Royal Wisdom with enough epidemic patients to know that sometimes, it's not about action. It's about intent. Perhaps you've doomed us both. Perhaps you've failed Rarakhi. But I know you aren't a bad person.

"Unlike you, I *do* have an inner darkness. My immediate thought was to kill Razarkha while I was caring for her, partly to protect you, yes, but also because I despised her. There are other selfish actions I've indulged in that even you don't know of. Speaking candidly, if Plutyn Khanas is able to extract favours from the Church of Eternity, then I fully intend to work closely with him."

Rakh managed to find a smile. "You're not evil, Erwyn. You just want to ruin people who deserve it. I'm no better than that."

"Perhaps we're idealising each other," Erwyn admitted. "What I know for certain is you're wasting time with this self-hatred. No matter what you said, I was going to help you the moment I saw you. We must move forward and figure out a solution. For now, let me inject you with some poppy milk. Sleep well and try not to panic when you wake up. A lot's going to be missing."

Before Rakh could say anything, he felt a prick in his upper right arm. It wasn't long before he was too mellow and confused to think anything at all, let alone speak.

* * *

Kasparov Manor was a sprawling estate nestled far from the gusty coasts of Zemelnya, sitting beneath the ever-present shade provided by the Plague Obelisk of the Isle. Most of the manor was surrounded by the Scruchen Forest, a community of trees that the obelisk had twisted into amalgams of flesh and wood. The grounds were the size of a large hamlet, while the manor itself was enough to house Pakhan Elki Kasparov and his many descendants.

The Kasparov patriarch sat in his games room, spending time with his favourite granddaughter, Anya. The room had windows facing the corrupted forest beyond and numerous game tables, including those for gambling. Of course, family never played for keeps against family. There were books stashed here as well, but mostly instructions for gaming; the most important texts was hidden behind his best mages at the library, not his illusionist progeny.

Elki Kasparov sat about an eight-by-eight squared gaming table with his granddaughter. He was silver-haired, his eighty years just barely showing through his pale makeup. He wore a blue and white robe in mockery of Fel'thuz, the damnable ancestor that left his family's true founder in the dust.

By his right hand was the Soulstealer of Craving, a hybrid structure of multiple gemstones enchanted by energies only the gods fully understood. Rose quartz twisted into aquamarine and carnelian at the top, while the lower half was bowl-shaped and made of deep blue topaz. Occasionally, this section would glow in the absence of light.

His granddaughter was lounging about in naught but a dressing gown, playing with her own enchanted gem; a recently-acquired ascension necklace. While Anya Kasparov did her best to appear Ilazari in public, within the house she preferred to dress like a Yukishiman. Fittingly enough, the grandfather and granddaughter were playing Wrenfall-style chess.

Anya advanced a pawn with clear intent to mobilise her queen and oppress Elki's relatively boxed-in king. When she hit her side of the timer's button, Elki grinned.

"Are you sure you don't want to take that back?" he asked.

"Why would I?" Anya replied. *"I know what you're planning, grandfather."*

"I don't think you do," Elki said. *"If you did, you wouldn't have done that."*

"By Conditor's infinite patience, if you've got me mated, you really ought to get it over with," Anya said with a sly smile. *"On the streets, people don't wait for you to finish gloating."*

"But in this game, I have, let us see..." Elki began, checking the timer, *"...two minutes remaining to talk about how you failed this game. To start, you grew impatient and made a premature gambit with your bishop, which while resulting in a technically even trade, still led to—"*

Elki's lecture was cut short by the appearance of his two youngest sons, Oleg and Yegor, along with Scholar Prismus of Sula, the librarian of the Grand Central Library. The ascendant's smoky form occasionally spilled from his armour, and somehow, the expressionless being was able to transmit its unease to all. Elki carefully pressed the clock so that both timers were frozen.

"*What is the meaning of this?*" Elki asked. "*I told you to save personal meetings for emergencies, Prismus.*"

The ascendant did not require a mouth to speak, nonetheless its transmission was shaky. "*This is an emergency, Pakhan Kasparov. The restricted histories section has somehow lost multiple items.*"

Anya spluttered. "*How? We have numerous pyromancers and cryomancers. The thief can't have been there long; what was stolen?*"

"*Numerous items of your personal stock, Captain Anya, but most worryingly, the Kasparov family tree, one of Kaspar's journals, and the Plague Emperor's records regarding the creation of the soulstealers,*" the ascendant reported.

Anya's fear halted her tongue, but Elki Kasparov kept his speech slow and deliberate. "*Were there any signs of chaos-speech or deathspeech? Were there any other unusual incidents at the time of the theft?*"

"*We never caught the thief, so I can only estimate the time, but the night before I did notice somebody shouting outside the library in the Common Tongue, but when I looked, there was nothing there. I think the Plague Obelisk may have disrupted my senses.*"

"*What about signs of chaos-speech?*" Elki asked.

"*There was daemonic residue upon the shelves that contained the missing books,*" Prismus confirmed.

Elki stroked his soulstealer. "*Can I trust in your discretion, Prismus?*"

"Of course, nobody knows about the missing books but the people in this room," he claimed.

"Thank you."

With that, Elki Kasparov put a hand on the Soulstealer of Craving and spoke to the god within it.

"Bold Individualist, the one who punishes those who run from expression and mortality alike, grant me this soul!"

"It's been a while since you last used the soulstealer, I was beginning to lose hope that you'd kill another ascendant in your lifetime," a dark divine voice replied. ***"Consider it done."***

Prismus already knew what was happening, but his attempts to abandon his armoured form and slip away were futile. An unholy vortex trapped the ascendant, and though it looked as though the gaseous librarian was swirling within a typhoon, the rest of the room remained still. As the artefact completed its work, its victim filled the air with distorted babbling.

"Please, Pakhan, I beg of you, I've done everything you've asked, I've been loyal!"

Loyalty was not enough to save him. Pieces of armour clattered on the floor, and the magical cloud was no more. Elki's soulstealer glimmered and warmed his hand. Oleg and Yegor fixed their clothes, then gave their father a simultaneous bow.

"Very good, father," Oleg said, then the two brothers left the room.

Anya, meanwhile, lacked her uncles' sycophancy. *"That was short-sighted of you."*

"We can't afford for the people to know we've lost something precious," Elki said. *"Besides, if there's rebellion brewing, I will need every soul I can get."*

Anya folded her arms. *"Replacing the very distinctively ascended librarian in the most visited library in Ilazar will be noticeable enough. The best course of* action would be to downplay the significance. The knowledge would inevitably become public. What if Oleg or Yegor get captured by the War'mals and have the information pulled out of them?"

"If the public will inevitably know, it is better to buy time so that we can plan our next move. You're still young, Anya. You haven't learnt to consider every possibility like I have."

Anya sighed. *"Make your move, grandfather."*

Elki started his timer and swiftly checkmated Anya with a bishop. "See? You were so focused on securing you own victory that you failed to notice I was one turn from mating you."

Anya played with her ascension stone, then moved her queen, regardless of her mated king, checkmating her grandfather simultaneously. "Life is not chess, grandfather. The unexpected may happen, and if I'm honest, I think it already has."

Elki scoffed. "Your little demonstration doesn't negate your loss."

"No, but some people don't care if they lose if their enemy loses too. There are only two chaos-speakers in Zemelnya. One of them has been bedridden for months. The only other one is—"

"Yes, his son, the polite, on-time debtor. He must have betrayed us."

Anya nodded. "And I believe the Common Tongue ranting is the result of his new lover, Razarkha Fel'thuz. There's nothing behind her eyes, grandfather. She is the woman who will destroy us even if she loses."

"Fel'thuz? She's a mere illusionist like us. What threat could she pose?"

"With a chaos-speaker who could uncover the soulstealers' limitations on her side, she's more than threatening enough."

Elki put his chess pieces away. *"You make a good point. We mustn't startle them, lest they accelerate their plans."*

"I'll covertly investigate the situation while I'm making a routine visit to collect Weil's payment," Anya promised. *"The moment I have confirmation, I'll make him a cup of tea."*

"That's the Anya I trusted to be captain," Elki said. *"As for the Fel'thuz girl, kill her if you must, but I am interested to see her in person."*

Anya raised an eyebrow. *"You want to conceive more pure illusionists to fill the house? Isn't she a little young for you?"*

"She is. My time as a stud is over, but Oleg could do with a consort."

Betrayal

Weil and Razarkha walked through the yellow-and-green eastern streets of Zemelnya, the former withdrawn while the latter strode with confidence. She would, like gnomish clockwork, rush ahead, then zip back to drag her chaos-speaker forward. Though Weil gave directions, he was hardly leading Razarkha to greatness.

"What's wrong with you?" she asked. "This is our moment! All we need to do is see War'mal and then our problems will be over!"

Weil shrunk under the gaze of the myriad passers-by. "Perhaps we should save this shouting for when we're in the Academy. Anya's informants are everywhere."

"Fortune favours the bold! There's nothing left to fear! She and her family are liars!" Razarkha said with a twirl of her body, then casually shoved a nearby aquamancer. "Do you hear that? Liars!"

"Shitcunt," the aquamancer spat, moving on without so much as a challenge to a duel.

Razarkha made to approach him, but Weil held her back. "What are you doing? I don't know what your plan is because you won't tell me. If you die, the plan doesn't happen."

The former countess kissed Weil's cheek. "You're adorable. Come, visit the academy, he's not worth it anyway."

Weil's voice wavered. "About this plan, does it rely on my participation?"

"Of course, you're my Plague Emperor!" Razarkha said with a smile. "Why, is there a reason you'd be unavailable?"

The young man stopped in the middle of a small square, a sea of spellbinders moving about him in a whirlpool. Razarkha's heart sank and her tone sharpened.

"Don't tell me you have something better to do. This is your one chance to free yourself! Why would you give up when you're so close? Has our time together meant nothing? Answer me, Weil! Do you hate me? Are you going to give up on me after everything?"

"No!" Weil blurted. *"It's nothing like that. You're the only person who feels like a friend to me. I don't want to lose you, but after seeing my father reading that scroll so lucidly, I think he might finally be able to talk to me. I want to be there in his final moments."*

"And squander everything? The Bold Individualist wouldn't want that, would he? He'd want you to unleash your wrath upon your enemies. Don't waste time saying goodbye to the very reason you're indebted. Fight for freedom, don't imprison yourself!" Razarkha begged. *"You have so much potential. Don't waste it as a pawn to your own feebleness."*

Weil pointed to the northern side of the square. *"Go that way, then turn left. After that, ask for War'mal of the Plagueborn. I don't know anything else about them. I'm sorry, Razarkha. You're welcome in my home, but I need to be with my father."*

The boy turned his back on Razarkha and walked off. She stammered, she reached, but nothing effective escaped her mouth. By the time she could speak, Weil was long gone, so she opted to scream instead.

"I don't need you! I'm my own woman! I'll show you! Don't leave me!"

He was lost in the crowd, and people were looking at Razarkha. One slick-looking man with jet-lined pauldrons and a spiky pair of wristbands spoke to her.

"Excuse me, strange woman, could you refrain from—"

"Go away!" she yelled, vanishing moments after.

As a solid wind, Razarkha drifted through the streets, filling the air with under-the-breath ranting about

Weil's ingratitude, insincerity, and inability to see things from a greater perspective. He wouldn't be wasting time sinking ships if he erased his lenders. He'd be able to see his stupid father as much as he wanted if he shut up and did as Razarkha asked. A thought crossed her mind, and her hatred disappeared as swiftly as Tei did. Razarkha would liberate her friend one way or another, but for now, she had to secure her way to Elki Kasparov.

With Weil's directions, she found the Zemelnya Academy of Higher Magical Learning. It was generally wider than it was tall, except in the places where towers with bulbous domes sprouted from the building. Stripes of various colours gave the academy a distinctly Plagueborn aura.

Standing taller than the rest of the towers was a domeless spire which spellbinders could be seen leaping from, before using their powers to attain flight or stability of some sort. Pyromancers used localised explosions and fire-streams to propel themselves, cryomancers froze the air before themselves to skate across temporary airborne paths, and aeromancers extended kite-like clothing to harness artificial winds that enabled true flight. Razarkha shed her cloak and approached the door guard, a spellbinder with folded arms, along with five pairs of metallic arms floating about him, along with bladed weapons that orbited his body.

"Do you speak the true tongue?" the man asked in pure Plagueborn.

"I know Plagueborn to a small, but it is known to me," Razarkha said. *"I am Razarkha, descendant of Fel'thuz of the Plagueborn. Liberated Galdusian blood flows through my... blood-tubes."*

"Veins, that is the word you wanted to say, Razarkha of Fel'thuz's blood," the guard corrected. *"What is your purpose? Do you wish to better yourself and become part of the War'mal Group?"*

"A thing akin to that. I want to speak to War'mal with directness," she said in broken Plagueborn. "I contain information he would enjoy to hear. War'mal is a man, yes?"

"He is," the guard said. "And fortunately for you, he's able to speak Isleborn. He shall be with you shortly, but I warn you, if he thinks you're wasting his time, he will add you to his taxidermy collection."

"Half of those words were not understood, but the message is. I comfort you, this message is one War'mal cannot exist without."

The guard paused, then raised an eyebrow, sliding the stony door of the building aside. Without hesitation, Razarkha walked into the dim room on the other side, prompting swift entrapment as the door shut behind her. As a result, she was left in total darkness, her dim illusory light the only means to see.

There was no door on the other side, no blocked-off windows, no signs of cracks or openings. She read some of the Old Galdusian runes that were painted on the walls; most of them were generic proverbs, such as *'flesh is limitation, and limitation is what highlights power'*, *'death is what makes life worth living'*, and *'the Plague comes for all that pervert the sacred darkness'*.

"You are most amusing," Razarkha called out. *"You can let me see War'mal, now."*

A white-and-black portal opened upon the wall, occasionally letting out pale wisps and disembodied murmurs. A voice from within spoke fluent Isleborn, albeit with some manner of magical distortion.

"Razarkha Fel'thuz, am I correct?"

"You are," Razarkha replied in Isleborn.

"I am Bookkeeper Mal'dar. Your request to speak to War'mal has been temporarily deferred. I shall speak to you in his stead and decide if you are worthy of a further meeting. War'mal does not like his time to be wasted."

Razarkha looked to the portal. *"I have to step in there, correct?"*

"We are speaking now, are we not?" Mal'dar replied. *"You are certainly fearless for considering it, however. I cannot think of a person who stepped into our sealed entrance so swiftly, and not one has stepped into a deathly portal without being urged to. People with no fear are like everflame; they burn bright, but not for long."*

"Enough pleasantries! Hear this, Bookkeeper," Razarkha began. *"The Kasparovs are mere illusionists. They're the same blood as I, albeit half Isleborn. Then Kaspar, their founder, bred with a Nortezian necromancer! They're illusionists, hybrids, and fakes!"*

"Yes, yes, we already knew that," the disembodied deathspeaker said. *"Did you think this was revolutionary news? The only Kasparov regularly in the field is Anya, and she's always surrounded by pyromancers and cryomancers. Their personal weakness was always obvious, and we've already had our arcanologists investigate. Your information is worthless."*

Razarkha's voice faltered. *"That's— well, why haven't you attempted to overthrow them? I saw your people practising their magic by diving off a tower nearly as tall as the Plague Obelisk!"*

"It's the damnable soulstealer in Elki's possession. If we raided Kasparov Manor, even if we overcame their mage forces, Pakhan Kasparov need only say the words, and the soulstealer would consume all mages in the area."

Razarkha's uncertainty washed away, and mania flooded into the void it left behind. *"You're joking. You mock me for bringing you useless information, yet you're oblivious."*

"Oblivious?" the voice asked. *"What are you talking about?"*

"The Soulstealer of Craving is worthless in Ilazar. These runes upon the walls, the wisdom of those brave

Galdusians who refused to give up their bodies? The soulstealers were made with such philosophy in mind!"

"Do not tease me further. I have a harvester with your name in mind."

Razarkha chuckled. *"Oh, I'll tell you if I must. The soulstealers were made to kill ascendants, not mortals. It absorbs unbound souls and converts them into magical fuel, but it can't tear souls from a body. Only ascendants and the recently deceased can be taken."*

The portal rippled, and a long pause preceded Mal'dar's next sentence. *"You're bluffing. There's no way that can be correct. We wouldn't have been so easily fooled. We've seen Elki Kasparov perform lumomantic spellwork with the soulstealer, clear proof he's sapped power from a soul before."*

"Perhaps he absorbed a dying family member. Perhaps he sucked up an ascendant, it's not as though there aren't any in Ilazar. There's one in the central library," Razarkha argued.

"If we raid the manor, we risk a disproportionate number of troops on a hunch from a woman we cannot even call an associate."

Razarkha shrugged. *"You don't need to believe me. All I propose is that you start whittling down Kasparov troops so they have less security detail, carve a path towards the manor, and allow me and an associate to do the rest."*

"And what is the 'rest'?" the Bookkeeper asked.

"Once I get to Elki Kasparov, I'll challenge him to an honour duel on the Battle Isle of Azraiyen. I'll even allow him to use his soulstealer. When I inevitably dominate him, his bluff, and the soulstealer's true insignificance will be revealed. From there, the Plagueborn will be able to retake the city. Isn't that what you want?" Razarkha asked.

"What would you want in exchange for all this? You volunteered to do most of the risky operations. There's a Plagueborn proverb that says if you're freely given something, something of yours is freely taken."

Razarkha put her hands together. "And how right that is. Still, you'd be surprised at how little I want. I want you to erase the debts my associate owes the Kasparov Family even if you pick up the rest of their extortion rackets. It's a few thousand credits, no doubt a pittance to an organisation with monetary flow such as yours.

"In addition, I want clemency from your group as an associate, and ownership of the Soulstealer of Craving once Elki Kasparov dies. Seeing as I'll prove its uselessness by beating him, I can't imagine that will be a problem."

"I shall relay these terms to War'mal," the voice said. "Is there anything else you would ask of the War'mal Group? If your information is correct, it is most useful."

Her mind danced about, then made a cautious leap. "I have one small request. I want to make a good first impression with dearest War'mal. Are there any hitmen who have angered him lately? I would be glad to assist in some erasure."

* * *

Rakh crutched through the slushy streets of Moonstone, Erwyn by his side. The weather didn't know if it wanted to be sleet, snow, or hail. Somehow, the count's frailty made him feel the grim precipitation even more. Even his missing hand stung from the cold.

"This is it. The day we possibly die," Rakh said. "After what I've survived, it would be something of an anti-climax."

Erwyn sighed. "If only life were a story. As it is, we must accept our deaths as a possibility. I still think it's less likely than you imagine."

"You realise Khanas is mob boss—"

"Of course I know that. I also know he takes his noble name seriously. The Khanas in the Crystal Palace, Rowyn, is a knight who from all reports is a perfectly honourable fellow. Regardless of what he is on the inside, he has a reputation to maintain. Is there honour amongst thieves? I can't truly say. What I can say is some want to act as though there is."

"You haven't seen what I've seen, Erwyn. Former members of his group are nothing but corpses for him to experiment on."

Erwyn chuckled. "I'm offended, Rakh. What do you think *I* do with spare cadavers? I'm a biologist, he's a necromancer. People like us never squander a fresh body."

Rakh shuddered. "It appears we'll be safe after all. You and Plutyn Khanas seem to be made for each other."

"I wouldn't quite say that, but I appreciate the faith," Erwyn said, his pale face reddening.

They made it to the Khanas Estate, and when they walked through the winter garden, the usually listless, gardening zombies stopped their work and stared at Rakh's crippled attempts to navigate the icy path. Erwyn slowed his pace too, though whether it was fear or dutifulness to his count, Rakh couldn't say.

"Perhaps we should turn back."

"Plutyn already knows we're here, if these undead are any indication," Erwyn stated. "If we run, we're confirming that you've turned cloak."

"You make a good point," Rakh admitted. "Forgive me if I'm still afraid."

"It's good to be afraid. Fear is what keeps us alive."

They reached Bloodmetal and Notongue, the latter of which snagged Rakh by the collar with a hiss.

Bloodmetal, meanwhile, hoisted Erwyn over his shoulder and spoke.

"It's nice of you to come back, Count Fel'thuz. Lord Khanas wants to speak to you, and honestly, it ain't looking good. We were discussing options this morning."

Rakh wriggled in Notongue's grip. "We wanted to speak to him. Clear things up."

Bloodmetal chuckled. "You're a braver man than I, Fel'thuz. I ain't your pal, but I ain't your enemy either. If Lord Khanas sent me after you, I'd hurt for a moment."

"I'll take that as a compliment," Rakh said as Notongue slackened his hold. "Erwyn wishes to discuss matters with Lord Khanas too. We don't want this to be a bloodbath."

"Nobody does," Bloodmetal claimed. "But we can't have associates acting out of line."

"Let's just get this over with," Rakh muttered.

The pair were carried into the marble manse to a room Rakh had never visited before. It was a bare, extremely clean space with naught but a hard, rocky floor and several green-burning braziers. Within, Plutyn Khanas stood with enforcers of multiple races, his eyes glimmering as his revenant orcs dumped Rakh and Erwyn on the floor.

"You're honourable for returning, but it looks like you visited somewhere else first," Lord Khanas said. "You've been a helpful associate, Fel'thuz, but I don't believe Erwyn Yagaska pledged his discretion to me."

"Lord Khanas, I can explain—"

"Men, make a point," Plutyn said with a click, and immediately, the enforcers got to work.

Rakh's body was already in a constant state of aching and nausea; somehow, this sharp pain was more bearable. A missing tooth, a jab to the chest, and a winding knee to the stomach were somewhat refreshing in the most agonising sense of the word. He almost laughed, but then looked beyond himself. Erwyn was wailing, curled up and shaking. He wasn't some mad snake like Rakh was.

"Yield," Rakh blurted. "Yield, please, for Erwyn's sake."

Plutyn held up his hand, giving the pair respite, then slinked to the downed Rakh, crouching so he could meet his eyes. "Why would you protect Yagaska? That upjumped Sanguinasi count is the problem. You were almost a made man, Fel'thuz. I considered making you an official part of the family so you could be with your son. But you turned on me."

Erwyn finally broke his silence. "He did nothing of the sort. He emerged from the catacombs, bedraggled and afraid. He *begged* me not to take him in. I had guards carry him to the castle against his will. If this is a truly pressing concern, kill me!"

"No!" Rakh begged. "Don't say that, Erwyn! You saved my life, don't die for me too."

Plutyn stepped back and put his hands together. "How touching. Well, if you're both so eager to die for each other, I'll gladly assist—"

"No!" a young man's voice echoed, before immediately degrading into babbling. "Shit, shit, shit, shit, shit, shit—"

"Rarakhi," Plutyn broke in. "Reveal yourself. You won't be punished. You've hidden Plutera with you, haven't you? Come out, both of you."

The young lovers appeared in a dark, lantern-free corner, Plutera standing in front of Rarakhi.

"Father, please forgive Rara's outburst—"

"He's free to speak," Khanas replied. "I'd like him to make the case for his father's survival."

Rakh's hope evaporated. Even if the boy had made a heart-warming attempt to save him, Rarakhi still knew little about Rakh. What could he say that Plutyn didn't already know? The necromancer's expression was indiscernible in the dim light, but something told Rakh it was the same cold gaze as usual.

Rarakhi made a few false starts, then finally articulated himself. "When I asked if I could see my mother, you said I could. You respected my father's final wishes when you thought he was dead and now you're turning on him? Now that I know he's alive I want him to come with me! You think I'm not going to make him answer for leaving me in that orphanage? I need him alive!"

Plutera stammered a few words of her own. "If I may interject, the spies told us Rakh tried to stop Erwyn from taking him in. He obviously didn't want to reveal his affiliations. I know I'm biased, father, and I know you have the power to overrule me, but please consider his efforts. He didn't *want* to betray you. If anyone needs to die, let it be the wisdom."

"Intent is meaningless," Plutyn stated. "I need to know how many people have found out about your injury and how many people understand its significance. Even if your disgraced mentor taught you the finest tricks in the business, I *know* you can't measure that amount accurately, Yagaska."

Erwyn steadied his breath and made his case. "I don't know how many people saw Rakh's injuries, this is true. But I know how many people can link the injuries to you; Rakh and I. Painstaking efforts were made to ensure the lady never knew Rakh was in the castle, let alone ask about how he got his injuries. As for servants who've seen them, they've been given a small bonus to disincentivise gossip."

"What about the commoners you passed on the way? You can't pay off everyone," Khanas pointed out.

"I don't need to," Erwyn said. "They only know Rakh was hurt fighting some monster, and Lady Selenia is hardly going to speak to peasants. Aside from that, they know nothing of your family's involvement. I can easily spin a story to sway the people. If I disappear, on the other hand, *that's* when tongues will start wagging. Lady Selenia views me as a father. Imagine how she'd use her guard force if I went missing."

Plutyn clicked his finger. "Men, make a point."

A nearby enforcer stamped on Erwyn's crotch, and the necromancer loomed over the writhing wisdom.

"Do not presume to threaten me. You may have valid arguments, but you must watch your tone in the presence of old nobility."

Erwyn whimpered in pain, so Rakh did the speaking for him. "Please don't kill him. He's done everything he can to keep our connection secret. He kept Rarakhi's location concealed for twelve years; he's good at what he does. He even expressed interest in working with you."

Plutyn raised an eyebrow. "He wants to work with me? You'd find a way for that idiotic brat in the ilmenite spire to treat me as a noble? Is that what you're proposing?"

Erwyn finally found his voice. "I have information you may desire and positions you may enjoy. I'm willing to extend the hand of friendship between the houses of Selenia and Khanas. Are you enemies with the Church of Eternity, by any chance?"

Lord Khanas turned from Erwyn and walked back to his enforcers. "After discovering some of their perennial activities, yes. Stand this fellow up. He is to be treated as a guest unless I order otherwise. As for you, Fel'thuz, your life is in your son's hands. He demanded you visit his mother with him, so that's your duty. If you disappoint him, my mercy will become fury."

With that, the men helped Erwyn up, and left the room along with their lord. Rakh's ever-loyal wisdom looked back and tried to say something, but whatever it was, it was muffled by the commotion. The only people left were Rarakhi and Plutera, the latter offering her hand.

Rakh smiled and took it, pulling himself up. "Thank you, Plutera. You too, Rarakhi. Without you, Erwyn and I would be dead."

Rarakhi covered his sling. "I wanted to catch up with Erwyn anyway. As for you, like fuck I'm going to let you get away."

Rakh chuckled. "Tell yourself that if it helps you sleep at night. Lord Khanas told you where your mother is, correct?"

"She's working in Deathsport," Rarakhi answered. "Lord Khanas has a cousin in the Crystal Palace who's friends with this ascendant guy. The ascendant said they felt her presence in Deathsport, an' even read her thoughts. She's a spymaster for the Crown. She even visited Moonstone when you fought Aunt Razarkha."

The mere pronunciation of Razarkha's name brought the day's events back to Rakh. The hooded, child-sized woman with a tail serving Quira Abraxas was Tei after all. If knew at the time, what would he have said? What could he have said? It didn't matter. He had a train journey to think his questions over.

Desolation

Muffled bumps and clacks acted as gentle background noise to Rakh and Rarakhi's train carriage. Outside their window, the lush green plains of the Sanguinas Territories rushed backwards at an alarming rate, while the varnished tables of the interior stayed fixed. Populating the carriage were numerous travellers, most of them rich enough to afford sachets to hide the oily aroma of the chugging machinery they occupied.

Rakh and Rarakhi sat opposite each other, both wearing acceptable levels of eye makeup and hair dye for once. Picking at pieces of a pork pie, they chatted with one another. Unlike Rakh's previous conversational efforts, Rarakhi was talking as much as he was.

"I tried going to a jazz club in the Yookietown on the night you killed the daemon," Rarakhi said. "Some bar that pretended to be café. Do all Yookies love tobacco so much? What's wrong with bhang-weed?"

Rakh shrugged. "I think it's something about showing off their imperial might. Tobacco doesn't grow naturally in Yukishima."

"Where does it grow, then?"

"Na'lima, in Northern Amerist, though I might be wrong about the country. Anyway, it's Ameristian, so to Yookies, it's essentially smoking a trophy of conquest."

Rarakhi smirked. "Why do you like Yookies so much? They seem like a bunch of imperialist fucks."

"Not every Yookie is like that. The Park Pals have been nothing but humble in the years I've known them," Rakh said. "Besides, I don't need to like Yookies to like their music."

"Sounds like denial to me."

Rakh chuckled. "By that logic, you have all the stereotypes of a man who enjoys horticulture. Perhaps I should inform Plutera of what truly sways you."

Rarakhi's face creased. "Are you calling me inverted?"

"If you can take a musket-ball to the back, you can take a bit of banter," Rakh said. "Does it feel good to be free for a while?"

"You mean away from Moonstone and the Boss?" Rarakhi asked.

Rakh nodded. "It can't be good for a boy your age, working for a man like Plutyn Khanas. He's respectable in many ways, but you saw what he did to Erwyn and I."

"I dunno," Rarakhi said, stuffing the last piece of pie into his mouth, continuing to talk as he chewed. "I kind of like icing fools. Not in the creepy way torturers do or anything, just soldier to soldier, you know, killing a person who wants you dead. Feels good to me."

Rakh gazed out of the window. "In another life, you could have been a knight or a guard."

"What's the difference between what I do and what an 'official' soldier does? Isn't it all killing for some person who calls themselves lord or lady?"

Rakh couldn't provide an unhypocritical answer. This was a breed of incisiveness Rakh lacked; only Tei could shut him up so easily.

"Well? What's the difference?"

"Nothing significant," Rakh admitted. "I know that guards are at least limited by the law."

Rarakhi scoffed. "Nah, they're not. They're the ones with the weapons, and 'cause of their secrets, the Boss controls a lot of 'em. Erwyn and that lady may pay them, but they got different concerns."

Rakh's voice staggered. "At least a guard can quit his job any time he likes. If he doesn't want to kill and apprehend criminals for a living, he can stop and start his career anew. As you've seen first-hand, people don't leave the underground life."

Finally, the boy was quietened. "I guess. All the folks I iced had family, probably. Still, if they were part of the underground, they were probably bad folks like me."

"I can see how you'd think that. It's not killing to you, it's business."

"I'm like you in a way. I need an excuse too, just not a moral one."

"Whenever a person dies, they're leaving someone behind. That can't be avoided, no matter how we rationalise it. It takes a rare family to withstand the destruction the underground brings," Rakh said.

"I think we're doing all right," Rarakhi remarked, but his expression shifted as his father raised his stump of a forearm. "Sorry."

"It's fine. The Fel'thuzes were shambolic long before I discovered who you work for."

Following this statement, the pair stewed over their thoughts. Beyond the train, the scenery had shifted to a thick set of blurred trees, all landmarks obscured by their trunks. Rarakhi played with his tangled, overgrown hair, then broke the silence once again.

"Aunt Tei is my mother, but you were married to Razarkha. What happened?"

Rakh closed his eyes. "I was wondering when you'd ask that. Please promise not to take this personally."

The boy held his sling to his body. "It's how I came into this world; how else do I take it but personally?"

"My apologies. I'll try to keep this short," Rakh began. "Razarkha and I had been married for five years or so. We tried to make it work, and even she wanted to raise an heir. She kept miscarrying, and while she was already twisted, her failure to have children, best me in arguments, or do anything productive embittered her.

"Bitter people become bullies, and there was always someone for Razarkha to torment if she was feeling bad that day: Tei. She's what people call an imp, that's— that's when a spellbinder comes out deformed and stunted. Erwyn knows the name of the condition, but my point is, she was different, and Razarkha exploited that."

Rarakhi turned his gaze to the table. "The Boss says blood purity is its own biggest weakness. We're all illusionists, but we're all at least a little fucked up."

Rakh gave a sad laugh. "Razarkha is broken mentally, Tei is broken physically, and I've been a terrible husband. I could have tried to mollify Razarkha, but instead, I focused on comforting Tei. Every time Razarkha went too far, Tei would ask to speak to me alone, and I would always make time for her.

"One night, she told me she was hideous. She dropped her usual facial illusion and cried over some comments Razarkha made regarding her disfigurement. I told her that reasonable people would look past it, and that she was lucky to be free of the marriage Razarkha and I endured. It wasn't enough. She told me her biggest fear was being alone for life."

Rarakhi's voice shook. "So you comforted her by —"

"Yes. It was wrong of me. She was a girl of eighteen, I should have known better," Rakh said. "Razarkha made us both miserable, but we had each other. She wanted to be with someone who looked past her deformities. I'm sure Tei looks back with regret too."

"I'm just the result of two scared siblings fucking," Rarakhi muttered. "An accident that everyone regrets."

Rakh's chest filled with fear. "No, no, that's not— *you're* not the regret here, the affair is the regret. If your mother and I regretted *you,* don't you think we'd have taken an easier route? Tansy tea is inexpensive. Instead, Tei cast constant illusions to hide her baby bump. She avoided

Razarkha however she could and trained in magic just to ensure she was never attacked by our mad sister. She thought you deserved to exist."

The boy's voice only tightened. "If that's true, why did she put me in an orphanage? Why carry me all that time just to throw me away once I was born?"

Rakh shook his head. "I wanted to keep you, but Tei and Erwyn were right. Hiding a pregnancy was one thing, but hiding a screaming baby was another. I'd trained daily, done what research I could to suppress sound using illusionism, but at the time my knowledge wasn't extensive enough to hide a baby. So Erwyn and Tei spirited you away, keeping your location to themselves. They knew I wanted to see you but didn't trust me not to give it all away."

"Then my mum fucked off to Deathsport, leaving only Erwyn to visit me."

"I'm sorry, Rarakhi. I could have done so much more if I tried. Perhaps in a way I took an out by accepting your fate. Perhaps I did abandon you with my inaction," Rakh admitted.

"Yeah, you did," Rarakhi said, his young voice scratching a tad. "But Tei abandoned me more. At least Erwyn tried to keep me happy, but Tei held me in her belly, then threw me away when she realised I'd be inconvenient. Know this, dad. When we see Tei, we're not gonna be a happy family. I want answers, and I don't care if I have to beat them out of my mother. I want her to answer me, I want her to acknowledge me, and I want her to apologise to me."

Rakh offered his hand. "I understand, Rarakhi. This visit will uncover answers, not happiness. Perhaps, with time, we can find reconciliation."

* * *

The time was slowly approaching. Razarkha lay alone on Weil's couch, staring upwards at the ceiling. After everything, she was still his guest. She'd worked on such an assumption, but it wasn't the behaviour she wanted from her Plague Emperor. She needed an equal to sow destruction with; fortunately, that person would soon come to be. All she needed to do was give the signal. It was amazing what a pilfered crate and projected glittering could do.

Upstairs, the ceiling rumbled with pacing and the air shook with Weil and Vi'khash arguing. Razarkha sat up and strained her ears to pick up any remarks she could use later.

"Your father is improving, thanks to me. I think I should be appropriately compensated!" Vi'khash said in her rough dialect.

"Weren't your wages compensation enough? What was I paying you for if not the healing of my father? I'm starting to think Razarkha was right!" Weil spluttered.

"That brown-necked moron is nothing but trouble for you. She's like the bull at an Elarondian festival, heedlessly charging about and goring whoever she touches," the healer replied. *"You can pay me another two thousand for my continued service or we can end this deal today."*

Weil's voice grew despondent. *"You know this is the day Anya comes to claim her monthly payment. Why today, why now?"*

"If you can't afford it, you'd best find some more money."

There was a lengthy pause, before a set of heavy steps crashed down the stairs. Razarkha opened the front room door and stopped Weil as he headed through the hallway.

"Weil, what's happening? Where are going?"

"I'm going to 'beach comb'," Weil said with a tired tone. "Vi'khash is asking for even more money. I'm sorry for letting you down. Right now, my father is all that matters."

"Of course. Best of luck finding some credits," Razarkha said.

"Aren't you going to come with me? Normally all you do is follow me."

"Not today. I want to read some more of Kaspar's journal. After a little beauty sleep, of course," she said with a sly grin. "Go forth, my Plague Emperor. Even though you occasionally disappoint me, I'll be here, believing in you."

Weil paused. "That's kind of you to say. Thank you, Razarkha."

With that, he moved on and left his home, slamming the front door behind him. Once Razarkha heard him lock the door, her plan was set in motion. First, she vanished, second, she unlocked the door from the inside, and third, she moved back to the front room. From the window, she watched Weil move through the streets of Zemelnya. Once he was sufficiently lost in the crowd, Razarkha projected an image of a dancing, younger Tei into the streets, tripping over her tiny legs like the idiot she was.

In moments, a black-clad pyromancer jumped from a nearby roof, slowing his descent with his flames. Razarkha grinned; this was Han'jazar, the Plagueborn hitman she'd found skulking around War'mal's territory. According to Mal'dar, he was partially trained by the Group's academy yet was expelled for killing 'fellow family'. He may have been an accomplished killer, but he was terrible at noticing illusory credits.

The door opened, and Razarkha slunk out of the front room, still cloaked, to watch Han'jazar quietly close it behind him and edge up the stairs. He was quite unlike typical Ilazari; while most saw it as a point of pride to wear the impractical, handicapping clothes, this man wore simple, black wrappings that covered most, if not all of his body. She retrieved a dagger from her garter and followed him until he stopped outside Weil's room, where he and Razarkha alike listened to the healer and patient within. Vi'khash was quietly ranting to herself, while Ivan made the occasional loud outburst.

"I don't want you to treat me," the old man said in plain Isleborn. *"You're trouble. You're evil. You're not kind to Weil."*

"Weil likes the abuse. Look at your son. He's a failure. He has no spine, and that's why I'm prosperous. He's taken everything you've built up and funnelled it to me. Why are you defending him? He somehow managed to ruin your death."

"He trusted you, he— oh. The end is finally here. It ends, it ends, it finally ends."

Vi'khash laughed. *"Ah, he's back to not knowing where he is. I was worried for a moment."*

At this point, the hitman rushed into the room and unleashed a stream of fire directly at Vi'khash's glittering clothes. She screamed as her hair and clothing caught fire but found enough wherewithal to form a shield of ice, chilling the air to prevent further burning. While Ivan babbled incoherently, Razarkha stayed hidden, lying in wait for her opportunity.

"Someone wants you dead, little girl," Han'jazar said in a dialect even rougher than Vi'khash's. *"I'm about to become a rich man, and it doesn't seem like anyone would miss you. Don't make this harder than it needs to be."*

Vi'khash chuckled in a rasping tone. *"That Arkheran bitch finally made her move. I think you'll find I die hard, friend."*

The ice wall extended to brandish multiple icicle-like spines, then with a gesture, Vi'khash 'pushed' the wall towards Han'jazar. He was quick to blast through the area that would impale him, leaving nought but sodden floorboards in front of him. Razarkha, meanwhile, had to dive directly behind her hitman to avoid becoming collateral damage.

With the wall melted, Han'jazar slowly walked towards his mark, flames dancing about his hands. In a panic, Vi'khash conjured an ice bayonet and made to charge him, but the hitman put his hand out, blasting her in the chest with enough pyromantic power to knock her to the floor. The once-proud healer was practically nude, her once-flowing hair as burnt and tattered as her ruined clothing. She struggled to breathe with her blistering, seared chest, and somehow managed to force out some words.

"She... can't... pay you. If that... Arkheran bitch... sent you... she's tricking you."

Han'jazar hesitated just long enough for Razarkha to act. She leapt invisibly towards the hitman and stabbed him cleanly between the shoulder blades, downing him, then upon his fall, pierced the back of his neck, just to be sure. Once he stopped moving, she revealed herself.

Vi'khash stared at her 'saviour', wheezing between words. "Razarkha? I don't... understand. Didn't you... send him? Why... did you save me?"

"Finally, the timekeepers have announced our end," Ivan babbled. "The harvesters shall reap what is theirs, and I shall be free."

Razarkha watched the hitman's blood pool onto the floor, then met Vi'khash's eyes. She couldn't help but smile.

"Vi'kara... no... this isn't over. Send for a healer, Razarkha. If... you're here to save me... send for a healer..." Vi'khash begged.

This caused Razarkha's smile to bloom into uncontrollable laughter. She sniggered, she guffawed, she giggled, and she chuckled. Finally, she wiped the tears off her face, and knelt to address the charlatan.

"Silly Vi'khash. There's a healer in this very room. You can give me advice. Don't worry, I'll pay for the privilege."

Vi'khash's eyes widened. *"No..."*

Razarkha moved to the bedside table and picked up a set of essential oils. *"Oh, would you look at that, the heat didn't light them up. Your cryomancy truly is remarkable."*

"No, no, you don't... if you're serious, stop! *My... treatments aren't... effective—"*

"It's all right," Razarkha said, taking the set and moving closer to Vi'khash. *"I know how to follow instructions, unlike Weil. Don't worry, I'll inform him of how weak you think he is."*

"Please, please, not like—" Vi'khash began, but was cut off by hacking violent enough that Razarkha expected her to expel half her throat.

"If I recall, it's chamomile to put you to sleep, and then after that I can really *get to work,"* Razarkha said with childish glee, rubbing indiscriminate oils upon Vi'khash's blisters.

The healer could no longer speak, only scream. Razarkha eventually tired of slow rubbing, and so experimented with directly feeding her some likely inedible oils, then she opened her burn wounds and applied oils to the deep flesh within. Eventually, she tired of Vi'khash's noise, so she swapped a bottle of oil for her dagger.

"I'm so glad Han'jazar burnt your chest. A simple stab wound will be indistinguishable amidst all this mess. Have fun navigating every hell there is!"

With that, Razarkha plunged her blade into Vi'khash's heart, quickly removing it and pondering over her agenda. She moved to the bathroom to wash her hands and fill a bucket, then searched the house for a set of matches. After moving the essential oil set back to its place by the bed, she lit a match and burnt away any oils that stuck to Vi'khash's body, hiding both her torture and her stab wound, then used the water to prevent the fire from spreading beyond the corpse.

Once everything else was arranged, she moved to Ivan himself. Despite it being the easiest job of all, something slowed her. He wasn't an enemy, but what else could be done with him? He wasn't doing right by his son, and he wasn't doing right by himself. She stood over the old man and took a pillow from beneath his head.

"There she is. The mortal harvester. I've seen you before. You're here to change my son's world. You're here to change everybody's world. Yet all bright flames are short-lived."

"This bright flame is here to stay. I hope wherever you go, you find your mind permanently," Razarkha said. *"Is there anything you wanted to tell your son?"*

"I'm sorry I was a burden. He should move forth and change the world by your side. This house will soon be no more. The Rakh'vash destroys all orderly perversions of nature."

Razarkha sighed. *"Part coherent, part nonsense. I'll relay what I can to him. Sleep well, Ivan."*

She pushed the pillow onto the old man's face, and though he struggled, he swiftly succumbed. This was the most crucial part of the plan, yet Razarkha wasn't satisfied. She raised his limp head and put the pillow back in place, then slumped into a chair with a malaise she'd never experienced before. This was supposed to be the removal of all her obstacles. This was the triumph her attempt to kill Rakh should have been. She laughed like a jester while going off-plan with Vi'khash, yet finishing the tasks left her dreading the future.

The door opened once again, and Razarkha jumped. She scrambled out of the room, and in a pained tone she didn't have to force, yelled downstairs.

"Weil! Weil, there's— somebody came in, and Vi'khash— everyone's dead."

Without pause, the young man charged upstairs, the air distorting around him as he moved. He pushed past Razarkha and beheld the carnage for himself. The crime scene was exactly as Razarkha had planned, but nausea clung to her nonetheless.

Weil's shoulders slumped, and he held his head in his hands. Tiny portals opened and closed around him, and all Razarkha wanted was for him to speak. If she broke the silence, she would have given herself away. She was liberating him, so why did it hurt so much?

"Who is the man on the floor?" he asked in a monotone.

Razarkha looked down. *"Han'jazar. The War'mal Group talked about him; he's killed a few members. He probably works for the Kasparovs."*

"Did he say anything?"

"Just that somebody wanted Vi'khash and Ivan dead."

Weil's legs became weak, and he caught himself with one hand as the portals around him grew bigger. He started muttering in Chaostongue, while tentacles writhed within his Chaotic Realm.

"I'm here for you, Weil. I'll help you get revenge however you can—"

The door knocked, and Weil stood with disconcerting speed, speaking in a lifeless drone. *"Ah, it's Anya Kasparov, here for a collection. Of course."*

Razarkha watched Weil's portals close, and he quietly walked downstairs, his welling eyes the only outward indicator of turmoil. She followed him, and he opened the door to see that yes, Captain Anya was there, along with her entourage. Around her neck, her malachite trinket glimmered with arcane energy.

"Hello there, Weil. I'm just visiting to make the monthly collection."

Weil's tone remained flat. *"Yes. Come in, I'll make some tea for you and your men."*

Anya entered with her muscle, and Razarkha stayed still, too terrified to question Weil's actions. He was too quiet, like a dog moments before it lunged.

"You look perturbed, Weil. Is there something weighing on your conscience?" Anya asked, offering a disarming smile.

"No, nothing of the sort. Please, get comfortable," he said, heading into the kitchen.

Razarkha rushed after him in a panic and whispered, *"What's going on? Why are you inviting her in, you should give her the money outside, or—"*

"Shut up, Razarkha."

She'd seen his expression before. It was the one Rakh wore whenever she'd gone too far with Tei. Had he figured her out already? If he had, why wasn't he attacking? All she could do was evaluate the situation in silence. He started a fire on his stove, though not before squinting at the matchbox. He put a kettle upon it, then moved with Razarkha into the front room, where his guests awaited.

"Dearest Weil, we're friends, are we not?" Anya asked as he entered.

"We're associates," Weil muttered.

"Associate or friend, it doesn't matter," Anya said. *"I'm glad you and I have such a fruitful business relationship. You're a reliable borrower, and I just want you to know how heartbroken I'd be if—"*

"You killed him," Weil interrupted.

"Excuse me, killed whom?"

"My father. Don't feign obliviousness."

Anya's face twisted with pure, animalistic fear, and Razarkha began to enjoy the situation again. She projected a worried face to hide her grin.

"Think about this, Weil," Anya spluttered. "You're a loyal debtor, why in the world would I kill your father? He's the reason I'm profiting so much from you, it makes no sense for me to—"

"You know we stole from the library, don't you?" Weil accused.

Anya started to back off. "Now Weil, I don't know what you're talking about, but if your father is dead, that's not what I—"

Her words were cut off by a tentacle lunging through her stomach. Before her guards could react, Weil opened a set of portals around him and Razarkha to protect them from the impending assault, accidentally breaking and absorbing parts of the ceiling with stray tendrils. He dragged Anya over his wall, skewered upon a tentacle, and began to scream.

"I should have known it wasn't a perfect crime! I should have known you'd send someone! Hear this, Kasparov! I'm done licking your boots, I'm done being your servant! I'm going to fight you, and I'm going to win! Do you hear me?"

Anya wasn't looking at Weil. She instead stared at Razarkha as her life steadily drained. Finally, she spoke, a wispiness to her voice.

"You poor fool. I didn't have your father killed, and if you haven't got the brains to find the true culprit, I won't spoil the fun. I'll be watching when you finally figure it out, and I'll enjoy every moment."

With that, Anya's body dissipated into a fine magical dust, which gathered itself into a cloud that dragged her malachite necklace upwards while the rest of her clothes fell to the floor. Razarkha panicked and pointed upwards.

"She isn't dead! Open a portal, make sure she doesn't— no!"

Unfortunately, the cloud had already escaped the portal wall. Weil raised his hands and screamed his grief as portal after portal opened around him. More of the house became split by his irresponsibly placed portals, but Anya's new form weaved between them as her entourage found themselves yanked by tentacles or bisected by rifts.

"No! She can't get away with this!" Weil yelled.

Razarkha grabbed hold of him. *"Weil, stop! Focus on killing her men, at this rate you're going to destroy the —"*

"I don't care!" he shrieked, opening a massive portal beneath himself.

Razarkha desperately took hold of him, and the portal kept growing amidst the cacophony, sucking up the floorboards, the stairs, the bannisters, all the unsold books and paintings within the manor, along with the bodies of Ivan, Vi'khash, and Han'jazar. Beneath them, a great beak surrounded by eyeballs opened to consume all.

Even as the Kasparov men screamed to their deaths, Weil and Razarkha floated in the purple-and-red space, locked in an embrace, and finally, the young man wept. Between sobs, he conveyed his true thoughts.

"I'll kill them all, Razarkha. I'll kill them all."

Razarkha stroked his hair. *"I know you will. And I'll do everything I can to help."*

Disruption

The Chaotic Realm's exit dropped Weil and Razarkha amidst the screaming winds of the Sudovykly cliffs. While the latter was quick to pick herself up, the former stayed face-down in the mud, with only the rise and fall of his back indicating he was alive.

"Get up!" Razarkha yelled. *"Do you know what you just did?"*

"I know."

"Now we have no choice but to crush the Kasparovs or die trying," Razarkha said, hoisting him up by the shoulders. *"We need to tell War'mal our plans have accelerated."*

Weil finally came alive and met Razarkha's eyes. *"Thank you for staying strong for me. I don't know if I have the backbone."*

"Of course you do, you just stood up to Anya Kasparov! Yes, she escaped as an ascendant, and yes, we're probably wanted by every Kasparov man there is, but that's why we must finish what we've started. Come, to the Academy!"

Razarkha took Weil's hand then cloaked him along with herself, dragging the listless chaos-speaker back to the civilised parts of Zemelnya. As they neared the city square, they noticed mages in blue and white roaming the area, shaking down anyone and everyone for information. While some citizens gave sheepish answers, the closer they got to the Academy, the more they witnessed people taking the aggressive questioning as a provocation, resulting in destructive magical street brawls.

The pair worked their way around pyromantic explosions and deadly lumomantic rays, before a bulbous-headed tower crumbled directly above them. Razarkha let go of Weil and dived, but there wasn't enough distance cleared. In a panic, she screamed for her friend, drawing nearby gawkers, but the boy had matters under control.

He opened a portal and unleashed a tentacle as wide as the spire itself, catching and suspending it above himself, Razarkha, and numerous Plagueborn onlookers. There was no point cloaking after her scream, and she could hardly make the suspended spire vanish from the memories of the people around her.

Upon Razarkha revealing herself, a pair of Kasparov men, one pyromancer and one telekinete, elevated so they were hovering above the crowd. Razarkha covered her eyes, Weil struggled to keep hold of the tower, and the other citizens were too busy saving themselves to defend them. Razarkha closed her eyes and cursed her need to cause conflict and strife. For a moment, she bemoaned that she'd destroyed everything her only friend cared about for nothing.

Two yelps and the sound of tearing flesh were heard, and Razarkha opened her eyes to see that the formerly flying Kasparovs were skewered above the citizenry, staining the icicle running through both their hearts pink. Perched atop the roof of the Zemelnya Academy of Higher Magical Learning was an old spellbinder with flowing white locks, icy blue eyes, and shifting ice armour.

He allowed the massive icicle to shatter, causing the Kasparov men to fall with a wet thud. Weil was muttering in urgent Chaostongue in an attempt to convince his tentacle to dispose of the tower safely. The people surrounding the Academy made room for the armoured cryomancer, who cast a path of ice towards the ground that he quickly skated down.

"Clear out," the man said in Plagueborn. *"If you see any Kasparov men, do not cooperate. Their wounds have been exposed, and you shall not fear them."*

Razarkha couldn't fully glean the meaning, save that this man wasn't her enemy. *"I am sorry, know only small Plagueborn. You speak Isleborn?"*

"Regrettably, yes," the cryomancer said in fluent Isleborn, walking over to Razarkha. *"I believe my bookkeeper spoke with you. Please have your chaos-speaker swallow that tower."*

"Swallow? What do you mean?" Razarkha asked.

War'mal shoved Razarkha aside in response, and put a hand on Weil's shoulder and took a stern tone. *"You are asking the wrong thing of the Rakh'vash. You cannot prevent chaos with chaos. You can only give your god an offering."*

"You want me to take this tower into my Chaotic Realm? But where will it go?"

"That is for your god to decide," the cryomancer said. *"If you do not do this, destruction is guaranteed."*

Weil closed his eyes and muttered incomprehensibly. Shortly after, a massive portal opened mid-air, slicing the already-extended tentacle and dropping the tower into the Chaotic Realm. He swiftly closed both the portal his tentacle came from and the mid-air one, falling to his knees in exhaustion.

"Well done, boy. Weil, I presume?"

"Yes," Weil said with a puff.

The cryomancer turned to Razarkha and gave a low, theatrical bow. *"And Razarkha, blood of Fel'thuz, the broker. Come, both of you. We must discuss… recent events."*

"Who are you?" Razarkha asked.

"War'mal, the voice of the Plagueborn. Will you be burned by a Kasparov pyromancer, or will you come with me?"

"We'll come, won't we, Weil?" Razarkha replied.

Weil rose with an almost undead slouch. War'mal walked back to the Academy without bothering to match pace with the pair behind him, gestured to the door guard, and opened his academy's entrance. Instead of the dark, sealed room Razarkha experienced, the entrance instead revealed a fully-lit foyer filled with glass displays of historical magical artefacts.

Magitech devices lay mounted upon the walls, along with a painting of the Plague Emperor, clad in wyvern-scale armour, raising a soulstealer into the air amidst a swirling vortex of souls. Curators stood by their assigned displays, explaining their relic to any interested students. There were two sets of stairs at the end of the room, and War'mal headed to the right.

"You may speak poor Plagueborn, but I know for a fact you can say 'thank you' in Isleborn," War'mal said as he started his ascent.

Weil was still in a state of torpor, so Razarkha did the talking. *"Of course. Thank you, Great War'mal, for saving us. I assure you; we didn't deliberately accelerate—"*

"Be quiet," War'mal commanded, reaching the top of the stairs. *"We can discuss details in my chamber."*

Razarkha shut up and followed, keeping an eye on Weil. His eyes were glazed over, and the space about his head was continually distorted by fleeting rifts the size of walnuts. She attempted to perk him up by linking arms with him, but he swiftly unlinked them in response.

After a walk through the halls of the academy's first floor, they reached War'mal's chamber. It was a large room whose air was continually chilly, with glass displays akin to the foyer's. Instead of containing artefacts, however, they contained people, taxidermised in a mockery of lifelikeness. There were numerous labels with Old Galdusian runes upon them, which Razarkha could easily make out. Amongst them were the words *'Disappointment'*, *'Monstrous Betrayer'*, *'Incompetent'*, and *'Kasparov'*. The flesh was poorly fitted to its stuffing, but remarkably well-preserved.

War'mal took a seat behind a desk flanked by a couple of taxidermised elves labelled as *'Foreign Interloper'* and *'Arrogant Wyvern-Rider'*. There weren't any other chairs, so Razarkha and Weil were left to shiver on their feet.

"*Kasparov forces are in quite the panic due to your unexpected actions,*" War'mal said in calm, deliberate Isleborn. "*What in the world were you thinking?*"

Razarkha looked to Weil, who remained pensive as ever. She played with her hair and began to bargain for their lives.

"*We weren't thinking. Anya Kasparov miscalculated. She found out about our heist of the library and decided to send Weil a message by having a hitman kill his father.*"

"*Odd, weren't you looking for enemy hitmen to kill? That's what Mal'dar told me. Who was your mark?*"

"*Han'jazar,*" Razarkha answered. "*I never got the chance to plot his death, but by coincidence, he was sent to kill Weil's father. I took the opportunity and stabbed him in the back.*"

"*Then your friend consumed his own house,*" War'mal said, gesturing to Weil. "*What do you think of this, boy? You seem tired.*"

Weil's conscience flitted back to his body. "*I've lost everything. All I want is vengeance on the Kasparovs.*"

"*Due to your actions, we have no choice but to engage in hot warfare with them. We were at a steady cold war, but that could never last. I'm still unsure of the claim Razarkha made regarding Elki Kasparov's soulstealer being ineffective against non-ascendants. However, given the Pakhan hasn't left his manor despite the commotion, you may be correct.*"

Razarkha butted in. *"Greatest War'mal, please put me to the test. Spare Weil and leave this to me. I'm confident in my claims and fully believe you can raid Kasparov Manor. If his soulstealer is more than a bluff, feel free to kill me for treachery. Otherwise, allow me to challenge Elki Kasparov to a duel."*

War'mal raised an eyebrow. *"If you're wrong, we're all doomed regardless. Pakhan Kasparov's dearest granddaughter is dead. He will not take this lightly."*

"Then why bother killing us for this indiscretion? Kasparov will do your work for you!" Razarkha said. *"If I'm right, however, and you let me duel Elki Kasparov as a mere illusionist, my life is betted, your men's lives aren't, and most importantly, I'll prove the Kasparovs' weakness to all, giving your takeover of Zemelnya legitimacy. Think about it—"*

An icicle flash-formed from War'mal's hand, stopping an inch from her neck. The Plagueborn mob boss held it in place, maintaining frosty eye contact with Razarkha.

"You consider yourself a genius, but got caught stealing those classified books, and you let your chaos-speaker brute escalate this conflict unnecessarily. Your plans are not as amazing as you think."

Razarkha's face flushed up. *"What's your point? If you're going to kill me, do it!"*

War'mal chuckled. *"Ever so brash. The Plague Emperor would have liked you, no doubt. Given you're betting your own life, feel free to join the raid on Kasparov Manor."*

Weil's eyes widened, and Razarkha breathed more freely as War'mal's icicle melted.

"What do you mean, 'join the raid'?" she asked.

"The Kasparovs made the mistake of intimidating people under our protection while chasing you. Honour demands we go for the throat. We already had a raid

planned. If you're wrong, as you said, we're doomed. But if you're right, I will look forward to your antics. However, if you betray us once you have your soulstealer, know that I'm not opposed to taxidermising women."

Razarkha inclined her head. "Of course, Great War'mal. We're in awe of your mercy, aren't we, Weil?"

"Thank you," Weil mumbled.

"Then it's settled," War'mal said. "Get out of my sight. Stay in the Plagueborn side of town until summoned; I won't let you die until the raid."

* * *

Putting faces to words was Tei's greatest strength and weakness. She could glean a personal motive for every report she received, see the person behind the political issue, yet she often felt the skill was wasted once she relayed her findings to the King's publicly visible advisors. She sat alone in her house, watching Deathsport's train station from her window while trying to focus on the notes her spies had provided.

The city stank of scummed-over seawater and sewage, along with the ever-present musk of the overcrowded peasantry. She was glad she lived close to the train station; the scent of oil and machinery was often a welcome respite. A steam engine from the northern provinces had just arrived, tooting its whistle and venting as it came to a stop. Tei tore her mismatched eyes away and focused on her notes. Scanning through, the gist was absorbed within minutes.

Lord Verawyn Verawor of the Crystal Palace was making deals with Wrenfall via Jadeport, likely to curry favour with the Soltelle Empire, naval superpower that it was. In the north, Lady Marissa Gemfire and her cousin, Genna Oswyk, were on the verge of armed conflict due to the former's irresponsible handling of the Gemfires' ancestral home, the Rainbow Fort, while Moonstone's organised crime appeared to be becoming more efficient due to the Khanas Family pushing ahead in the local gang wars.

Tei rubbed her eyes. To her, organised crime was a necessary evil, a means to economically benefit from resources the Crown couldn't publicly approve the sale of. If gangs were busy fighting each other, none would ever consolidate enough power to prove a threat to the nobility. It was when a crime family won their war for good that the real trouble began.

King Landon, by contrast, despised crime in every form. A woman could kill an abusive husband in self-defence, and he would insist upon the woman's execution for the crime of murder. Tei considered it odd that Landon didn't call for the death of his prince-cum-executioner, Komekk Axol, but it was likely he saw enforcing the law as the ultimate exemption from it.

The Moonstone Khanases didn't need to be brought up. It would be wasting royal resources to try and clear every influential crime family from the Kingdom, especially one connected to the old necromantic remnant. Conversely, she would need to speak to Wisdom Robb about the Verawors.

She dropped from her chair and threw on her garb. She'd shed the official and unofficial colours of her family, preferring to instead wear gold and red, along with the blues, blacks, and whites of the Shearwater king that took her in. Personal heraldry seemed to be a pattern within her family; both of her siblings avoided the Fel'thuz blue and white, so she saw no reason to display the family colours herself.

Taking the documents related to Lord Verawor and the Gemfire dispute, she slipped into invisibility, headed downstairs, and entered the paved streets of Deathsport. She obfuscated the motion of her door and took most wide-open path possible; as goblins and gnomes knew well, frequenting tighter-packed areas as a halfling was asking to be trampled.

She moved along a terrace, past a flower-beset obelisk known as the Cheegal Massacre Memorial, and the Carminium Music Hall, a necromantic-style marble theatre. From there it was north-west through the noble district, where Shearwater Manor, the Axol Estate, and Aranathar Manse resided. Peasants of varying fortune passed her by; in the noble district most wore clean clothes and at least one form of eyeglass, if only to show off their relative wealth.

Eventually, she reached the Royal Palace, a tall, monstrous affair which persistently avoided its own origins. It stood behind worked metal gates, numerous engraved spiders dotting its upper window frames, whereas on lower floors these spiders were covered by bold banners depicting a black-and-white sword on purple quartered opposite a pied shearwater on blue.

The gates were shut, but Tei had her own ways of getting in. She walked along the fencing's perimeter until she was right of the palace's entrance, slipping straight through the 'ground' nearby. The truth of the illusion was a trap door disguised as paving; its false nature was obscured by Tei's powers whenever she was awake. She lit the dank surroundings beneath the trap door with her illusionism and headed through, emerging from the tunnel by sticking her head up beneath a rug in the Royal Palace. She clambered out, repositioned the rug, and took note of the guards.

They were mostly elven and orcish, clad in heavy armour with purple cloaks. The troops outside bore muskets and pikes, but within the palace, they almost exclusively wielded swords. Tei slipped by them whenever they marched by a fork in the hall. While it was her duty to be a myth to all but the highest authorities, that didn't mean she couldn't have fun with her status.

One time she caught a guard trying to sneak a peek at the Royal Advisor undressing, promptly resulting in his dismissal, another time she caught Prince Komekk distracting the guards by offering to arm-wrestle them for money. After minutes of labyrinthine navigation, she found the chamber she was after: The workspace of Royal Wisdom Robb Stagg.

She opened the door while obscuring the sight and sound of it as best she could, but somehow, the squint-eyed young man looked up anyway. Gnomes were an odd people; short and stout, just like her, with tiny, light-sensitive eyes and stubby limbs. What they lacked in sight they made up for in hearing; even emulating Rakh's sound manipulation wasn't enough for Tei to successfully hide from Robb. After she continued her entrance and closed the door, the pale, blonde halfling huffed with annoyance.

"I-I-I-I— I can hear you, T-T-Tei. J-just come up with a sp-special knock or something, I could have b-been doing anything," Robb said, twitching throughout.

Tei revealed herself with a curtsey. "I should hope you weren't doing anything requiring privacy in your crown-allotted workspace."

"W-well, no, I-I have a house— f-f-forget I s-said anything. W-what do you have f-f-for me?"

Tei placed her carefully curated reports on his already cluttered desk. "I'll leave the details for you to read over, but in short, Verawyn Verawor seems to be making passive-aggressive jabs. In response to our requests to renegotiate tax rates, he's currying favour with the Soltelles. Also, the Gemfires are having a family spat. It may come to war, but it's up to His Majesty to intervene."

"Th-thank you. Are there any that y-y-you, um, y-y — that you trimmed?" the gnome asked. "N-not that I'd t-tell the King, I just— f-forget I said anything."

Tei narrowed her eyes. This man wasn't half the wisdom his predecessor, Melancholy, was. She couldn't trust him to speak a coherent sentence, let alone trust him with secrets. She still had to assuage his suspicions. Wisdoms, regardless of competence, asked questions.

"The usual. Minor gossip, spies with too much free time on their hands, 'he saids' and 'she saids'."

"Oh, I s-see. Quira w-was asking about you, she s-said you've b-been avoiding her since you returned f-from Moonstone. How are you taking y-your sister's exile, is it…"

The wisdom trailed off as Tei's glare found its way into the short-sighted fellow's head. Tei rubbed her temple, then turned from Stagg.

"I'm not avoiding Quira; I've just been busy. Why, is there a pressing matter she has for me?"

"A-as far as I know she's j-just worried about your wellbeing."

"Then I suppose I need to quash those concerns. But not today. I have to befriend a spellwork book on chaos-speech."

Robb cocked his head. "D-d-don't you get lonely, b-being unseen all the time?"

"Not at all," Tei said through clenched teeth, vanishing and making a muted getaway.

She traversed the halls once more, reached the same rug, moved it, entered the passageway, pulled the rug to as she closed the trap door, lit her way, exited through the false paving, and strode as well as her stunted legs allowed. She'd almost made it home when, upon passing the train station, a pair of spellbinders caught her eye.

One was undoubtedly Rakh, crimson-eyed, tall, toned for a spellbinder, but something was off. His right hand was wavering, and with a little counteractive distortion, a stump was revealed. Beside him was a slightly shorter spellbinder, a boy of thirteen or so with teal eyes and his father's features. Around his right arm was a sling, and his hair was a great long tangle.

Tei stood in place as her breathing fell into disarray. Was Rakh here for her, or were the Selenias sending him to make a petition to the King? When had he lost his hand? Most importantly, why in the world was Rarakhi with him, and how did he get injured?

She couldn't afford to follow them; Rakh was too good at spotting a poorly maintained cloak. She remembered all the times she'd sneak into his bed, thinking she'd fooled him, but he would always lift the sheets and her cloaking at the same time. She instead made a panicked dash back to her home, slamming the door and locking it with three chains and her key.

As far as the public knew, she was just a shut-in with inherited money lucky enough to live on the richest terrace in Deathsport, some girl who paid for easy access to the trains but lacked the confidence to explore the kingdom. Without context, nobody would suspect Tei Fel'thuz of Moonstone lived here, not even Rakh.

She stayed cloaked and moved back to her bedroom, staring down from her window to track her kin. They roamed through the crowds, almost pantomiming a search effort, their motion suspiciously smooth. They were so tall, so noticeable, so much better than Tei. Her eyes welled up just watching the healthy, albeit injured boy she'd birthed. He wasn't deformed, he wasn't short, he was physically perfect, just like his father.

Tei was so lost in her memories that it took her a moment to realise that the two men had vanished. Her eyes darted about as she tried to find them again, then somebody knocked on her door, shocking her out of her chair.

She couldn't pretend nobody was in. Rakh could probably detect the distortions her magic made through the window. Perhaps he'd seen her running from them. What kind of Royal Looking Glass was she if she couldn't hide from her own family? Biting her lip in frustration, she moved downstairs and opened the door, remaining invisible.

"Come in. Shut the door."

Rakh and Rarakhi were so much taller than her, looming over the family freak without trying. Their tails were so straight, their faces so ordinary. Once Rarakhi shut the door, Tei dropped her cloak.

"Explain yourselves."

Confrontation

Rakh stood before his former lover, the little sister who'd endured everything. She was shorter than her adolescent son yet stood resolute. Silence clung to the air, forcing Tei to destroy it with prejudice.

"*Well?* Explain yourselves! Erwyn and I worked to ensure you *wouldn't* do something stupid like expose our son. What in the world happened?"

Rakh attempted to form an adequate response, which allowed Rarakhi to overtake him.

"He said 'fuck it' and actually tried to see me, which is more than you ever did!" the boy yelled. "If what he said is true, then you're responsible for everything. Me growing up in a shithole, Erwyn stringing me along, *everything!*"

Finally, Rakh found his words. "Tei, I— I didn't blame you for anything, I just told him what I knew. I want us to reconcile now that Razarkha's gone, and—"

"My dad's been making excuses, but guess what, ma, we found you! Seems like the King can't keep you hidden all too well when Khanas eyes are on you," Rarakhi ranted, striding towards his mother, who tripped over as she backed off. "I want to know why you kept me. Why you *forced me to live!*"

Rakh used his remaining hand to grab the back of Rarakhi's collar and pulled him back. "Don't you *dare* physically threaten your mother. We're going to talk about this like civilised people, am I understood?"

Tei lay prone on the floor, breathing heavily as her son stood down. "What happened to you, Rarakhi? Why are you injured? Why are you so hateful? Gods, you mentioned Khanas, didn't you? What have you two been up to?"

"Lead us to your guest room," Rakh said. "We need somewhere to sit and discuss matters calmly."

Tei nodded, then scrambled into a side room. Rarakhi glared at his father once she was out of sight.

"Why are you protecting her? She knows what she did."

"You're not going to get answers if you hurt her," Rakh said. "Is what you want your first impression to be? A mother-beating thug? She'll continue to hide the truth if you do that. She kept you secret from her big sister for years. Do you think she's the loose-lipped type?"

"Shut up."

"No, the time has come for you to be quiet so she can give you the clarity you say you want. Are you looking for answers, or vengeance?"

Rarakhi took a long, seething breath. "I don't know what I want now that I'm here."

"Calm down, think about what you want, and don't bully my sister. Am I understood?"

"Fine."

Rakh joined Tei in her living room, a dusty affair with a single couch and a large cushion lying upon the floor. The only decently maintained fixture was a game table with an eight-by-eight checked board, perfect for *Wraiths and Wyverns,* chess, and draughts. Two plates lay on the floor, one with crumbs and another with a half-eaten fairy cake.

"Sorry about the mess," Tei muttered, hiding the plates beneath the table. "Please take the couch, I'm happy on my cushion."

Rakh's throat stung a tad. "Are you sure? I thought you'd appreciate the—"

"I insist," Tei said as she sat. "I know I'm short, Rakh. You don't need to pretend I'm normal or beautiful. I'm stunted, I'm deformed, and I'm cowardly."

Rarakhi wasted no time sitting on the best seat in the house, and Rakh remained stood, unsure of how to comfort this new Tei. The three Fel'thuzes lingered in the room, waiting for someone else to break the silence, but there was no social protocol for the trio's situation.

"How did you both get injured?" Tei asked.

"I got shot," Rarakhi said matter-of-factly.

Rakh, meanwhile, tried to spur further conversation. "I lost my hand fighting a daemon. It was huge enough to block part of Moonstone catacombs. According to reports, it appeared out of nowhere; I'm not sure how something that big sneaks underground."

Tei's brow furrowed. "These injuries are connected, aren't they? I know you're bold, Rakh, but I can't see you taking up daemon hunting to make up for the lack of a daemon at home. This came after discovering Rarakhi's whereabouts, didn't it?"

Count Fel'thuz grimaced and put his stump against the back of his head, forgetting there wasn't a hand to play with his hair. "Sharp as ever, Tei. I didn't want you to worry, but Rara has joined the Khanas Family. By the time Erwyn gave me his location I was too late. I had to do some favours for Plutyn Khanas—"

"And now you're effectively a Khanas associate," Tei concluded. "I'm sure he appreciated your self-sacrificing nature, but this will have long-lasting consequences. Does Erwyn know the hole he's put you in by giving Rarakhi's location away?"

Rakh paused. "He does. He saved my life, and now he's negotiating with Plutyn—"

"For pity's sake, Rakh, how much ground have you ceded to a criminal? I've been tracking the situation from here, and do you know what happens when the careful equilibrium of crime families starts to skew in one's favour? You get Ilazar, where the ruling class means nothing but being the winning family's—"

"Will you shut up?" Rarakhi butted in. "You're acting like the Boss is a monster and that Moonstone's gonna be shit 'cause he's gaining power. He's a better parent than you'll ever be. He loves his daughter, and fuck it, he loves me too!"

Tei closed her eyes and shook her head. "I'm sorry, Rarakhi. This shouldn't be about politics. This should be about you. If you truly feel that I'm worse than an organ smuggler and blackmailer, I'm sorry."

"You're 'sorry I feel this way', right?" Rarakhi scornfully remarked. "Sorry I can't just look at my kin and accept them without question. Dad's told me about how he treated Razarkha. She did shitty things, and blood didn't stop him hating her."

Tei's voice levelled out. "You're right. You're free to hate me."

The boy's voice wavered. "But you— why aren't you sad about that? Why are you just— you— *why are you accepting that?*"

"Because I failed you. I was only a girl when you were conceived," Tei admitted. "I was scared. I thought if I drank bitterwater, I'd be a monster, a baby-killer."

"So that's it, you forced me to suffer just so you could feel better? Where's the genius dad bragged so much about? Why are you so *stupid?*"

Tei composure collapsed, and she began to sob, prompting Rakh to intervene.

"Rarakhi, I told you to stay quiet and let Tei answer your questions. If you're just going to interrupt her whenever her answers aren't ideal, what's the point?"

"Please stop defending me, Rakh," Tei broke in. "I've always hidden behind you, and when you couldn't stand up for me, I'd run. Rarakhi's right to be angry. I need to hear his hatred. I need to know what I've done to the innocent boy we created."

"But Tei—"

"I can't run forever, Rakh! You've demonstrated that more than ever. All it took was my curiosity regarding your stump and a few poor cloaking decisions for you to track me to my home. I've hidden long enough. It's time to confront my failures."

Rarakhi's eyes started to leak. "That's what I am? A failure?"

"No. You were an innocent I allowed to suffer. My failure was my neglect, not your existence. I know it's stupid of me, Rakh, but when I was a little girl, I had this terrible, evil dream that always left me smiling," Tei said, emitting a broken husk of a laugh. "I dreamt that you pushed Razarkha out the window. Just like how Razarkha was never tried for pushing Waldon out the window, you got away with uxoricide. Then we married, we took Rarakhi in, and we would be free to be a family."

Tei wept once again, and Rakh moved from the couch to kneel by his sister. He took her into his arms, momentarily believing that he had two hands to hold her.

"It's an understandable dream, but it could never be."

Tei trembled in her brother's embrace. "I saved a baby's life, and now he's a criminal."

"I wrongly spared Razarkha's life. Rarakhi is no Razarkha, I assure you."

Rarakhi remained on the couch while his parents whimpered, groaned and rocked in each other's arms. Eventually, his apparent patience for self-pitying adults vanished.

"You're both failures. But I fucked up too. Joining the Khanas Family was a bad choice I made on my own. You didn't force me to do that. But you know what, I had fun 'cause of that decision. I killed some evil fuckers, I made my own money, and I even fell in love with Plutera! It's not like your lives have *always* been complete shit 'cause of your failures."

The Fel'thuz parents stopped their blubbering and released each other, staring at their son. Rakh wiped away his tears and allowed a moment of genuine laughter.

"I suppose I always loved my verbal sparring with Razarkha. And even if my womanising was primarily to cope with Tei's disappearance, the women I've met over the years have expanded my perspective. Even meeting Plutyn Khanas has been an enlightening experience."

Tei smiled. "I would never have risen to Royal Looking Glass and met people like Quira Abraxas if I hadn't exiled myself. If it wasn't for Razarkha running roughshod, I'd have never met Erwyn. Life's terrible, but beauty accompanies the misery."

Rarakhi stood. "I didn't know what I was gonna do here. I hated you, ma, I really did. I wanted you to beg and cry. I wanted you to fear retribution for everything you did wrong. But now I know *both* my parents are pathetic people who hate themselves for their decisions. You morons are punishing yourselves enough. I just want to go home."

"Wait!" Tei said. "When do you hope to depart?"

Rakh swallowed. "Tei, you're not hoping to—please don't resign because of us."

"I'm not going to resign. If you think that my stupid fantasy of us being a perfect family is ever going to happen, you're mistaken. But while Razarkha is languishing wherever she is, I want to visit Moonstone and perhaps negotiate with your Lord Khanas. Meet the man Rarakhi considers to be his father. Saying hello to Erwyn would be nice too."

Rakh tried to pat his sister on the back, but instead clubbed her with his handless wrist. "Best of luck getting some time off. Rarakhi, are you happy if she comes home with us?"

"What am I going to do, stop her buying a train ticket?"

Tei smiled wholeheartedly, then obscured her form. "I'll be right back!"

* * *

Within a training room of the Zemelnya Academy of Higher Magical Learning, Razarkha and Weil were mere cogs in the magitech device that was the War'mal Group. Pyromancers, lumomancers, cryomancers and geomancers stood in line, awaiting orders from their glorious leader.

Weil was to Razarkha's left, and just beyond him was a black-haired spellbinder in a simple white robe. Bones adorned this peculiar fellow's necklace and a wyvern's skull acted as his helmet. He turned to Weil, keeping his hands behind his back.

"*Ah, here is the one who pushed us all to this point. You haven't seen me in person, but I'm Bookkeeper Mal'dar.*"

Weil frowned. "*I'm sorry, I don't know who you are. Did Razarkha discuss matters with you?*"

"*I did,*" Razarkha said. "*You're a deathspeaker, if I recall correctly. You threatened to summon a harvester. Will you be able to summon any today?*"

"*If the Inevitable Harr'khel wishes it, yes,*" Mal'dar replied. "*Today many offerings shall be given to them. They should be in a good mood, I imagine.*"

Razarkha smirked. "*That's good to know. I myself have a few—*"

"*Enough,*" Mal'dar said. "*I would like to talk to the chaos-speaker. It appears you have trouble controlling your chaos portals if you're sucking up entire houses with your powers.*"

Weil closed his eyes, and distortions appeared around his head. "*I usually have no issues summoning daemons, though the type is left to the Great Rakh'vash. I cannot, however, choose where in the mortal realm I enter from the Chaotic Realm."

"What happened with your manor, then? Why was the portal so destructive?"

"Because I lost my father to a Kasparov hitman, then Anya visited to gloat. Magical incontinence would be expected of anyone," Weil muttered.

"Of course. Try to stay focused when taking revenge. We don't want to endanger our troops. For everyone's good, be sure to unleash daemons a good distance from allies, if at all."

"What use am I if I don't summon daemons?"

"You could block incoming magical projectiles with portals, drop people into your rifts, cause structural damage to the manor with tentacles. Get creative, and your powers will reward you."

Weil smiled, and Razarkha faced the floor. This stranger had succeeded at cheering Weil up while everything she'd attempted since the death of Ivan had only made him miserable. What good was she if she couldn't inspire her allies? She straightened her back and tightened her grip on her dagger. She knew who she was. She didn't make people feel better, she made people *be* better. Weil's potential was limitless, and his grief-stricken outbursts were just the beginning. Under her, the boy would become a potent weapon, and she would wield him.

War'mal walked into the wide-open room, silencing all preceding chatter. Once in front of his troops, he formed a pillar of ice beneath his feet, elevating himself in a more than figurative sense. He cleared his throat, then addressed his people in Plagueborn.

"Men of Zemelnya, liberated blood of Sula, our time has come. We have reason to believe that the Isleborn's hold over Zemelnya is little more than an illusion, and that the strong have yet to dominate this great isle. We shall take Zemelnya, and from there we can secure the inner cities of Kaosukryl and Osvobozhden. For now, we shall focus on the task that will enable all these future feats: Raiding the Kasparov Manor.

"Those who attended the elite briefing will already know that while any Isleborn can join the Kasparov Family, biological Kasparovs are mere illusionists, much like our associate, Razarkha of Fel'thuz's blood. This, along with light hair, blue eyes, and white and sky-blue robes is how one shall recognise blood Kasparovs.

"All adult Kasparovs shall not be spared our wrath, save Elki, the family's Pakhan. As for their children, they shall be spared and kept as involuntary guests at the Plague Emperor School of Healing Arts for analysis. Being able to replicate the delicate balance of lumomancer and necromancer required for illusionism will be useful knowledge indeed."

Razarkha cringed at the pieces of information she could properly translate. Something about sparing children for experimentation didn't sit right with her. Killing them made the most sense; it would end the Kasparov line, rid them of any vengeful future enemies, and wouldn't exploit the weak. The strong didn't need help from weaklings; the Plague Emperor knew this, and so did Razarkha. She kept silent, however; protesting was likely to result in an extended stay in War'mal's office.

"Geomancers, you shall take the front line. Clear the way through the Isleborn side of town and the Scruchen Forest, then destabilise the foundations of Kasparov Manor. Pyromancers and lumomancers should focus on defending us with focused fire on any Kasparov men foolish enough to attempt a flank, while cryomancers and our two godspeakers should add to this defence by walling off Razarkha of Fel'thuz's blood."

Razarkha's eyes lit up as she recognised her name amidst the Plagueborn blur and spoke up in her broken rendition of the language. *"I think you no defend me?"*

"We shall see you to the manor. From there, it's up to you to find Elki Kasparov. Bookkeeper Mal'dar is in consultation with a harvester tracking your life force. If you die, he will know. While we occupy and kill every Kasparov we can, you shall move through the manor and find the Pakhan. From there, challenge him to a duel. With any hope, Pakhan Elki's humiliation will be complete as he loses to Razarkha."

"And if she dies before challenging him?" Mal'dar asked.

"Then we shall kill Elki ourselves. There is one caveat to this attack," War'mal admitted. "It assumes that his soulstealer is ineffective against fleshly beings, as Razarkha has informed us. If she's wrong, we shall quickly realise it, and will retreat any way we can, then flee Zemelnya. We would also kill Weil, the chaos-speaker who forced this escalation."

Weil remained silent and didn't take Razarkha's hand when she offered it. She pled with her eyes, prompting an uncomfortable smile from him before he reversed his rejection.

"I comfort you, Elki Kasparov's power is as nothinged as brother kin's proudness. I defeat him on Battle Isle Azraiyen, and many see weakness of Kasparov," Razarkha attempted to assure the group.

"Forgive her terrible Plagueborn," War'mal continued. "Given she's also in mortal danger, I have no reason to think she doesn't believe her information. What is yet to be tested is if she's correct. Until a conclusion is reached, you have your orders. Plagueborn of Zemelnya, blood brothers, move out!"

The soldiers cheered, and as a squad, they left the academy. Weil was herded to the back line, while Razarkha moved to the centre of the formation, within a group of cryomancers. She looked back, desperate to call out to him, but she didn't know what to say.

Marching through the Plagueborn part of town elicited encouragement from the surrounding citizens, but once they reached the richer parts of Zemelnya, Kasparov men came out of cover. Pyromancers hovered and attempted to firebomb the back line, but Weil and Mal'dar opened portals to swallow the fireballs as they came.

Abruptly, a tentacle emerged from Weil's portal and grabbed one pyromancer, flinging him into another, sending both careening to the ground in a bloody heap. The portals closed and the onslaught continued. Geomancers levelled the Kasparov establishments; first came the Kasparov House of Chance and Dreams, then the Nacre Evaluation Centre.

When the time came for Kasparov Financial Solutions Limited to fall, Weil opened a portal, personally launching a tentacle through the building despite the geomancers' efforts being easily enough to demolish it. The portal unexpectedly cut off, and the disembodied tentacle fell upon the gutted building, writhing atop its ruins. Razarkha couldn't help but grin; her Plague Emperor was finally showing himself.

The march continued to the rural, northern side of Zemelnya. Though a few geomancers and cryomancers were lost in the approach, the formation War'mal had settled on was effective and terrifying. They passed Duke Mayenev's personal ranch without so much as its guards questioning them, so official interference was unlikely.

Once within the Scruchen Forest, War'mal's pyromancers got to work torching the bizarre, flesh-infested trees, lighting the way amidst the darkness caused by the nearby Plague Obelisk. The formation stopped as they waited for the fire to spread ahead, then deployed the cryomancers to put out the closest fires and form icy shields. During this brief break of formation, more Kasparov soldiers attacked, this time assisted by illusionism. Razarkha finally had a place beyond being escorted.

"*There are people that cannot be seen!*" she warned in her special rendition of Plagueborn. "*I shall cast a shadow upon us!*"

Razarkha raised her arms, took a deep breath, and cloaked the entire formation. Pyromantic bombing by the Kasparovs still proved successful despite her efforts, due to the formation's lack of mobility compared to the zipping, invisible pyromancers above them.

The remaining cryomancers weren't enough to hold the line. Their icy blockades were close to giving way, and the godspeakers' portals was the only alternative line of defence they had. Kasparov Manor was visible through the remaining flames, and so she turned to the cryomancer directly next to her.

"*Make noise for them here. I move ahead.*"

"*No. If you leave, we'll be revealed! We cannot hold forever!*"

"*As you say, not eternal holding. I therefore move ahead.*"

Razarkha pushed through the formation, not looking back, even for Weil. The geomancers raised muddy walls that dampened some of the Kasparov volleys, and Razarkha dropped the formation-wide cloaking. Instead, she snuck away under a personal cloak while the Kasparov troops' focus renewed against the squad.

With the Kasparovs distracted by the War'mal Group's final stand, she moved through the trees, seeking out any biological Kasparovs as she approached the manor. The first she came across accidentally, bumping into thin air mid-dash. A feminine voice heightened in shock, and Razarkha used the noise to estimate a stabbing point.

She hoped to hit the woman's heart, but instead hit a shoulder, which was more than enough to reveal her properly. She was but a teenager, a copy of the late Anya

Kasparov in all but height. Razarkha kicked the girl away, dislodging her knife, then stabbed her where she first intended. After that, she checked behind her to find a good portion of the Kasparovs' pyromantic bombers revealed and being juggled by Weil's tentacles.

Before she could continue, a screaming young man came charging after her with a sword in hand. Razarkha left an illusory copy of herself staring like a startled mouse while her true self stood to the side, leg outstretched. When the boy inevitably tripped, she stomped on his back and delivered a fatal stab to the back of his neck.

She chuckled and spoke to her trusty dagger. "I really ought to give you a name. Even when I get my soulstealer, I won't forget you."

She kissed the hilt and advanced, happy to see that the tide of battle was turning in the War'mal Group's favour. She produced numerous decoys to lure out other illusionists, keeping her true self focused on the path ahead. At the gates, a set of cryomancers stood, maintaining a wall of ice about the manor.

Razarkha had no choice but to wait for the others. She approached the least dangerous-looking flesh-tree she could find and hid behind it, resting her magic and gasping for air. She eyed the Kasparov cryomancers, then turned to check on the War'mal Group's progress. They had finally started to put out the forest fires closest to the manor. To her joy, one of Weil's tentacles flung a pyromancer who dying explosion that blasted an opening in the ice wall as well as the gate it protected.

This was her moment. She cloaked and dashed through the hole before the geomancers started their assault on the manor's foundations, traversing the Kasparov grounds in a desperate sprint. She couldn't hold her cloak forever, but she maintained it long enough to slip through the surprisingly unmanned front door. Razarkha grinned at the apparent convenience until realising that the manor was an illusory maze.

Doors led to empty rooms, halls led to dead ends which, when turned around in, resulted in completely different halls materialising before her. Occasionally, Razarkha came across illusionists armed with musket pistols or daggers of their own. Most were adults, with some children following along. As she made it to the first floor through aimless trial and error, she noticed a little boy wandering alone with tears in his eyes.

She put on an illusory disguise that resembled Anya Kasparov, then crouched by him, speaking in perfect Isleborn. *"Hello, little one. Don't worry, I'm here."*

"Cousin Anya, I thought you were dead!" the boy said, hugging Razarkha with fervour.

Razarkha prepared her dagger beneath her disguise. *"I fear grandfather thinks the same. I need to tell him something important. Can you lead me to him?"*

"Your voice sounds funny, Anya."

"I'm just afraid," Razarkha lied. *"Please show me where grandfather is."*

The little boy took her hand and led her through the manor, guiding her through numerous illusions the Kasparovs had set up. Razarkha withheld her urge to hoot with laughter, and on the highest floor, Pakhan Kasparov stood in a regular bedroom, staring out of the window. He wasn't a grand, immortal monster; just an old man in blue and white.

"Who is it?" the patriarch asked, turning around to point a musket pistol at Razarkha. *"Watch out, Nikita!"*

She was already prepared for this. She dragged the boy towards him, put her dagger to his throat, and dropped her disguise.

"I'd be careful where you point that," Razarkha said. *"War'mal intends to spare the children, but my blade could slip."*

"*Who are you? Why did you pretend to be Cousin Anya? Grandfather, help!*" Nikita babbled.

"*There is one way you can help little Nikita,*" Razarkha said. "*You know what I'm after.*"

Elki Kasparov kept his gun level, squeezing a crystalline structure in his off hand. "*Why are you after my soulstealer? Its true power is intimidation, which you've successfully erased.*"

"*Your problem is a lack of vision. I'm not after Ilazar. I have greater dreams.*"

"*Then I cannot allow you to have it.*"

Razarkha pressed the knife against Nikita's neck. "*Think carefully. You can save Nikita and stop the soulstealer from falling into my hands. All you need to do is broadcast this exchange to everyone outside the manor.*"

Elki lowered his gun. "*I'm listening.*"

Once these words echoed from outside, Razarkha lifted the knife a touch. "*Now that everybody else is listening too, I hope they understand Isleborn. I, Razarkha Fel'thuz, challenge you, Elki Kasparov, to an honour duel on the Battle Isle of Azraiyen!*"

The old man stroked his soulstealer and slackened his posture as he broke into a smirk. "*You're joking. You wish to duel me? You don't know what you're up against.*"

"*Neither do you. I presume the answer is yes. You're not afraid of the woman who killed your beloved Anya, are you?*"

"*I do not fear my enemies; I hate them. I accept your challenge, Razarkha Fel'thuz. You'll regret your kinslaying ways. When a man kicks a bee's nest, it is seldom the bees who grieve later.*"

"*Know that if you have me assassinated before the duel, the War'mal Group shall know. Your cowardice will be plain for Ilazar to see.*"

"*If you release Nikita, your request shall be honoured.*"

Razarkha let the child go, allowing him to run to his grandfather in tears. She put her knife in her garter and slouched on Elki Kasparov's bed as the manor began to rumble.

"Soon this manor will be no more, but if you beat me, at least you'll have your pride. Did you use your soulstealer to absorb that foolhardy granddaughter of yours? Is that why you're so confident?"

"What are you talking about? Anya never returned to the manor."

Razarkha's eyes widened. *"That's— what?"*

* * *

Baron Giles Oswyk lay awake, a smile on his face and a beauty in his arms. He wasn't in his manor and the woman may not have been his wife, but what were morals in the face of ecstasy? His secretary, a starry-eyed half-Malassaian human named Verra, nestled into his chest as the moonlight caressed her light brown skin. Nothing could ruin this moment. As if to refute this thought, a clothed wisp of magical smoke pushed the window open and echoed in a feminine, accented rendition of the Common Tongue.

"Baron Oswyk. I'm only here because I owe you my life," the cloud claimed.

Verra screamed, holding an equally terrified Giles. He tried to stay calm, and in a shaky voice, asked the most pertinent question.

"What are you talking about? Who are you?"

The cloud moved the cloth covering what a humanoid would call their collar, revealing a glowing, green-and-black gemstone hovering within the magical mist.

"Anya? Is that you?"

"Yes. Thank you for giving me this ascension stone. It was quite the timely gift. A woman from your kingdom is laying waste to my family. I want you to warn every noble who'll listen that there's a chance Razarkha Fel'thuz will return to this kingdom a much more powerful woman."

"If your family is in peril, why aren't you using your ascendant powers to help them?"

"I did some soul-searching. Without my body, it's the only self-discovery I'm capable of."

"And how did that result in you abandoning your family?"

"I concluded that my grandfather is desperate and isn't worth returning to. Zemelnya will no doubt be collapsing into gang war as we speak, and if that's the case, he'll take any soul he can capture. He's not taking mine."

"What good are you if you're not helping your family?"

Anya's wisp let out an odd noise that resembled a titter. *"Ask yourself the same question. Unless fucking your secretary is some service to your family that I'm unaware of. I'll admit I'm not versed in Arkheran nuptial culture. My motives are personal. I want to see Razarkha Fel'thuz fail spectacularly, and watch her boy realise the depths of her betrayal. Hence, I'm going to set up every obstacle I can. Promise that you'll warn your fellow nobles."*

"What's in it for me?"

Abruptly, Giles's body fled from his mind's control, and he was still capable of spectating his own actions. Anya's wisp was within him. She moved his arms against his will, stroked Verra's hair, and shocked her out of his bed.

"Giles? That isn't you, is it?"

Baron Oswyk couldn't speak. Anya pulled his hands towards his neck and made them squeeze lightly as she spoke directly to his mind.

"I could borrow your body to enjoy carnal pleasures for the rest of your life, then move onto your heir once you die. Consider me not doing this your payment."

Giles fervently tried to accept her agreement within his head, but it was only after he came close to fainting from self-strangulation that control returned.

"Thank you, Anya. I'll tell them. Overlady Selenia, Marissa, everyone. I promise."

"Good. If I find out you've been lax, I'll be back, missing carnal pleasures more than ever."

Ensnarement

The train to Moonstone slowed down, and the snows of the Forests of Winter brought a smile to Rakh Fel'thuz's face. The reality of his sister and son sitting around him felt illusory even now. If Razarkha hadn't made her hare-brained bid for power, this wouldn't have been possible. Mad as she was, her self-destructive tendencies had changed things for the better. While Rakh basked in his own warmth, Tei worked with her son, filling out relevant information on a form she'd retrieved from the King.

"Are you sure you want me to be a real Fel'thuz?" Rarakhi asked. "Ain't I too much of a thug?"

Tei shook her head. "Razarkha is as thuggish as they come, and she was honoured with the title of countess."

"Yeah, but when she tried to kill dad, she lost her title. I threatened you and treated you like shit, 'sides, I say vulgar words all the time. I don't think I'm ready to be a noble."

"Can you encourage him, Rakh?" Tei asked, rubbing her forehead.

Shifting from his bliss, Rakh stumbled over his words. "Sorry, what are we talking about?"

"Rarakhi's legitimisation, you idiot," Tei snapped. "Think about it, Rarakhi, you'll never have to kill again if you become a nobleman."

"Why would I want to give that up? Before all this I was invisible, I could do anything. If I become a nobleman, people will judge me for blinking the wrong way," Rarakhi said. "What if Aunt Razarkha comes back, won't she try to kill me?"

"If Razarkha returns, it's better you have the Selenia guard force protecting you given your identity is in the open," Rakh explained. "There's a much more compelling reason on top of that. Tei, you said you wanted to placate Plutyn, didn't you?"

Tei nodded. "First, we need to find out what Erwyn's given Khanas already—"

"That's Lord Khanas to you," Rarakhi butted in.

Tei continued without so much as a pause. "If *Lord Khanas* is in a position to topple the current order, we need a way to ensure he's happy with things as they are."

Rakh smirked. "What better way to do that than convincing him he's going to be part of the 'new system'? Rarakhi, if you become my heir, do you realise how eligible a bachelor you'll be? Plutyn won't want to wait. The moment you become a man grown, Plutera will be yours to marry."

Rarakhi fidgeted his fingers. "Well, I'd be marrying her anyway. 'sides, lords marry within their race. I know spellbinders and necromancers are close, but they ain't the same."

"That's not strictly true," Tei claimed. "In fact, the Royal Advisor, a ne— a spellbinder, nearly got betrothed to a seerish lordling. It's not exactly common, but there's some historical precedent for crossbreeding between similar races. Dark elves and high elves mixing in the Sanguinas Territories, spellbinders and necromancers in—"

"Fine, I'll become a nobleman," Rarakhi said. "But I ain't do that 'friend of the people' shit. I know the lower class, and they ain't all nice, shat-on innocents like dad thinks."

"Perhaps you can be a firm hand where I over-idealise," Rakh suggested. "I'm sure Razarkha would murder peasants for sport if she could get away with it, while I'll admit that I may have fetishised the lower class. You, however, have grown up within them. I think that makes you uniquely qualified to give them a voice once the time comes."

"I think you see too much in me," Rarakhi said. "I'm just an angry kid."

"You'll grow up. Everybody does," Rakh claimed, before swiftly changing his mind. "Well, most people."

Tei tapped their table. "Enough rambling. Rarakhi, finish the form, we're almost at Moonstone. If you need any help writing, you can dictate to me."

"I'm a spy, I know how to write," Rarakhi said in an indignant tone.

He scribbled out the appropriate details, then pushed the form back to Tei. When she read it over, she wore an odd, wistful smile.

"Your handwriting is terrible, but legible. Truly are a spy at heart."

"It's why I don't want my life to change. I know the Boss ain't a person you two approve of, but honestly, I don't care. He knows what I'm good at and lets me do it."

"That may be, but has he ever encouraged you to be *more* than what you think you are?" Rakh asked. "You're almost thirteen. You have a lifetime's worth of changes ahead of you."

"And I'm gonna change exactly how you want me to, is that it?" the boy asked, the train's stop unsettlingly synchronised with the subsequent pause.

"We just want you to have the best opportunities," Rakh insisted. "Lord Khanas will be overjoyed if you become my heir. We both know he craves noble authority."

Rarakhi cradled his slung arm and looked away from his parents while the train's passengers trickled from the locomotive. Tei clambered off her seat with a sigh.

"Let's get off before the train continues to the Rainbow Fort," she said. "I don't know what to tell you, Rarakhi. We're trying to make your life better."

"And use me in stupid political schemes."

"That was unavoidable the moment Rakh blindly— never mind. We're here."

As they alighted, Moonstone's snow ceased to be a fond memory. Instead, it was a chilly, shoe-soaking obstacle. Rakh had the family he loved by his side, but things were far from fixed. Though Tei wasn't here to stay, part of Rakh hoped that she would linger a little, at least until she and Rarakhi could discuss matters without bickering.

He'd figured out Tei's plan near-immediately after she'd conceived it; all it took was Rarakhi mentioning Plutera and the vaguest idea of the Khanas situation for her to see her own son as a resource. Rakh had considered similar notions, and while using people was ethical provided all parties benefitted, he couldn't help but see this as something Razarkha would do.

It was for the good of everyone. Rarakhi couldn't continue living at the mercy of a crime lord. He needed protection. He needed resources that could forge him into a thoughtful young man. He needed a father who could be there. As they neared the castle, Rarakhi's face shifted from relaxed to dreading, and once they were outside the castle gates, the boy was outright panicking.

"Are you all right, Rarakhi?" Rakh asked.

"No," the boy bluntly replied. "It's— it's the guards. They've got guns."

Rakh put a hand on his good shoulder. "Once you're legitimised, these gunmen will be your protectors. It'll be the same for Lord Khanas and Plutera. I'm not sure what arrangement Erwyn has with Plutyn, but once you become a Fel'thuz, you'll be safe."

The boy shook his head. "Yeah, I know they're not my enemies. I'm still afraid. Sorry."

Tei handed Rakh the legitimisation form. "Go in and catch up with Erwyn."

"Are you sure? Wouldn't you want to see him too?"

"I'll be waiting at the *Moon's Vein*," Tei said. "Would you like a drink for your nerves, Rarakhi? I'll give you a briefing on some castle etiquette, how about that?"

Rarakhi shook. "Why are you all being so nice to me? I was shit to you on the way here, now you're just gonna forgive me and not call me a coward?"

"I don't think being afraid makes you a coward," Tei said. "I think allowing fear to control you is true cowardice. Come, your father will deal with everything else."

The boy hung his head. "All right. See you later, dad."

Rakh nodded. "See you later. So, I catch up with Erwyn, then return to you?"

Tei nodded. "For now. We should only approach Khanas once we know Rarakhi is officially a Fel'thuz."

With that, Rakh watched his sister and son's backs fade into the winter mists. They weren't holding hands, they weren't even at a friendly proximity, but they were walking together. Count Fel'thuz was finally free to resume his role as a nobleman. The guards inclined their heads as he headed through the gates, and within the gardens, servants turned to watch his approach. Cloaking wasn't necessary anymore. Once inside Castle Selenia, Rakh thought to move upstairs, only to be ambushed by an extremely ineffectual tackle.

Holding onto him was Lady Selenia, resting her head against his chest while her unworked arms failed to so much as restrict his breathing. Rakh allowed warmth amidst the chilly metallic halls and put his hand on her raven locks.

"Hello again, Lady Kagura."

"Is that all you have to say? I missed you so much, Rakh! Erwyn told me you were going to see your son but then you disappeared for a month and then he told me that you went monster hunting and lost a hand and *why didn't you tell me where you were going?"*

Rakh returned her embrace. "I'm sure Erwyn was a good enough advisor for both of us."

Kagura abruptly let go of Rakh. "That reminds me, Count Fel'thuz, Erwyn has been ever so productive in your absence. He even hired a new councillor specifically to deal with criminal activity. Apparently, there's a lot of it, probably done by those filthy dark elves and necroma— actually, no, not necromancers, because they're our friends now."

"Necromancers are our friends?"

Kagura smiled wholeheartedly. "Yes! Our new Minister of Criminal Affairs, a title I came up with all on my own, is Sir Plutyn Khanas!"

Rakh needed a moment to hide his inappropriate laughter. "Sir?"

"Well, the cousin branch in the Crystal Palace are knights, and I was hardly going to give him the status of baron or count, was I? He's a minister, not a lord."

Rakh cringed. "I hope you haven't rubbed that in."

Kagura cocked her head. "Why not? According to my history books, the Khanases came to Moonstone as beggars. They stopped being lords the moment they failed to defend their city! Even his knighthood stems from my generosity!"

"I think you and Sir Plutyn ought to keep minimal contact. Hopefully he and I are on good terms."

"Oh, because ugly snake people naturally like other ugly snake people? Oh wait, no, that's not right, because you and Razarkha hated each other. Why are you two friends?"

"I've met him before. I like his manor, that's all. Anyway, I know your time is precious, so I'll leave you be. Is Erwyn in?" Rakh asked.

"Of course, he's upstairs, he's probably missed you more than me. No offence, Rakh, but even though I like you, spellbinders are really scary."

Rakh bowed with a flourish, though without his right hand to gesture it failed miserably. Kagura didn't seem to notice or care, so the count continued with his planned spiel.

"Farewell for now, my lady. Good to see you, as always."

Kagura's chest puffed up, and she rubbed her cheek. "Of course it's good to see me, I'm the most beautiful woman in the world."

Rakh softly smiled, then started his climb of the castle. Erwyn Yagaska was in his spire, writing letters to who-knows-where. When Rakh barged into his office, he immediately put his pen in its pot.

"You're back," the high elven wisdom said in a warm tone. "Did you find Tei?"

"Yes, but she's currently in the *Moon's Vein* with Rarakhi. He's still wary of guards, so he had a hard time approaching the castle. I can't blame him. Old habits die hard," Rakh said, raising his stump.

Erwyn's eyes creased. "I'm sorry I had to do that to you."

"You did everything you could. Tei wants you to notarise this," Rakh said, taking out the partially-completed form and handing it over.

"A legitimisation form? Heavens, I recognise that tiny, scattered hand; Robb Stagg wrote this," Erwyn remarked, adjusting his monocle as he read it over. "I suppose Rarakhi needs to get over his fear of guards swiftly."

"I heard you appointed Plutyn Khanas as Minister of Criminal Affairs. I imagine this is an investigatory position?"

"Investigators are simply blackmailers who work above-board and arrest people rather than extort them. Additionally, I'm envious of his comprehensive understanding of humanoid bodies. His skills and information network are transferrable and useful," Erwyn explained. "I won't pretend that he's completely trustworthy. He could attempt to overthrow us if Kagura continues with her 'knight, not lord' talk. While giving him an equivalent title to Lady Selenia is a ludicrous notion, reminding him of the fact is not exactly diplomatic."

Rakh grinned. "That legitimisation form may assure Khanas of this allegiance. Once you and the King approve it, it's binding."

Erwyn nodded. "I understand. For now, rest well. Bureaucracy takes time. I'll let you know when Rarakhi is officially a Fel'thuz."

* * *

The crashing waters of the Accursed Sea splashed against the hull of the *Osminog,* a caravel whose permanent crew consisted of a solitary female deathspeaker, Talsi. She covered her face with a long, pointed mask with shaded glass about her eyes, while the rest of her garb was loose and dark. The only sign that she was a woman was her soft, lilting tone.

Razarkha and company had taken a train to the whaling port of Ubiyscht Kashalot and sailed northwards from there towards the Battle Isle of Azraiyen. While most sailors didn't accept such a request, there was a group War'mal called the 'Servants of Harr'khel' that specialised in taking duellists to the famed isle.

Razarkha and Weil stood at the bow of the *Osminog,* far from War'mal, who chatted with Mal'dar on the starboard side, and Elki Kasparov, who sat at the aft with three of his remaining grandchildren, all younger than ten. While Razarkha wanted to snoop on them, Deathspeaker Talsi insisted that duellists remained separate until they reached Azraiyen. From the bow, the isle dominated the horizon. It was a snow-covered expanse that somehow glowed with geological fire, populated by evergreen trees and little else. The pines reminded Razarkha of the Forests of Winter and the brother-husband she'd get even with.

Azraiyen's increasing proximity ran jitters through Razarkha's back. She turned to Weil, opened her mouth, then stopped herself. She couldn't afford to admit anything. She intended to survive this duel, and if she did, she would need Weil by her side. Still, if she died, Weil would never know. He'd grieve her as though she was a friend, when in truth she was as monstrous as Vi'khash.

"*What's wrong?*" Weil asked, shoving Razarkha's thoughts into the churning seas beneath.

"*I was thinking about how much you mean to me,*" Razarkha improvised. "*I know I've been harsh and put you through every hell there is, but you're the most important person in the world to me.*"

Weil paused, and looked at the waters. "*Since my father died, you're all I have left.*"

"*Don't say that. Even if I died, you'd still have your vengeance. Promise me that if I die, you'll keep fighting.*"

"*Why?*" Weil asked. "*You won't be around to stop me disappearing.*"

Razarkha's throat stung. He was reliant on her, just as planned, but this wasn't right. Weil deserved a life beyond her; how else would he conquer in her name after she was gone?

"You would insult my memory. Promise that you'll avenge me and your father if I die."

"Fine. Once the Kasparovs are dead, will I be free to die?"

Razarkha paused. "No. After that, find another woman to love, someone who'll make you sigh and make comparisons to me, then you'll have little plague emperors with her and lead a crusade through Galdus. You'll become great and powerful without me. If I survive, the same will happen, only with a much better lover."

Weil looked away from Razarkha. "I wish I could help you. I know it goes against every Ilazari code of honour there is, but you've helped me so much. Without you I'd still be a debt slave. Now, people know me as the chaos-speaker that raided Kasparov Manor."

"Without me, your father would still be alive," Razarkha blurted.

Though taken aback, Weil remained calm, growing morose rather than angry.

"You forced me to take risks. Some led to my father dying, but perhaps it's what my father always saw. He always babbled about his end and how he was on borrowed time due to his forays into chronomancy. I can't blame you for how Anya reacted to our exploits."

Razarkha tripped over her own words as she desperately took the out. "I suppose you're right. Anya ordered the killing, even if I made you provoke her."

"I needed someone to change me. Strong people make changes to their miserable lives alone, but you helped me despite my weakness. I want to make it up to you. Is there any way I can help in this duel?"

"*I'm unsure. I imagine the Servants of Harr'khel are strict about duels being between the participants alone. I'll ask a relevant question, and if the answer is positive, you'll know what to do,*" Razarkha promised.

The isle was close enough to make out its frost-covered beaches grooved with blackened trails of solidified volcanic rock. Hardy dune grass persisted amidst the chilly sea breeze, and the *Osminog* anchored itself just shy of shallow waters. Deathspeaker Talsi approached the Kasparovs first, arranging the first pinnace out of the ship, then she approached War'mal and Mal'dar for the same, and finally she approached Razarkha and Weil.

"*Please take your boat to the Battle Isle. Know that once you step onto Battle Isle's grounds as a duellist, you have taken an oath to kill the other or die.*"

"*That isn't a problem to me,*" Razarkha said with a scoff. "*How many people lose their nerve before the duel?*"

"*More than enough. Harr'khel always takes their due, however. Know that the End of Mortality comes for all, especially on Azraiyen. In duelling your opponent, you give another to Harr'khel in place of yourself.*"

"*Yes, yes, death comes for us all, just show me to the boat and let's kill this old man,*" Razarkha said with a dismissive wave of her hand.

Talsi cocked her bird-like head towards Weil, who shrugged in response. Once the deathspeaker tired of her arbitrary tension-building, she readied a pinnace and gestured for the pair to get in. Once they did, she spoke again.

"*Godspeaker Deus will be with you shortly. Once he meets the duellists in person, they may only talk to him or each other.*"

Razarkha rolled her eyes. "*If you say so.*"

As the rowboat lowered, Razarkha ruminated over the decision that led to this; her simulacra of an Ilazari honour duel with Rakh. There were no restrictive rules or pretentious godspeakers in her little game, just one illusory rule that claimed the duel wasn't fatal. If she hadn't lied, she could have killed Rakh without consequence.

She was better than Rakh. She was always better than Rakh. She would reach Galdus with Weil, soulstealer in hand, massacring all and being lauded for doing so. She would finally have viable children and prove to her brother that it wasn't her fault she miscarried. Weil rowed the pinnace diligently while she remained lost in thought. One day, she'd return to Moonstone and show Rakh how wrong he was. The boat reached the sand and Weil got out, having to wave his hand in front of Razarkha's eyes to get her attention.

"Are you sure you're all right?"

"I'm thinking, that's all," Razarkha said as she left the pinnace.

"What about?"

Razarkha stood and gave Weil the longest hug she'd given someone. Her chest shook as she breathed, and she released just enough that she could kiss him modestly on the lips.

"If I die, remember me."

"I will."

"If you commit suicide, you won't remember anything. Remember *me."*

Weil's voice became stringent. *"I will!"*

"Good. Now, watch for my question."

The pair walked to where the other visitors of Azraiyen had gathered. Elki Kasparov played with his soulstealer and whispered to his grandchildren while War'mal used the nearby water to form an icy lookout post. Mal'dar, meanwhile, kept his beady eyes on Razarkha.

"I still have a harvester with your name in mind," Mal'dar remarked in a harsh rendition of Isleborn. *"We'll know if you've let us down."*

"Do you have one with Elki Kasparov in mind?" Razarkha asked.

"Yes. I'm going to use them to track who's won from afar," Mal'dar said.

"Would you be able to tell me too?" Weil asked. "I don't want to be left wondering."

The deathspeaker shrugged, rattling his bone necklace. "I see no reason not to."

Portals of varying colours opened about the beach, each projecting the same voice, filtered through several languages both comprehensible to mortals and otherwise. Amidst the cacophony, Razarkha detected a rendition of the message in the Common Tongue.

"Dearest visitors to the Battle Isle of Azraiyen. You come regarding the duel between Elki, descendant of Kaspar of the Isle and Cythria of Nortez, and Razarkha, descendant of Fel'thuz the Plagueborn and Rina of Arkhera. Once the duel's rules are adequately explained, the participants must ascend the nearest dune to meet me.

"From this point, duellists must not return to the other visitors until one has killed the other. Duellists must not be assisted by allies; however, all natural and neutral hazards are free to be used as part of the duel. The first one to die loses. Are there any questions?"

Elki spoke first. "Grand Godspeaker Deus, is it fair to use previously captured souls as magical sustenance during the duel? They don't technically count as allies, do they?"

"They do not," the disembodied voice said.

Razarkha cleared her throat. "And what about any immortals that happen upon us? Would they count as a neutral hazard?"

"As neither of you are godspeakers, yes. Do not consider yourself safe because you have a chaos-speaker as an ally," Deus advised. "If an immortal is summoned on Azraiyen, they shall behave as they wish. No mortal can *compel them here, due to my protection of their will. All you can hope to do is summon and unsummon."*

Weil mouthed fearfully to Razarkha, but she gave him a small, confident smile, mouthing a single Isleborn phrase.

"*Do it.*"

Godspeaker Deus appeared to wait for Razarkha's little conspiracy, then continued. *"If these are the only questions, then the duellists may ascend the dune and join me."*

With that, Razarkha Fel'thuz and Elki Kasparov walked ahead of the group. The sand gave way as they climbed, and though the pair kept a healthy distance from each other, Elki still eyed his opponent with what she assumed to be scepticism.

Standing before a pine forest on the other side of the dune was Godspeaker Deus himself. He wore what seemed to be four cloaks stitched together: One black, one white, one orange and one red. His face was hooded over, but what could be seen of his chin was bony and decrepit. His mouth was permanently agape, but despite this, his portals projected a clear, authoritative voice.

"Come with me. You shall fight by the Battle Gorge."

Razarkha's hope shrivelled and died as the old spellbinder drifted through the forest, further and further from Weil, until the beach dune was no longer visible. Elki covered his mouth as amusement brightened his eyes.

"*Oh, it seems the great Razarkha's plan to cheat with daemons will be foiled after all. Your pet chaos-speaker won't be able to find our battleground. Even if his daemon does, you're not safe from it either. What else do you have in your arsenal? A knife? Illusionism that would make a child look proficient? You made a grave mistake when you roused the anger of the Kasparov Family.*"

"*Anya hasn't returned to you,*" Razarkha replied. "*It seems even Kasparovs don't want to associate with you if you have a reason to betray them.*"

"*You act as though you haven't betrayed your friends. Anya's death reeks of a false flag operation. I took the liberty of researching your life. You're despised by your family, despised by your nation, and the only boy who doesn't despise you* would *if he knew the truth.*"

Blood rushed to Razarkha's head. "*Perhaps I'm despicable. That's still better than dead.*"

"*Tough words. A shame that's all they are.*"

"*You're not offering much beyond words yourself.*"

Elki gripped his soulstealer. "*You're an infuriating case. You're not intelligent, you're not well-intentioned or idealistic. You're just a child, bashing a chess board and rumbling the pieces without thought. I briefly considered marrying you to Oleg, but now he's dead, like every son of mine. You're nothing but a mad dog that doesn't understand the world they savage.*"

"Shut up! Just shut up!" Razarkha yelled in Common, prompting Godspeaker Deus to stop moving.

"*If the duellists' banter exceeds my threshold of tastelessness, I shall take both lives for the glory of Harr'khel. Are my words heard?*"

"*Of course, Glorious Deus,*" Elki said.

"Sorry," Razarkha muttered.

The group reached a clearing, where cracks veined through the ground and emitted red light that rippled the air. The largest was enough to count as a gorge, with numerous footholds and crags stacked atop a bed of glowing lava. Surrounding the ravine were boulders and geysers, periodically spurting steam while the ground rumbled. Deus took Elki's hand and led him towards one vent, and once he was done led Razarkha to another. He then floated so he was between them and opened a portal beneath himself.

"Once I enter this portal, the duel shall commence."

Razarkha awaited further monologuing, but as the godspeaker descended, she realised there was nothing else. Hastily, she projected a false copy in her place, cloaked, and dived behind a boulder, fumbling for her dagger. Deus and his portal vanished, prompting Elki to casually walk around the turbulent expanse. He smirked, pointed his soulstealer at Razarkha's illusion, then spoke.

"Do you think I'm stupid, Fel'thuz? A decoy illusion is the first trick any decently trained illusionist is taught. Then again, Arkhera is hardly known for its intellectual resources. Your brother taught himself well despite the setbacks of being born Arkheran, but you couldn't. Stop embarrassing yourself with worthless illusions and I'll make your death quick."

Razarkha stopped projecting and cursed herself. She couldn't beat Rakh, what chance did she have here? She thought Weil could skew the match, but instead she was stuck in an even more doomed match than her first. Elki continued to mosey, then abruptly disappeared.

Breathing had just become a luxury. Neither illusionist was visible, and a loud step would give one side or the other away. Out of thin air, an orb appeared, which subsequently birthed a massive ray. It blasted a boulder yards from Razarkha's hiding spot, shattering it with heat alone. A projected voice continued Elki's rant.

"You're stalling, after all your bold talk? Where's the Razarkha Fel'thuz that threatened Nikita? It seems you're willing to put knives to children's throats and murder the ill, but when it comes to opponents who fight back, it's a little harder, isn't it? Show yourself!"

Razarkha stood, hoping to approach the probable origin of the beam, but as she made her first step, she was snagged upwards by a bizarre appendage wrapped around her waist. She screamed, dropping her cloak and dagger alike in the confusion, desperately attempting to evaluate the creature that picked her up.

It was a daemon, mostly humanoid save for the many tentacles in place of its limbs and its 'face'. Instead of a proper mortal façade, the beast wore a bizarre, shifting mask. Its current expression was an exaggerated depiction of confusion.

"Weil, you *idiot!*"

Matters worsened as a glowing orb appeared a good distance in front of her and the daemon. Razarkha closed her eyes and braced for death, however she was lifted out of the way by the beast. The orb's next beam tore through the monster's torso, leaving an even, cauterised hole half a yard in diameter.

Razarkha attempted to ask the daemon why it saved her, but before she could it flung her towards a geyser and leapt towards the source of the orb. She landed inches away from the vent, which summarily erupted, searing Razarkha's left hand and causing her to scream. This wasn't the time to cry. That could wait until she was reunited with Weil. She needed to prove she was worthy of glory and heroism. She needed to bring a nation to its knees. She was powerful, she was unfeeling, she was composed. She was the monster the world needed.

Once her arcane incontinence subsided, she cloaked herself and stood, watching the daemon's attack on Elki. It had successfully removed Elki's cloak and shook the old man about with its tentacles by the gorge, trying to work around the Soulstealer of Craving. Elki took advantage of this and muttered some Old Galdusian words, resulting in a small pulse of light from the artefact that rendered the beast a pile of black goo from the waist up. As the daemon's lower half fell apart, Razarkha charged forward. Elki kept his soulstealer pointed at the collapsing octopoid, failing to account for an invisible woman bum-rushing him. She may have been a child hitting a chess board, but sometimes, that worked.

The impact knocked Elki to the edge of the gorge, where he teetered and waved his arms to keep balance. It was at this point Razarkha revealed herself, grabbing the hand Elki's soulstealer was in.

"Don't worry. I've got you," she claimed.

Elki smirked, moving his free hand to a holster behind his back. *"How very honourable. Did you decide using daemons was in poor taste?"*

Razarkha returned his expression, snagged the Soulstealer of Craving, then kicked him into the gorge before he had a chance to shoot her. As he fell, he screamed in Isleborn.

"Not now! Please, not in there, I don't want to be in there! Not while she *wields it!"*

The yells stopped with a wet thump, and after a delay, the soulstealer glowed. Razarkha made to walk away, before the pile of inky sludge abruptly reformed into a haphazard mass of half-formed appendages, wearing a decidedly enraged mask.

"Oh."

Unfortunately for the creature, a portal opened beneath it. It was soon slipping into the Chaotic Realm, its mask shifting to a confused expression as it shrugged its six shoulders.

Razarkha took a moment to process the situation, then burst into laughter. "Weil, you *genius!"*

Once she was done basking in her glory, she sought out Godspeaker Deus to little success. She started to walk back to the pine forest, but a whisper in the air stopped her.

"Congratulations."

"Who's there?" Razarkha asked. "Is that you, Deus? You sound different."

"I'm not a godspeaker; I'm a god. The Ilazari call me the Bold Individualist, the Yukishimans call me the

Sovereign, in Na'lima they've taken to calling me the Disharmony. Arkherans don't have a name for me but know my influence nonetheless. Call me what you wish. I'm the one who owns this soulstealer, and you're the latest borrower."

"If I make a deal with you, the soulstealer is mine, correct?"

"In the same way renting a property from a landlord makes the property yours. Your tenancy ends with your life, at which point your soul will linger within the soulstealer until the following owner perishes. Then your soul will be mine to do with as I please."

"I don't intend to perish. There are spellbinders who've lived for *centuries* without ascending."

"Use of the Soulstealer of Craving comes with a price. As well as your soul's extended stay, you will be consumed by the craving that every previous owner succumbed to. Your dissatisfaction will inevitably shorten your life, and I will get a return on the investment I give by allowing you to consume the souls of cycle-violators."

"I've bucked a lot of trends in the last few weeks. I'm willing to take my chances with this little trinket. How much more could I possibly crave power?"

"I suppose we'll both find out. Do you wish to become the Soulstealer of Craving's wielder, then?"

"Without a doubt."

"Then the deal is made."

Commitment

Crying children polluted the soundscape of the train to Zemelnya, and worse still, there was no way Razarkha could head somewhere quieter. The cause of the crying, War'mal, had insisted that she and Weil remained in his sight until they reached the capital, and following the duel, she was too exhausted to protest.

Since escaping immediate danger, Razarkha's body had allowed her left hand to feel its burns. She could still grip with it, but it was a coin toss whether she'd feel excruciating pain or nothing at all when she did. She'd also left her dagger on Azraiyen; in the panic, she'd forgotten where the daemon made her drop it. In its place, she gripped the Soulstealer of Craving.

Its form was curious, a bizarre mixture of a three-cord rope and a ladle made of gemstones. Pink wrapped into cyan and scarlet, opening at the bottom into deep, dark blue. Razarkha had her hammer, now she needed passage to a nation of nails. Weil offered an alternative noise to the weeping Kasparov children, which she gladly listened to.

"What's the soulstealer like? Does the Bold Individualist speak through it?"

Razarkha frowned. *"Possibly, though he's been silent since the first time I picked it up. Perhaps when I'm close to its intended targets, he'll train me."*

"Were you able to reply to the Bold Individualist when he spoke to you?" Weil asked, his tone probing.

"Yes," Razarkha said. *"Why, what's significant about that?"*

"It means it's somehow able to grant the holder the ability to speak its creator's tongue," Weil explained. *"It's almost insulting to the years godspeakers put into learning such languages."*

Razarkha grinned. *"You should know by now that I don't care who I insult. I'm a heroine. I toppled Elki Kasparov and changed a nation!"*

"I hope my daemon assisted."

"It nearly killed me, but aside from that, yes."

Weil slipped his hands under the table. *"Now that you have the soulstealer, are you finished with me? You thought of me as a great weapon, but now you have a greater one."*

The insinuation pained Razarkha for reasons she couldn't comprehend. She took Weil's hand beneath the table and met his eyes.

"Weil, when I told you I want you by my side, I meant it. Unless you have something on this isle to stay for, you and I will always be together. You're my Plague Emperor."

"You're not your own Plague Emperor now that you're armed?"

Razarkha smirked. *"I'm better. I'm a Plague Empress. I make this look good."*

Weil exhaled, untensing his body. *"Thank the Dark Four. You've been worrying me."*

"What do you mean?"

"You've been far too kind. This Razarkha is the one I'm familiar with."

Razarkha released his hand. *"My hand may be burnt, but it can still act as a blunt instrument."*

The train came to a stop, and an attendant yelled through the carriages.

"This is Zemelnya, our final stop. All alight at this station, I repeat, all alight at this station."

Razarkha stood and faced War'mal and Mal'dar, who were accompanied by the miserable remnants of the biological Kasparovs.

"What now, Great War'mal?"

The cryomancer put his hands together. *"I am most pleased with recent developments. I prepared for several possibilities, but thanks to you and your pet chaos-speaker, the best outcome has arrived. Elki Kasparov will forever be known as the deceptive failure who lost to a mad foreigner."*

"I'll try to take that as a compliment," Razarkha muttered.

"What are you going to do, consume my soul?" War'mal said, allowing himself a raspy, harsh chuckle. *"Jests aside, you and your pet must come with us to the Academy. We work hard, but we must celebrate our victories."*

Weil edged into the conversation. *"My name's Weil, and I'm not just a—"*

"I know what your name is," War'mal said. *"Your efforts are appreciated, and without your unpredictability, our assault on the manor would have resulted in far greater losses. You are still this woman's pet. Come, there is revelry to be had."*

He led the pair off the train along with his bookkeeper and the Kasparov children, greeted by jubilant Plagueborn citizens. Repairs to damaged buildings were underway, largely conducted by geomancers and aquamancers, while pyromantic glassblowers slaved away at on-street workshops, preparing stained glass for fresh onion domes.

Once inside the Academy, War'mal led his guests to the foyer. He gave Mal'dar a nod, prompting the deathspeaker to open a portal and speak into it. A few sharp Plagueborn words and a closed portal later, the mob boss addressed the group.

"Nikita, Kirill, and Vladlena," War'mal said to Kasparov children. *"You shall leave with my bookkeeper, Mal'dar. His directive is to keep you safe, so do not attempt to escape."*

"*Why should we trust you?*" Nikita asked. "*You killed father, you killed grandfather, you killed everybody!*"

War'mal crouched to his level and stared the illusionist boy in the eyes. "*Therefore, if I wanted to kill you too, your blood would already be pink crystals upon my icicles. Your alternatives are limited. You could roam the streets as a beggar and hope enough Kasparov supporters remain to give you shelter. If you did, we'd have to treat you as a future problem. Even a boy as young as you should know this is folly. Will you cooperate with us?*"

"*Yes. Sorry.*"

"*Kirill and Vladlena?*"

These were children that couldn't have exceeded five, so naturally, they nodded along with the grown man's demands. Razarkha's hands trembled, but she'd seen War'mal's power. For the moment, they were friends, even if he intended to exploit the weak. Inaction was her only choice until she gathered the necessary souls.

"*Good. Mal'dar, open the portal and take them away. As for Razarkha and Weil, you shall come with me.*"

After Mal'dar herded the children through one of his portals, War'mal led Razarkha and Weil to the foyer's leftmost set of stairs.

"*You two have brought Zemelnya into the hands of its deserving rulers. Is there anything I can offer as thanks?*"

Weil sighed. "*Unfortunately, what I want is already gone. Even with a deathspeaker at your beck and call, you cannot give me my desire.*"

"*As you wish. Razarkha?*"

It didn't take long for her to decide upon her reward. "*I would like a ship capable of travelling to Nortez. Now that I have a soulstealer, I intend to absorb some ascendants.*"

War'mal's voice tremored. "*You're more ambitious than I expected. I had assumed your attitude was compensatory. You shall certainly not grow lazy as Elki Kasparov evidently did. Consider it done. I shall tell you which ship is yours in the coming weeks."*

With that, they reached a decadent ballroom, filled with Plagueborn students picking at the buffet ahead of their host. Golden trim lined portrait frames across the walls, a four-tiered crystal chandelier assisted the sun in making the room sparkle and adding to the revelry were telekinetic bards playing balalaikas, bayans, banduras, cornets, and korobochkas. They played a jovial piece with the signature claps and calls of Ilazari folk music, something apparently shared between Isleborn and Plagueborn.

War'mal appreciated the music for four bars before he squatted and began a kick dance, bursting into an unnervingly jovial laugh as he clapped to the beat. He moved into the middle of the ballroom while continuing his dance, occasionally supporting his body with his hands between claps to achieve an extra high kick. Other students joined him, and the cryomancer started to sing in a rich, soulful rendition of Plagueborn. Razarkha stood by the edge of the ballroom and sighed.

"What's wrong?" Weil asked. *"War'mal seems happy with us. This party's in our honour, is it not? We should dance!"*

Razarkha kept her back against the wall. *"I don't know how to dance the Ilazari way. Do you?"*

Weil squatted. *"Here, I'll show you. Be aware that you'll have to humiliate yourself before you get it right."*

"I'm not interested," Razarkha snapped.

"Then I'll dance on my own," he said, starting a basic squat kick, folding his arms as he maintained his position.

Razarkha watched for a few painful moments, before finally caving in and squatting. *"Fine. Show me how to dance."*

* * *

If it wasn't for the sling over his son's arm and the absence where his hand should have been, Rakh would have grown nostalgic over Khanas Manor's grounds. The undead gardeners weren't nearly as intimidating as they initially were, and he almost smiled when he spotted the two orcish revenants by the door.

Rarakhi looked to his father. "This is just to stop the Boss killing that stupid lady, the one who talks like a kid, right?"

"Essentially," Rakh said. "It's not as though you plan to keep your marriage options open."

"I guess, but it didn't take long for you to see me as a political tool."

Rakh's voice became strained. "I was forced to marry Razarkha. As far as Fel'thuz duties go, you have it easy."

"I could always go back to killing people in the underground if you think I'm spoilt," Rarakhi threatened.

"Stop griping. It helps nothing."

The boy fell silent. When they arrived at the manor's door, Bloodmetal folded his arms and leaned against the wall.

"Well I'll be, it's Rakh Fel'thuz. This time I can say hello without manhandling your ugly snake body. How do?"

"Is Lord Khanas in? I've got an interesting offer for him."

The undead orc made an odd gurgling noise. "That's funny, there's another politician in here making 'er own offers. Chancellor Vult or something, an old human woman."

"I think you mean Enva, Chancellor of Vaults," Rakh suggested. "May we come in?"

"Absolutely. Lord Khanas has a gift for you."

Rakh suppressed his urge to flee to another province and waited for the orcish revenants to step aside before he entered with his son. There, a dark elven servant in a black-and-green suit gave Count Fel'thuz a nod.

"This way, Fel'thuz. Lord Khanas has been expecting you."

The dark elf led them to a smoker's lounge, where the self-appointed necromantic lord slouched on a settee, filling the air with bhang-weed fumes. Opposite him, the Chancellor of Vaults sat straight, holding onto a suspiciously full cup of tea. Plutera was knelt by a table, guarding a tea set, but upon seeing Rarakhi, she stood and rushed over.

"*Rara!* My scary ghost, you're finally back!" she said, cuddling her crippled lover. "How was it? Was your mother a good person after all?"

"You'll be able to see for yourself if you want, she's in the castle," Rarakhi said. "Have you been there yet? It's too big for my liking—"

"Oh, I love it!" Plutera interrupted. "And Lady Kag'nemera, she's ever so sweet. A little lacking in the head, but it's forgivable when she's so open-handed with fellow women. She commissioned a Wrenfall kimono just for me, I'll have to put it on for you at some point."

"Yeah, the castle's fantastic," Rarakhi stammered.

Plutyn took a long hit from his smoke and tapped the ashes into a tray. "I believe our discussion is over, Chancellor. You'll increase my salary to fifty gold a moon. Whether you approve or not, within weeks of attaining ministerial duty I exposed a child trafficker within the Church of Eternity, improving the city's finances and moral fibre alike. I should be appropriately compensated."

Chancellor Enva put her cup down, her voice shaky. "Of course, Minister."

"I'm glad to hear it. Now, off with you. Count Fel'thuz and I need to talk."

The Chancellor of Vaults ran off, no doubt headed for somewhere with as few necromancers as possible. Plutera and Rarakhi were already making sweet nothings with each other, leaving Plutyn as the only person Rakh could conceivably address.

"Lord Khanas," he said with a bow.

Plutyn sucked on his smoke once more, then opened a nearby chest. He retrieved a box the size of a large whisky bottle then presented it to Rakh.

"Here you are, Fel'thuz. I imagine your current state is maddening, so this is a small consideration for what you've lost serving your lord," Khanas said. "Open it."

Using his stump as an awkward balancing point, Rakh opened the box to find a model hand, complete with a harness to attach it to his forearm. It was painted the colour of flesh, but its weight and texture implied it was wooden.

"You didn't take this from any of your fallen allies, did you?" Rakh said with a chuckle. "Thank you, the thought is appreciated."

Plutyn rolled another smoke. "I'm quite enjoying my new position. Still, Lady Selenia is insufferable."

Rakh took the free chair the chancellor left behind. "Speaking of the lady, I have a gift for you too. I heard about the gaffe regarding your official title."

Sir Khanas's relatively sunny disposition returned to its familiar ghastly one in moments. "I'm not resentful. My cousin branch in the Crystal Palace are mere knights according to the new system too. What matters is the glory of our family, and no new system title can accurately represent that."

"Still, I can't imagine you'd be opposed to your daughter becoming a countess."

Plutyn raised an eyebrow. "I knew you had a hidden monstrousness but cuckolding your own son with a girl half your age is despicable."

Rakh panicked and took a piece of paper from his inner pocket. "No, no, that's not my meaning at all! Look at this."

It was the completed legitimisation form. Signatures from Erwyn Yagaska, Rob Stagg, Landon Shearwater, and Rakh himself all acknowledged Rarakhi as a trueborn Fel'thuz. As the form detailed, this made him his father's heir.

Lord Khanas inhaled so deeply that he coughed. "Plutera, this concerns you."

The girl tore herself away from Rarakhi to read the form over her father's shoulder. The moment her eyes stopped scanning the page, she squealed with joy.

"Rara, you didn't tell me you were a Fel'thuz now! That means when we're both of age, you *will* marry me. I won't take no for an answer. I want some of Castle Selenia's courtyard for winter-flowering plants, as well as gifts from Lady Selenia, and oh, everyone will call me 'Countess Plutera'! Father, aren't you excited? Your grandson's going to advise whatever silly Selenia is in power at the time!"

Rarakhi laughed falteringly. "I didn't realise you'd be so happy about this. What about me being your dangerous underground ghost?"

"Oh, you still are, but once your dad gets out of the way you'll also be my count. You can wear fancy Ilazari clothes like your Aunt Razarkha and I'll get to show you off to all the women who don't get to have you!"

The two young lovers jabbered between each other with similar refrains, but Plutyn Khanas was not in the same celebratory mood. His long forehead wrinkled, and he gave Rakh a chilling jade stare.

"Do you want me to beg your lady to authorise this betrothal? Before he was legitimised, he was a nobody who I could easily secure for my daughter. Now you've made him *harder* to marry."

"But with more perks. Consider the betrothal already brokered on your behalf."

"And what, exactly, do you want from me in return?" Khanas asked.

"Aside from not trying to kill Lady Kagura for her tone-deaf nature, this is a favour, man to man. A thank-you for your understanding and allowance of Rarakhi's new life."

Plutyn reignited his smoke and puffed. "I appreciate the thought, but I'm not satisfied yet. No matter how many gifts I receive, this city, under my guidance, will change."

"If those changes include the removal of traffickers and... non-vetted criminals, we'll be friends," Rakh said. "No facetiousness, no threats. I hope one day we can all get together as extended family and drink at a tavern."

"You misapprehend me as a commoner, but your sentiment is pleasant. For now, leave us. I cannot trust these two to remain chaste in their current state."

Rakh shrugged. "Chastity's overrated between families who know each other. Rarakhi, can you hear me?"

The boy was bragging to his lover about something Rakh could only glean the end of.

"Anyway, Deathsport looks like it's full of suckers. So many homeless folks too, I bet the Order's constantly recruiting over there. If you want to use your position as countess to expand operations, I say control Deathsport. Maybe we can get your cousin in on it. He's somewhere in the south, right?"

Plutera fanned with her hands. "Oh, no, he's not part of the underground life. He's a knight, a proper one. Father calls him a 'serf to the new system', but Rowyn doesn't care— oh, Rara, I think your father wants you."

Rarakhi groaned. "What is it, dad?"

"Time to return to the castle. Ready yourself however you need, and remember to kiss Plutera goodbye," Rakh said with a smirk.

"Like I need telling," Rarakhi said, before clumsily sucking on the girl's face.

At first Rakh was mildly amused, then his discomfort reached similar levels to Plutyn's, until eventually he was uncomfortable enough that it amused the Lost Lord.

"Let's go before matters get out of hand," Rakh commanded, seizing Rarakhi's wrist the moment his overly affectionate face consumption was over.

"Hey, I was gonna go back for more!" Rarakhi protested as he was dragged away. "Plutera, let's have some wine together, I think Lady Idiot has some in stock!"

"Only if father—"

Plutyn immediately shook his head.

"Sorry, my father won't allow it."

"We'll meet tomorrow, Petal!" Rarakhi called as he continued to be dragged away.

Once beyond the Khanas grounds, the boy glanced at his father. "You don't have any right spoiling a guy's fun. I know how to keep my cock in my trousers, unlike you."

"Yes, you haven't sired any bastards, but at your age, I'm not sure if you can—"

"Believe me, I can."

Rakh's eyes widened. "That's something I didn't need to know."

"Get used to it, you're a dad now. Isn't that what they do, know all sorts of horrid shit about their children? You weaselled out of changing my swaddling clothes, so you're gonna suffer through this."

"I suppose I walked into this sort of thing."

In a twisted way, this was bliss. If the worst thing Rakh had to remark on was overexposure to his son's state of puberty, then life was turning around. Father and son arrived at the castle, and the guards slung their guns over their shoulders upon seeing Rarakhi. Once they got past the door guards, Rakh smiled widely; Tei was waiting by the entrance for them. He opened his arms for an embrace, but she shook her head.

"I'm sorry, Rakh. I know you two are in a good mood, but Erwyn and I have received some terrible news."

Rarakhi frowned. "This better not be about my legitimacy. Turns out my girl likes me being a Fel'thuz, I'm not gonna give that shit up now."

Rakh knew Tei's expression all too well. Pervasive dread, uneven breathing, hands close to her body; she'd practically reverted into a child.

"Don't tell me this is about—"

"It's about Razarkha," Tei said. "A letter arrived from Baron Oswyk. She's apparently taken on a crime family in Ilazar and stands a chance at winning. What's most worrying, however, is the artefact the family has."

"You're joking," Rakh said. "If they have one Razarkha doesn't stand a chance."

"We both know Razarkha," Tei said. "This was a possibility the moment your worthless honour spared her life. She's like knotweed, Rakh. Cut her down and she'll grow back, stronger than ever. We need to prepare for Razarkha returning with a soulstealer."

Rarakhi clenched his fists. "What now, then? Am I going back into hiding?"

"It's too late. If she returns, she'll find out about you almost instantly," Tei said. "Use the protection the castle guard offers. I'm going to return to Deathsport as soon as possible to relay the message to the King. I'm sorry to leave so soon, but—"

"No, it's fine. This shit's important. All you two go on about is how bad my aunt is."

Rakh swallowed. "What worries me is that she's likely worse than ever."

Tei shook her head. "If I were you, I'd worry about how she *exceeded* your expectations."

Epilogue

The crackling of a needle descending upon a fresh long-playing record filled the cabin of Hildegard Swan. The vessel she was on, *Marya's Glory,* may have been military, but owing to her status as the genius behind any weapon used in Yukishima's Ameristian and Galdusian campaigns for the past three years, she was afforded a room with creature comforts such as threadweed, a double bed, and the very phonograph she was listening to.

Hildegard lay naked, smoking a pipe and enjoying *The Swing Sisters'* latest record, arm around her bodyguard-lover, Ana, a thin, red-haired woman with freckles covering most of her face. While she was a competent soldier with a thousand ways to kill an intruder even in the nude, as a lover she was a hapless child in constant need of correction and punishment, which Hilda was all too ready to provide.

"We're almost here," Hilda estimated. "I've heard no reports of storms getting in the way, so we should meet up with the Lunscar Fleet soon enough."

"I wish we had more time," Ana remarked.

"Don't start wishing or you know what'll happen," Hildegard said. "We ought to meet High Admiral Dennick with our clothes on, wouldn't you agree?"

"Of course, mistress."

Hilda left her bed and checked the mirror. Her blonde hair's perm had held despite the recent tousling, so all she needed was a quick soap wash. She put on a rich blue dress with embroidery defining everywhere above her thighs, and presented Ana with a white, low-collared dress.

"You will wear this today."

"You're letting me present as non-military?"

"While we're surrounded by allies, I believe Jensen can pick up the slack," Hilda explained. "Now wash and get dressed."

"Or what?" she asked in a teasing, excited manner.

"Or I won't slap you."

Ana's face contorted with frustration, and she begrudgingly did as her mistress commanded, earning the slap she was promised. After that, they waited in silence for another ten minutes, until a fuzzy voice came from the ship's announcement system.

"Marines on the Marya's Glory, *prepare to escort Imperial Engineer Swan and the ANF array to the* Celestia, *repeat, prepare to escort the Imperial Engineer and the ANF array. Imperial Engineer Swan, report to starboard."*

"That's our cue," Hildegard said. "Let's find Jensen and get on the boarding steamer."

Ana picked up a rifle, Hilda picked up a pistol, then the two moved above-deck, where Yukishiman marines were clambering down a ladder on the starboard side into a Hildegard Class-Seven Armed Boarding Steamer. A crane was deployed, steadily lowering Hilda's latest innovation; a metallic, nasite-and-redstone-lined device with numerous dials and switches.

This was the Arcana Nullification Field Array version five, invaluable for securing wide areas of Sula in future campaigns. All it needed was a few wet runs before a full-scale production and delivery cycle would be approved by Empress Marya. Standing by the guard rail was Hilda's other bodyguard, Jensen, a man who was armed to the teeth; in addition to a rifle and three holstered pistols, he had a belt of grenades prepared.

"Mistress," he said with a curt nod.

"What's the status?"

"Dennick Lunscar hears us loud and clear. He's preparing for our arrival as we speak."

"Good to hear it," Hilda said. "I suppose all I need to do is wait. I don't think I'll need to sell this invention to the good admiral. The results shall speak for themselves."

"Yeah, about that, there's a no-ANF-activation rule on the *Celestia,*" Jensen explained. "They say Admiral Lunscar's made some ascendant friends while protecting Quattrus."

"Ah, what a shame. Still, our official purpose is keeping the peace, not waging war," Hilda said. "Even if prolonged peace would lead to everyone on this boat's redundancy."

Once the device was securely lowered, Hilda and her bodyguards climbed down to the boarding boat, settling on the fore. Before them lay a fleet of at least a hundred steam battleships, with the flagship staying at the back, anchored amidst the blackened seas of Nortez. Further still was the distant port of Quattrus, Nortez's westernmost major city.

"Making friends with the ascended," Hilda remarked as the *Celestia* grew closer. "I never thought the admiral would be capable of it, given how many men we've lost to them."

"Seems Nortez's surrender has been more successful than we anticipated," Jensen remarked.

"Sula will still need your weaponry," Ana said. "Admiral Lunscar wouldn't make you come all this way just to turn your ANF down."

"I know that already, I don't need your comfort," Hilda snapped.

"Sorry, mistress."

They finally reached the *Celestia,* a monstrous, outdated steam ship with barnacles encrusting its lower hull and rust surrounding its circular window frames. A ladder lowered from its port side, with the High Admiral personally looking over the guard rail at the approaching visitors. He was a broad-shouldered old man with a thick grey beard and clothes that rendered him indistinguishable from his fellow crew members, save small blots of colour from his numerous medals.

"Ahoy-hoy, Imperial Engineer! When you get up here, I got something to show you. I think you'll find it interestin'. I know I did!"

"Mother's Mercy, whenever naval sorts find something interesting, I prepare for the worst," Hilda called back. "I'll be with you shortly."

The marines preceded Hilda in their climb, as did Jensen and Ana, but eventually the Imperial Engineer made it to the *Celestia's* port side. The High Admiral offered a hand, which Hilda briskly shook.

"Good to see you, Admiral Lunscar. Prepare your cranes. The latest ANF array may be lighter than the previous versions, but it's still a hefty device."

Admiral Lunscar looked to the bodyguards, then back to Hilda. "You three may want to follow me to the brig. On the way, you can tell me about the changes you've made."

The old man waved Ana and Jensen along, and together they descended into the bowels of the floating metal hulk. Hilda put her hands behind her back and smiled as threadlamps activated in their presence.

"I hear you've made friends with ascendants."

"There's a friendly ascendant on board from Quattrus. Her name's Quissera, and she's been an invaluable diplomat between us and Eternal Duke Weldum. What I wanted to show you, though, is a not-so-friendly ascendant. I say that, she's closer to unascertained. At any rate, we don't want either dying, so for now, no testing your array on the ship. Unfortunately, we'll need to wait for deployment to Sula for a proper run."

"I'm sure on the day you'll be impressed. Its start-up time has been reduced by ten minutes, and its range has been increased to a radius of sixteen-hundred yards."

"So, we're covering more than a mile diameter now?" Dennick asked.

"Provided the on-field tests are as successful as the dry runs in Wrenfall," Hilda said. "Colour me interested, though. I want to see this not-so-friendly ascendant. I presume she's contained?"

"I've made Nortezian friends, but don't frame me as stupid. 'course she's contained."

When they reached the brig, the only occupied cell contained one of Hilda's oldest inventions: The Swan Ascendant Imprisonment Chamber, SAIC for short. It was a mostly clear chamber, with numerous thread-fuelled nodes at the end of small airlocks, propped up on a column that held a spherical glass pod and transmitted sonar frequencies within it.

Occupying this SAIC was a malachite-based ascension stone, along with a mostly controlled arcane cloud, dotted with pale green magical embers. Through a voice modulator used to maintain the device's air-tight nature, a woman could be heard.

"Here to show me off again, Lunscar?"

"Sorry, lass. This girl claims to be part of the Kasparov Family," Admiral Dennick explained. "She's been going on about some Arkheran woman. I started off thinkin' she was mad, but she came from the west, not the east, so if she's from anywhere close, it's Ilazar. She didn't try to attack us, just politely asked for passage to Quattrus."

"Then you denied her," Hilda said with a laugh.

"Even then, she didn't get aggressive, just desperate. She said that Nortez needs to know about 'her'. Didn't attack us, but we couldn't take any chances."

Hilda folded her arms and addressed the ascendant. "And who's this 'her'?"

"Razarkha Fel'thuz. I warned Baron Oswyk of Arkhera that she was likely to overthrow my family, and since then I've confirmed it. The woman has a soulstealer,

and likely hopes to harvest Galdus's ascendants. I know you Soltelles have little love for the ascendants of Galdus, but whatever you do, don't allow someone like her to gain power."

Dennick looked to Hildegard. "I've promised that I'll at least look out for ships from Ilazar, but I don't know what to do with her 'sides from keep her prisoner."

Hilda frowned. "I think she's telling the truth. I'm going to stay with this fleet for a while in case we find this brown-necker. Soulstealers are, from my research, Sovereign-assisted ancient magitech designed specifically to kill ascendants. This Razarkha woman, if she's got the resources this ascendant claims, could prove useful."

Appendices

Appendix I: Map of the World

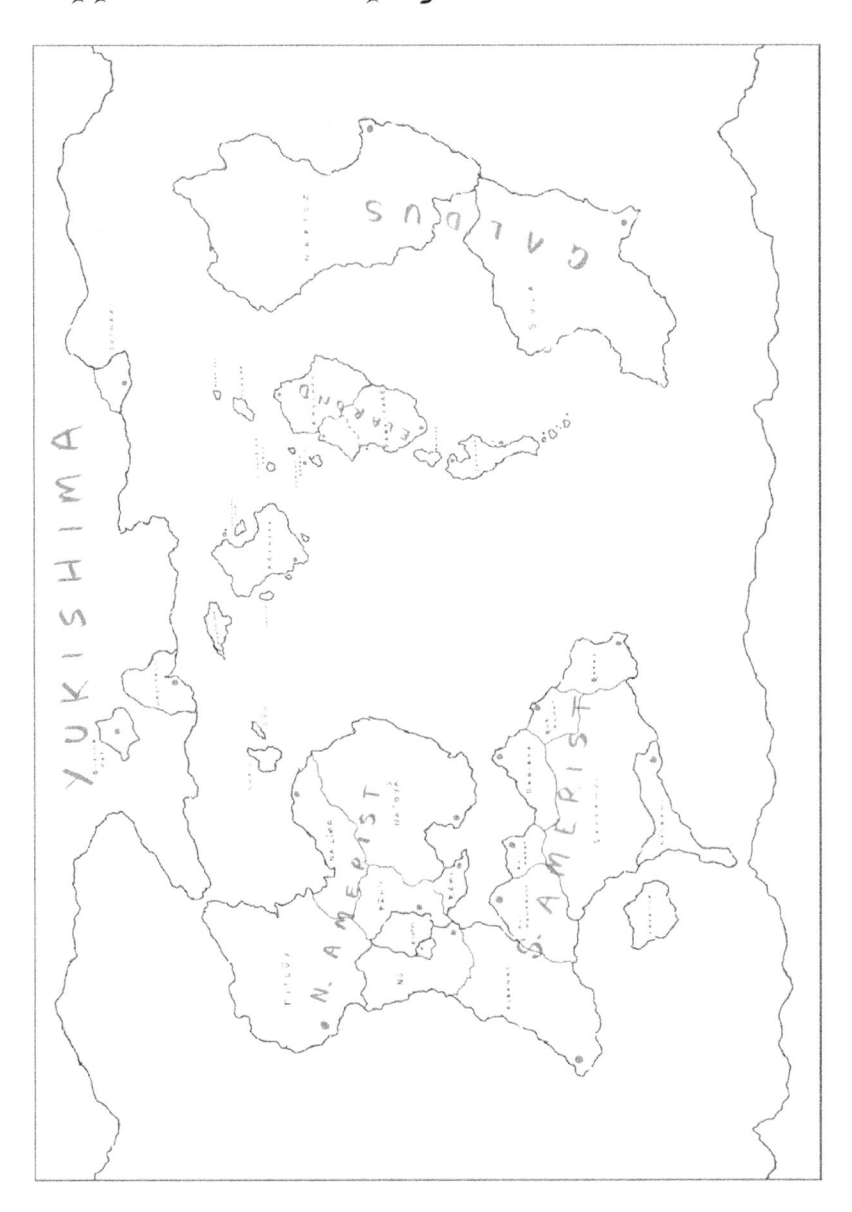

Appendix II: Races of the World

Humans: Humanoids much like the reader of this novel. Capable of magic in semi-rare cases, tend to be hairier than most other races save orcs. Populate most of the world and come in a variety of colours and cultures.

Elves: Beautiful, tall, dextrous humanoids who have long, pointed ears, youthful looks, and tend towards being non-magical. They have multiple subraces and cultures, such as pale-skinned high elves, charcoal-skinned dark elves, diminutive and red-haired forest elves, and the highly magical, mostly identical Kakajuan elves. Like humans, their presence is widespread.

Spellbinders: Willowy, pale, small-nosed humanoids who, while fragile, perform their natural magic with the same ease as breathing. They have long, rat-like tails and two primary cultures: The conservative, disciplined Galdusians and the bold, expressive Ilazari, both of which also populate Arkhera.

Necromancers: Cousins to the spellbinders, they are slightly shorter in both stature and tail length. Their magic, as their moniker implies, largely centres around control of the dead. An endangered race that is largely endemic to Galdus and Arkhera.

Orcs: Non-magical, apelike humanoids whose body hair makes them resemble sentient yetis. They are the dominant natives of Arkhera; the land is named for the Old Orcish for 'Orc Home'. Despite their lack of magic, they are tall, strong, and surprisingly quick.

Goblins: Green-skinned, scaly, and short beings who have more in common with monkeys than the apes most humanoids resemble. Bearing protractible claws, they are gifted climbers with large eyes they use to see distances other races cannot. Native to Malassai, though a healthy population exists in Arkhera.

Gnomes: Short humanoids with highly light-sensitive, myopic eyes and a sense of hearing that enables them to hear infrasound, gnomes are well-adapted to life underground. Modern gnomes that work in above-ground cities tend to wear goggles or sunglasses to avoid retinal damage.

Seers: Diminutive, waifish people native to Sanguinas Isle named for their race's limited prescience. Their abilities usually manifest as visions, but others experience their abilities the same way other humanoids anticipate events. Though they've spread to mainland Arkhera, they are relatively endangered after enduring multiple genocides.

Beastmasters: An endangered humanoid race endemic to the Arkheran Isles. They can bond with animals and share minds with them, enabling a unique, collaborative approach to animal husbandry other humanoids can't achieve. Most exist in the Iron Hills of Arkhera and as tribal communities on the Isle of Wor'ghan.

Printed in Great Britain
by Amazon